Possessed

Book Seven in the Jenny Watkins Mystery Series

1. Driven
2. Betrayed
3. Shattered
4. Exposed
5. Trapped
6. Vindicated

Bill + Sarah,

A million thanks...
again :)

Copyright 2015

Dedication

As always, my undying gratitude goes out to my family: Scott, Hannah, Seneca, Evan and Julia. They are both my inspiration and my motivation.

Special thanks to my proofreaders Danielle Bon Tempo and Bill Demarest. Danielle is my editor; Bill is my fact checker. They both keep me on my toes.

Even more thanks go out to the Foote family, namely Christopher (my cover model) and Altony (my cover photographer.) When I saw Christopher at my daughter's Tae Kwon Do school, I just knew he was my Devon. I'm so glad his parents were receptive to the wacko lady who approached them with the offer for their son to be on a book cover. ☺

Lastly, my thanks go out to you, the readers, who have made this whole experience surreal for me. I am so grateful that you have stuck with me through seven books. I love to write this series, and I'm delighted that you continue to read it. Thank you, thank you, thank you!!!!

I hope you enjoy Possessed!

Chapter 1

"It's hot," Jenny muttered as she lowered the thermostat one more degree.

Zack looked up from his laptop. "Seriously? You're turning it down *again?*"

"It's hot," she repeated, fanning her face with her hand.

"It's not hot; you're just seven months pregnant."

"Okay then," Jenny replied without animosity in her voice, "*I'm* hot. Either way it needs to be cooler in here."

"What's it set at?" Zack zipped his jacket a little higher.

"Sixty-six," Jenny admitted with a giggle.

"Good Lord, woman. Are you trying to force me to move out by freezing me out of here?"

"I promise I'm not." She placed her hand on her belly. "It's just this baby is a giant furnace. It's like I swallowed a heating pad that's on stuck *high*. Besides, the way I see it, you can always put more clothes on if you're cold, but I can't un-pregnant."

"I'm not arguing with you," Zack said. "I know better than that. I just can't believe you're actually calling this place hot."

The ring of Jenny's phone disrupted the conversation; the number was unfamiliar and the area code indicated the call was coming from out of state. She hoped it wasn't a solicitor. "Hello?"

A female voice came through the phone. "Hi, I'm looking for Jenny Watkins."

Even though she had a new last name, Jenny responded, "This is," and then braced herself for a sales pitch.

The woman on the other end gathered her strength with a sigh, immediately causing Jenny to realize this was more than just a random phone call. "My name is Kayla Moore; I'm calling from Ashland, North Carolina." She paused, clearly trying to formulate what she was going to say next. "I got your number through a friend-of-a-friend; she knows the owner of an inn in Virginia that you once helped with your psychic ability."

Jenny remembered that case. "Yes, her name was Jessica."

"Jessica…that's right." The fear in Kayla's voice remained. "Well, the reason I'm calling is because I was wondering if you could possibly help me as well." She cleared her throat nervously. "Actually, I need you to help my son, Devon."

Realizing this was a serious call, Jenny walked into the other room so she could devote her full attention to the conversation. "Sure. What do you need me to do?"

"I don't know what I need you to do," Kayla admitted. "Provide me with some answers, I guess?" Another sigh indicated she was having a difficult time keeping it together. "Lately, my son has been saying some things…things that just don't make any sense. He's been claiming that his name is Matthew, and he keeps talking about a fire that he wasn't able to escape from."

Jenny felt a chill.

Kayla continued, "At first I just ignored it, thinking he had a vivid imagination or something. But it's been two months now, and he talks about it almost daily. The fire has even been the focus of many of his drawings at school, to the point where his teacher has contacted me to voice her concern."

Drawings? "Wait a minute," Jenny interrupted with a rapid shake of her head. "Just how old is your son?"

"He's five."

"*Five?*" Jenny couldn't believe he was so young.

"Exactly," Kayla replied, "and he's an only child, so it's not like he has an older sibling watching violent movies in front of him or anything. His father and I are very strict about what he sees on TV, and the only computer he has access to is a little tablet designed for kids, so he's not getting any horrible images there. I honestly can't imagine where this is coming from, so that's why lately I've come to accept that maybe something very real and very frightening is happening to him. And that's where you come in."

Jenny couldn't imagine the despair that this mother must have been feeling.

"I understand that you have the ability to receive messages from the deceased…and it sounds like, from what Devon describes, this Matthew person died in that fire. If there really *is* a Matthew, and he *is* trying to relay a message…" Kayla's voice became shaky, most likely due to tears. "I wonder if you can figure out what that is so he will leave my son alone."

"You said you're where?" Jenny asked. "Ashland, North Carolina?"

"Yes, that's correct."

Glancing at the clock, Jenny replied, "My husband and I can be there by sundown."

Jenny hadn't met Devon yet; his father had taken him out for dinner at one of those crazy, child-centered pizza parlors that housed an arcade. This allowed Jenny to have a quiet conversation with Kayla at the house so she could have a better grasp of what Devon had been experiencing.

Jenny sat in the center of the Moore's couch, flanked by Zack and Kayla. "These are some of his drawings," Kayla said as she handed over a small stack of papers. Once Jenny had a firm grasp on the pictures, Kayla went back to wringing her hands.

"My God," Jenny whispered when she saw the horrific nature of the drawings. Fire, indeed, was the prevailing theme in all of them, although Jenny noticed something different in one particular image. "Is that blood?" She pointed to a red crayon mark on the picture.

Kayla shook her head slowly. "I don't know. I guess I should have asked, but I've always tried to downplay these drawings. Instead I try to focus on the more appropriate pictures he comes home with."

Jenny covered her mouth with her hand and furrowed her brow; she could see why Kayla had been upset enough to call her.

"And look," Kayla continued as she pulled out another drawing. This one showed what appeared to be a young boy playing happily with an animal of some kind, although kindergarten artwork was often difficult to decipher. "In pictures like this, he draws himself as black—which he is, obviously." She pointed over at one of the violent drawings in Jenny's hand. "But in the ones that feature fire, he draws himself as white."

Zack spoke for the first time. "So, it appears this Matthew person was white?"

"That's what I'm assuming," Kayla replied.

As this case became odder and odder, Jenny's heart bled more intensely for this little boy she had yet to meet. "When, exactly, did this start? I know you said it was a few months ago, but when was the very first time he mentioned Matthew?"

Kayla sat up straighter. "It was on our way home from vacation. We went to Disney World in July, and we were driving home when I heard him say from the back seat, 'Hi, Matthew; I'm Devon.' He had been asleep, so I just figured he was dreaming and thought nothing of it. Then, when we got home, he said, 'Mom, did you know Matthew got burned in a fire?' I was disturbed by the comment even then, and at that point I didn't know just how much this would take over his life." She shook her head, looking as if she were battling tears.

A thought occurred to Jenny. "Do you remember where you were in the trip when he first said hello to Matthew?"

Kayla thought but ultimately said, "I'm afraid I have no idea. We were driving overnight, so it's not like I can even say it was lunch time or anything." She thought some more before adding, "I think it was near the end of the trip."

The sound of Kayla's ringing phone permeated the room. "I'm sorry," she said, "it's my husband; I'm going to get it." As she stepped into the kitchen for privacy, Zack turned to Jenny.

"This is some crazy shit, huh?"

Drawing in a breath, Jenny nodded in agreement. She didn't reply, her mind too preoccupied with her own unborn baby and the prospect that this child may have had a future that looked very much like Devon's.

Zack continued, "Do you think he may have *picked up* a spirit on the way home from vacation?"

Jenny could no longer dwell on her own worries; there was too much staring her in the face. "That's what I'm thinking, which is why I asked where they were, specifically, when the talk of Matthew first started. I figure if she knows the exact location, it could give us an idea of where to start looking for a Matthew who died in a fire." She stifled a shudder at the thought of dying so horrifically.

Kayla returned to the living room. "They're about two minutes from the house," she announced with a worried look on her face. "Are you ready to meet him?"

Jenny stood and smiled brightly. "I would love to meet him." Seeing the look on Kayla's face, Jenny walked over and placed her hand on the nervous mother's shoulder. "Don't worry," she said compassionately. "It's going to be okay."

The words seemed to have a calming effect on Kayla, albeit minimally. Jenny was reminded of her own first psychic experience, when a more seasoned medium named Susan had said something similar to her. Susan's composure had been comforting to Jenny—she'd need to keep that in mind when talking to Kayla.

The front door opened, and in walked a very tall man and an adorable young boy in a plaid, button-down short sleeved shirt. The boy stopped in his tracks immediately upon seeing Jenny, furrowing his brow and looking at her as if she had three heads.

Kayla seemed surprised by his reaction. "Devon, honey, what's the matter? These are my friends Miss Jenny and Mr. Zack." Kayla turned apologetically to the Larrabees. "I'm sorry about this; he normally is so friendly. I thought he was going to come in and talk your ears off."

"It's okay," Jenny said reassuringly. She knew why Devon was acting strangely, and his reaction was perfectly reasonable under the circumstances.

In an attempt to appear nonthreatening to Devon, Jenny walked in his direction slowly. Kneeling before him, she gently held out her hand.

Devon responded by taking a step backward and hiding behind his father's leg.

"Hi, Devon," Jenny said in her most compassionate tone. "I know what you're feeling is weird, but it's okay."

Devon continued to look at her skeptically.

"What's happening?" Kayla whispered.

"He can feel it," Jenny explained quietly. She never let her eyes leave the boy's face when she added, "He has the gift."

Kayla sounded short of breath. "The gift?"

Jenny nodded. "He has psychic ability...and when psychics are in the presence of other psychics, they know it. I imagine he's never met anyone else like him before, and he doesn't know what to make of what he's feeling."

Devon's father squatted down to be more at his level. "It's okay," he said encouragingly. "She's not going to hurt you."

"It feels funny, doesn't it?" Jenny said with a pleasant smile, fully aware that the words *déjà vu* would mean nothing to a five-year-old. "Almost like you've met me before, even though you haven't."

With his brow still furrowed, Devon nodded so slightly it was almost imperceptible.

"Touch my hand," Jenny said. "It'll feel nice; I promise."

Devon looked at his father for approval.

"Go ahead," his father said. "I'm right here."

With that, Devon reached out his little fingers and wrapped them around Jenny's. Affirmation surged through Jenny's veins, a feeling similar to the exhilaration of holding hands with a new love. She had just been touched by a fellow psychic; the sensation had no other explanation.

Devon relaxed his eyebrows, looking at Jenny with what could have been interpreted as the beginnings of a smile.

"See?" Jenny said with a smile. "It's okay."

Devon removed his fingers from Jenny's, only to look up at Kayla and say, "Mom, why are you crying?"

Jenny glanced over her shoulder to see that Kayla was indeed wiping a tear from her eye. "You're just a very special boy, that's all," she managed to say.

Jenny had to acknowledge that this couldn't have been easy for Kayla to watch. After all, it had been hard enough for Jenny to recognize the ability within herself; she couldn't imagine sitting helplessly by and watching the person she loved the most struggle with that realization—especially when that person was a five-year-old child.

"He *is* a special boy," Jenny said as she stood up, "and he's going to need some guidance. But I promise, Mom, with a little love and support, he's going to be just fine." She took a step closer to Kayla. "You'll notice I described what he has as *the gift*. If handled properly, that's what this is—a gift—that he will eventually learn to appreciate."

Kayla nodded, although her hands continued to shake.

Jenny introduced herself to Devon's father, who said his name was Randall. Zack also joined in the greeting.

They all resumed their places in the living room, including Devon, who sat on his father's lap in a recliner that matched the sofa. "So," Jenny said to Devon in her best teacher tone , "I hear you have a friend named Matthew."

Devon fidgeted all around, proving to be like many other boys his age who couldn't sit still. "Uh-huh."

"Can you tell me a little bit about Matthew?"

After more squirming, Devon announced, "He died in a fire."

"Do you know when he died?"

"It's been a long time now." He slid off his father's lap. "I take karate."

At this point, Jenny inwardly acknowledged this case was going to come with a unique set of challenges. Nonetheless, she emphatically said, "You do? Let me see some of your moves."

After a short display, Jenny and Zack both applauded. "Remind me never to mess with you," Zack said.

"Okay, see, now he's warming up to you," Kayla warned. "You will be hard pressed to get him to stop talking."

"I want to get a dog," Devon added, "but my mom says no."

"We have a ferret," Kayla told Devon. "The ferret and the dog might not get along."

"Yes, they will."

Jenny looked over at Kayla. "This isn't how the gift works. He can't see the future; that's just a five-year-old boy trying to talk you into getting a dog."

"Oh, I'm not getting a dog," Kayla said. "No worries there."

Jenny turned back to Devon. "Honey, do you know Matthew's last name?"

"Nope." Devon galloped in a circle. "All he says is that his name is Matthew."

"Is he a child?"

Devon stopped and looked at Jenny. "No, he's a grown up."

"A grown up. Do you know how old he is?"

"I don't know. Like, fifteen?" Devon resumed his circle around the room.

Kayla turned to Jenny. "Last week he told his teacher that his father was fifteen on an *All About Me* assignment. I think every grown up is fifteen to him."

Jenny released a deep sigh; this was a child after all. Accuracy was going to be hard to come by, even though brutal honesty would most likely flow freely.

Returning to the matter at hand, Jenny asked, "Devon, can you do me a favor?"

He once again stopped running and looked at her.

"The next time Matthew comes to visit you, can you ask him what his last name is?"

The little boy scrunched his face, as if trying to understand the request. "He doesn't *visit* me. He becomes me."

Jenny understood what he meant. "You see the stuff that he saw, don't you?"

Bouncing around as if he'd had way too much caffeine, Devon said, "I see the fire."

Jenny straightened her posture, recognizing that the visions this boy had were probably far worse than any of her own had ever been. "Is the fire all around you?"

Devon threw punches at an enemy that wasn't there. "Un-huh. I can't get out. There's no place that isn't on fire."

Almost afraid to hear the answer, Jenny asked, "Does the fire hurt you?"

"No. It doesn't hurt me...but it killed Matthew."

"How do you know it killed Matthew?"

Still swinging his arms, he said, "It goes black."

Jenny's eyes shifted to Kayla, who appeared to have aged a decade since they'd arrived. Kayla rubbed her eyes, wiping her hands down her face, ultimately revealing a plastered-on smile that was clearly insincere.

While Devon seemed like he could have continued the conversation forever, his mother did not; she looked as if even another minute would have been torturous. "Devon, if it's okay with you, I want to go into the kitchen and talk to your mommy for a while."

He didn't acknowledge the comment, choosing to head-butt his father in the stomach instead.

Kayla walked quickly into the kitchen, closing the door as soon as Jenny had entered the room behind her. She hung her head as tears freely fell; Jenny handed her the box of tissues that had been on the kitchen island.

"I know it's tough," Jenny said, "but he seems to be handling it well."

"He's handling it better than I am," Kayla admitted as she dabbed her eyes with a tissue.

"You understand the implications," Jenny noted. "For you, it's much bigger than it is for him. All he knows is that he sees memories that belong to someone else—you understand that he's in it for a lifetime."

Kayla let out a deep-rooted sigh. "So, what do you make of this? What do you think is going on?"

"Let's have a seat," Jenny said, remembering a similar conversation she'd had with Susan, where she'd been on the receiving end of the news.

Being seated had definitely been helpful; it prevented her from collapsing. "I know it's your house, but can I get you something to drink?"

After Jenny got Kayla settled with a glass of wine, she sat down and began to explain, "My husband and I think that Devon may have picked up this spirit on the way home from Disney. Perhaps you drove through the area where Matthew's spirit had lingered, and Matthew recognized the opportunity when it appeared in front of him." Jenny leaned forward onto her elbows. "I hadn't really considered this before, but I think spirits have the ability to seek out people who can hear them. I don't know what the draw is—how they know they're being heard—but I know one particular girl was able to find me just hours after her life had been taken, and she had lived about a half an hour away from me. Another spirit pulled me in while I was just driving through on the highway, kind of like you were."

"Well, didn't you say that psychics can recognize each other? There must be some kind of signal you send out."

"Indeed there must be," Jenny acknowledged. "I will say, though, that Devon is very lucky in the sense that this *Matthew*—whoever he is—is not inflicting any of his pain on Devon. At times, I have actually been able to feel the physical pain of the victims, and I imagine what Matthew went through must have been excruciating. The fact that he has spared Devon of that says something about his character—and his intentions, for that matter. He's not trying to harm Devon in any way—he most likely just wants to get a message across."

"But what is the message?" Kayla asked.

"That, I don't know," Jenny admitted. "And I will say that we face an extra challenge considering the go-between is a five-year-old child. Nothing against Devon or anything, but it might be hard for him to try to figure out what Matthew is trying to say. The issue itself might be too complicated for him to understand, so even if Matthew presents him with very clear clues, Devon may not be able to articulate what he's seeing."

"So then why choose Devon?" Kayla's despair had resurfaced. "Why tell your story to someone who won't be able to communicate it?"

Jenny smiled, placing her hand on top of Kayla's. "Do you know how rare the gift is? Who knows how long Matthew has lingered there, just waiting for someone who can hear him. When Devon drove through, I imagine Matthew was just grateful to have *someone* to listen." Jenny sat back in her chair. "Though admittedly not ideal, better to have a child tell your story than no one at all."

Kayla shook her head, once again saying, "But why Devon? Why did he get this gift?"

"I don't know," Jenny admitted. "In my family it's genetic. Do you know of anyone in either of your families that have this ability?"

Shaking her head, Kayla emphatically said, "No. Not at all."

Jenny thought about the other explanation, realizing it may be a difficult topic to bring up. Clearing her throat she asked, "Well, has Devon ever been near death himself?"

Kayla's eyes grew wide, her expression as serious as could be. "When he was born," she began, "he stopped breathing for a while. A long while. The doctors were able to revive him, and he's made a full recovery." She frowned as she added, "Although, they said he did defy the odds..."

Raising her eyes to meet Kayla's, Jenny explained, "That may be what happened, then. If Devon had stopped breathing for long enough, he may have started to cross over, only for the doctors to come along and bring him back. If that's true, it's possible that his connection to the other side is still open, allowing him to receive messages from people who have passed."

"But won't that overwhelm him? Hearing messages from all those people?" Kayla looked to be on the verge of tears again.

"Honestly, I don't think it will be that many people. Most folks cross over after they pass away because they are at peace. It's only the ones with a message to send who linger and allow themselves to be heard."

"So what have most of your messages been about?" Kayla asked.

Jenny didn't want to answer, but she knew she had to. Refusing to allow her reluctance to be visible on her face, Jenny plainly said, "They usually want their killer to be found."

Chapter 2

"Did you see his shirt?" Zack asked as he unzipped his suitcase at the hotel. "He looked like such a cool little dude in that plaid." He glanced up at Jenny and added, "I want our son to dress like that."

"She might prefer pink," Jenny replied as she ran a comb through her hair. When she noticed Zack had returned his attention to his suitcase, she reached up and lowered the thermostat a degree.

"You and your silly fantasies," Zack said. "Like that baby might actually be a girl..."

Jenny shrugged one shoulder and put her brush back in her toiletry bag. Picking up her cell phone, she pressed the series of buttons to reach the alarm feature. "The plan is to pick up Kayla and Devon at eight. What time do you want to get up?"

After thinking a moment, Zack announced, "Six forty-five sounds good." Getting dressed into his night clothes, he asked, "Does Kayla have *any* indication where Devon had first mentioned Matthew? Are we going to end up driving all the way to Disney?"

"I hope not," Jenny noted. "She said she thought it was later in the trip—which was a *return* trip—so that would mean closer to home. Either way, we should bring our suitcases with us, just in case we need to get a hotel somewhere else tomorrow. She is under the impression that it will be at least an hour away, and if we do end up finding something out, I'd rather stay closer to the action."

"Fair enough." Zack slid under the covers, with Jenny following suit shortly after. He cuddled up his body close to hers, tracing his finger up and down her arm.

Jenny knew what he was doing. "Sorry, chief, but I think you might be fighting a losing battle."

"Are you sure you can't be convinced?" He kissed her on the shoulder.

"I feel like I ate a bus and all the people inside it; I'm pretty sure I'm not in the mood."

Zack flipped over onto his back. "You sure were a lot different a few months ago."

"I know," Jenny said, "but, sadly, that ship has sailed. I think it was a second trimester thing."

"I liked the second trimester."

Jenny laughed. "I'm sure you did. But hey…do you remember you once said my extra desire was proof that I was having a boy? What does it say now that I don't want to be touched?" She smiled slyly. "Twin girls?"

"Larrabees don't make girls."

"Well," Jenny said, "I guess we'll find out in a couple of months."

Jenny had been driving the Moore's minivan for over an hour, with Zack in the passenger seat and Kayla and Devon in the middle row. The young boy had been talking and fidgeting the entire ride, exhausting every adult in the car. As the signs for Columbia, South Carolina started to appear on the highway, Kayla posed, "Now do you see why we drove home from Disney overnight? It's the only way we could make such a long journey in peace."

"Little man sure can talk," Zack noted.

"Yes," Kayla agreed. "Yes he can."

"The bad place is coming," Devon said nonchalantly.

Jenny looked in the rearview mirror as Kayla turned to her son.

"What do you mean *the bad place is coming*?" Kayla asked.

Devon focused on the toy truck in his hand. "The bad place. The place where the fire was. We're near it."

Feeling nothing out of the ordinary, Jenny wished there was a way Devon could have taken the wheel. "Should I get off the highway, honey?"

Jenny immediately realized that question was clearly above a five-year-old's head; he didn't reply.

How on earth was Jenny supposed to know where to go if Devon couldn't provide her with directions? Was this going to be a very long day of trial and error? Just as a bit of panic was about to set in, Jenny began to feel a slight pull. She gave Zack a nod and a thumbs up, wordlessly letting him know that she had received the signal and everything was under control. Putting on her blinker, she moved over to the right lane, although her urge to exit the highway didn't become strong until several miles later.

She took a right at the end of the exit ramp onto a road that had the typical restaurants and gas stations that flanked a major highway. After a quarter mile, the tourist-centered businesses stopped, replaced by suburban offices and shopping centers. The tug led her down some long and winding side streets that eventually turned rural. Houses and stores were replaced by hay bales and sparse farmhouses in varying states of decay. Some of the barns looked as if they were on the verge of collapse, weathered and splintered from decades without care.

Just before the narrow country road took a sharp left, Jenny listened to her instinct and parked the car on the side of the road.

Devon chimed in from the back seat. "You need to keep going."

"The road goes that way," Jenny replied, pointing with her left hand, "and we need to go this way." She shifted her arm to point in the opposite direction.

"We *do* need to go this way," Devon said, confirming Jenny's desire to go right. "But it's far...too far to walk. We need to keep driving."

Jenny glanced over at Zack; although the tug in her stomach was still strong, she recognized that she had no idea how far the destination was. Perhaps the kindergartener in the back seat had better insight. "You're saying we shouldn't bother trying to walk there?" Jenny posed.

"We *need* to go," Devon protested, sounding as if he were on the verge of a tantrum. "We have to get there."

Jenny liked it better when the divine inspiration came from within herself. "What's there?" she asked Devon. "What do we need to see?"

"The bad place," he repeated.

Jenny turned around to see his eyes reflected a sense of urgency. "But you said it's too far to walk."

"It is," Devon said. He shifted his gaze from Jenny to the window, looking longingly in the direction that Jenny herself wanted to go. The anxiety in his eyes turned to sadness as he added, "But we have to get there."

Jenny sighed in frustration, desperately wishing she could provide this boy with some answers.

Zack held up his phone. "I've figured out where we are, and it looks like Devon wants to head northwest of here. Maybe we can grab some lunch or something and do a little research on the area…you know, see if there have been any fatal fires in the past…three-hundred years."

Jenny focused on Devon's heartbroken face. "How does that sound, sweetie? We'll leave here for now, but we'll try to figure out what's the best way to get to the bad place." Jenny's face bore an expression of compassion. "I promise you, honey…we'll get you there. We will absolutely not go home until you've been to the place you want to go."

With one long last look out the window, Devon nodded slightly. Satisfied that she had helped him as much as she could at that moment, Jenny turned the car around and headed back toward civilization. She felt much better once Devon announced, "I want chicken nuggets. Mom, can we get chicken nuggets?" He seemed to be back to his old, carefree self.

"Sure, honey, we can go to a place that has chicken nuggets."

"Chicken nuggets," Devon repeated with swinging feet. "Chicken nuggets. Chicken nuggets. Chicken nuggets…"

Jenny pressed on the gas pedal, trying to make the trip just a little bit shorter.

Devon practically ran to the booth in the restaurant, climbing into his seat first and immediately tinkering with the wrapped silverware. Kayla took the knife from him, instead handing him a tablet that was encased in a thick, bright blue case. Jenny figured that was the child-friendly tablet that Kayla had referred to the night before.

Looking apologetic, Kayla said, "I guess you've figured out that he is hyperactive." She put her arm lovingly around her son, who had already busied himself with a video game. "The doctors seem to think that's a result of his inability to breathe when he was first born. His cognition is good; he just has a lot of trouble focusing and sitting still."

Jenny nodded. "A lot of kids have it. I saw it quite a bit when I taught elementary school."

"All things considered," Kayla continued, "I realize we are very lucky. He could have had brain damage or even died, had the doctors not been able to revive him so quickly." She smiled lovingly at Devon. "But instead I have a perfectly healthy, intelligent, squirmy little guy whose brain runs a mile a minute…as does his mouth."

"I've got to say," Zack noted, "coming from a family of mostly boys, he doesn't act that different from a lot of the kids in my family." He shrugged with one shoulder. "I had just attributed his behavior to the y chromosome."

Jenny turned to Kayla, announcing, "That y chromosome does do some strange things to people."

"Don't I know it?" Kayla replied with a chuckle. "But this little guy does have some bigger challenges to conquer than just being a boy." She glanced up at Zack. "No offense."

"Believe me," Zack said, "none taken."

After everyone reviewed the menu and placed their orders, Zack pulled his laptop out of his bag and placed it on the table. Kayla took that opportunity to check her phone; she looked pleased with the results. "Miss Thorton emailed me," she said to Devon. "You have a couple of worksheets to do tonight, but I can help you with those."

The day of the week occurred to Jenny. "Oh yeah—I guess he did miss school today."

Kayla nodded. "I sent a message to his teacher, letting her know I'd be keeping him out of school—and why. She agreed that it's more important to get to the bottom of what's happening to him. She's just as worried about him as I am."

Zack apparently hadn't been paying attention to the conversation. "I've got the location called up," he announced, "but unfortunately it looks like there's a whole lot of 'not much' to the north and west of where we were…the direction Devon wanted to go."

"Let me see," Jenny said as she leaned in. "Wow, you weren't kidding," she added with a curled lip. "It just looks like farmland and trees."

"And when I zoom out and put it on the map view instead of the satellite view," Zack added, "there's not even a town name anywhere near where we were. The closest one is Cumberland, but even that isn't very close. It's literally like the *bad place* was in the middle of nowhere."

Kayla chimed in, "Do you think a farmhouse could have caught on fire?"

"It's possible," Jenny said. "The hard part is we don't even know what time frame we're talking about. This sprit could be from the seventeen-hundreds or from last year. The landscape could have looked a lot different once upon a time."

"His name doesn't even help," Zack noted. "It's not particularly modern or anything to indicate it was recent, or a name like Ebenezer that would definitely be from a long time ago."

Ebenezer? Jenny shook her head rapidly.

Zack continued, "The name *Matthew* could be from any time since they settled Jamestown."

Jenny strummed her fingers on the table. "Maybe we should just do a general search for deadly fires that occurred in this area. A news article might be able to tell us what era we're talking about…and what happened."

As Zack typed buttons on his computer, Jenny asked to look at Devon's drawings one more time; Kayla had brought the pictures with her in a manila folder.

Using the skills she had learned as an elementary school teacher, Jenny tried to decipher exactly what was depicted in the sketches. Despite her best efforts, she was coming up empty. Flipping one of the pictures around so it faced Devon, she slid it over in the child's direction. "What is this a picture of, sweetheart?"

Devon glanced up briefly from his tablet. "The fire." He returned to his game.

Jenny looked at him intently. "What's on fire?"

"Everything. The whole room."

"Do you know what started the fire?"

Devon kept his eyes glued to his video game as he said, "It's a present." Jenny realized he must have been talking about something related to his video game. Devon's young age and short attention span were surely going to pose a challenge.

Jenny continued nonetheless. "Did someone you know start the fire?"

"Nope."

"Did a stranger start the fire?"

Devin pressed the screen of his tablet as he emphatically announced, "Click."

"Did a stranger start the fire, honey?"

"Nobody started the fire."

Nobody started the fire. Could it have been an accident? She picked up the picture and put it back in the pile with the others, flipping through the rest of the drawings until another one caught her eye. "Devon, can you tell me what this red mark is?" She once again placed a picture in front of him, pointing to the red splotch that she had noticed the night before.

With another quick glance, Devon announced, "It's blood."

"Whose blood, sweetie?"

"Matthew's," Devon declared nonchalantly. "He hit his head."

Jenny made eye contact with Kayla, whose expression showed the apprehension that Jenny felt. Looking back at Devon, she asked, "When did he hit his head...before the fire or during it?"

The young child looked up toward the ceiling, closing one eye and sticking out his tongue as he concentrated. "At the same time." He returned his attention to the tablet.

"Where did he hit his head?" Jenny asked. "What part of his head?"

Devon raised one hand and tapped the right side of his own head, just above his temple.

"How did he hit his head? Did he fall, or run into something, or did someone hit him...?"

"He fell."

"Was he trying to get out of the fire when he fell?"

Shaking his little head, Devon said, "He fell because someone knocked the floor out from under him."

"I can't find anything," Zack said long after their food had arrived. "When I search for fires, all that comes up are fire stations in the area, and maybe the occasional fire safety class."

Glancing in his direction, Jenny asked, "Do you think this may have been from a very long time ago—too long ago to be featured in an article on the Internet?"

"It's possible," Zack said with a shrug. "There's definitely nothing standing out on here as our incident, and I think if something had happened in the recent past, it would be popping up."

"Maybe we should go to a fire department," Kayla noted, "or even a police station. Perhaps they could tell us if something has happened around here recently…or maybe even not-so-recently. Even if the fire is from two-hundred years ago, there may be some folklore about it."

Jenny pointed her fork in Kayla's direction. "That is genius."

She shrugged. "Sometimes people can tell you things that websites can't."

With a humble smile, Jenny remarked, "I guess I need to be reminded of that sometimes."

Kayla turned to Devon as Jenny pulled the minivan into the fire station parking lot. "Do you want to see some fire trucks?"

Arms and legs immediately started flailing from behind the seat belt. Jenny couldn't help but smile.

The van came to rest in the space closest to the building. Before long, Devon had jumped out of the car and charged toward the open firehouse door.

About a half-dozen men and a woman sat around a table, all wearing navy blue t-shirts and matching pants. "Let me guess," a gray-haired man said to Devon as the little one bounded into the station. "You'd like to take a tour of the firehouse…and see a fire truck."

Devon stopped in his tracks, clenched his hands into fists, and screamed, "Fire truck!"

When Kayla finally caught up to him, she discretely corrected his behavior.

The firefighter who had addressed them turned to the youngest person at the table. "Rookie...go show this young man around, would ya?"

Without a complaint, the newest member of the department stood up and took Devon by the hand. "Come on, buddy," he said. "I'll show you the truck first." The two quickly disappeared from sight.

Jenny wrung her hands awkwardly and confessed to the remaining firefighters, "We're actually here for our own benefit more so than his."

The older gentleman laughed. "Do *you* want to take a tour of the truck?"

Jenny also giggled. "No, that's not it." She twisted her face as she posed, "I'm wondering if you can tell me if there's been a fatal fire in the area...specifically one to the north and west of Route 489."

"Recently?" one of them asked.

Jenny knew she looked foolish when she replied, "I don't know."

The gray-haired man spoke. "Well, there was that train fire back in the 1960s..."

Chapter 3

Devon's words flooded Jenny's mind: *Matthew had hit his head because somebody knocked the floor out from under him.* That certainly could have been a five-year-old's way of describing a train crash.

Kayla made a sound that caused Jenny to glance over her shoulder; she had her head in her hands, looking as if she was making every effort to keep her composure. Jenny placed her hand on Kayla's shoulder.

The firefighters all shared the same puzzled expression, which Jenny completely understood. She used her free hand to point in the direction that Devon had just gone. "That boy in there," she began. "He is a very special child, born with an amazing gift. He's been speaking of a man named Matthew who died in a fire, and he led us to a spot on Route 489, telling us that's where the fire was. It's a place where the road takes a sharp left, but he had told us that he wanted to go right. He also said the place he wanted to go was too far to walk." She looked at the crowd of faces in front of her. "Does that sound like it could be the area where the train crash took place?"

"Route 489 is a long road," the gray-haired man noted.

"I can call it up on my laptop," Zack offered, "and show you exactly where we're talking about."

After a painfully long and awkward computer boot, Zack was finally able to point to where they suspected the accident had taken place. The gray-haired man nodded in acknowledgement. "Yup. The fire was right about here." He pointed to an area of the screen that appeared to be frighteningly desolate.

"But it doesn't show train tracks there," Zack noted, looking at the computer. "Not on the map view or the satellite view."

"Those tracks don't get used anymore. They're all overgrown now, and I imagine they wouldn't appear on any current maps."

Zack glanced at Jenny. "I guess that explains it."

Jenny addressed the gray-haired man. "What happened in the train accident?"

"It was an explosion, actually, caused by somebody lighting a match too close to an oxygen tank," he explained.

"Somebody lit a match?" Jenny asked with surprise. "Why would someone do that?"

"Oh, young one," the firefighter replied with a smirk, "smoking was allowed on trains back in the sixties. Anyway, that explosion immediately started a fire, and the railcar was quickly engulfed in flames. Unfortunately, they were traveling at a high rate of speed when it happened, so by the time the engineer figured out what was going on and was able to get the train to stop, the fire had already killed eleven people."

"That's terrible," Kayla said breathlessly.

"To make matters worse, it happened in a desolate area. Crews weren't able to get there in time to do any good. All of the people who were rescued were done so by other passengers on the train. They pulled people out of the windows and the holes that were created by the explosion."

Jenny couldn't imagine the chaos. She determined that even those who survived couldn't truly claim they'd escaped—their dreams must have still been haunted by the sights, sounds and smells of that awful day.

Zack seemed much less affected by the story; he had simply restructured his search and announced, "Now that I know what to look for, there's a lot of information about the explosion."

"Does it give a list of the victims?" Jenny asked.

Taking some time to scan through a few articles, Zack finally announced, "This one does." He glanced up at Jenny. "It looks like our victim was named Matthew Ingram and he was thirty-nine years old."

Jenny's shoulders sank; somehow that extra information made it even sadder.

"Let me get this straight," one of the younger firefighters began, pointing to the door Devon had left through. "That boy in there knew that this *Matthew Ingram* had died fifty years ago on that train?"

Kayla said, "I don't think he knew it was a train; he just knew that someone named Matthew had died in a fire. We're not even from around here...we drove down from North Carolina specifically to figure out who Matthew was."

The man looked with awe at the door. "That's amazing."

Zack nonchalantly referred to Jenny with his thumb. "She has the gift, too. She's just not getting contacted by this particular spirit."

Overcome with awkwardness, Jenny rolled her eyes and smiled. "Yes," she confessed, "I do have it, too, and one thing I've learned over the years is that the deceased don't bother to contact one of us unless something is terribly wrong. The ones who are at peace just cross over and are never heard from again."

"Most of the time," Zack added, "the sprits who linger want us to find out who killed them, but in this case, it sounds like his death was an accident." He looked curiously at Jenny. "I wonder what he could want, then."

Jenny shrugged and shook her head. "I guess our next job is to find that out."

With Devon and Kayla taking advantage of the hotel's indoor pool, Zack and Jenny sat in the restaurant in the lobby and conducted their research.

"It looks like what that guy said is true," Zack noted. "The accident happened on March twenty-fourth, 1961. They determined the explosion must have occurred when someone lit a match. They found the remains of an oxygen tank on board, and they concluded the tank and the open flame were most likely too close to each other."

At that moment, Jenny's phone rang, and she was pleased to see Kyle Buchanan was the caller. "Well, hello, world's-best-private-investigator."

"Hello to you, world's-best-psychic."

"I'm not so sure about that," Jenny said with a smile. "There's a little boy in a swimming pool not so far from me who might give me a run for my money." Preparing a pen and paper, she asked, "Were you able to find anything out?"

"Sure was. It appears Matthew Ingram was from Terryville, South Carolina, which is about sixty miles south of the accident site."

Jotting that down, Jenny smiled and replied, "That's good information. Thanks."

"No problem. Hey, I also discovered he was buried in a family plot in Landover, Ohio, in case you want to visit him for any reason."

"We just may want to do that," Jenny said, even though the thought hadn't occurred to her before. "And knowing where he lived, now we can see where he most likely caught the train. The site of the accident is apparently too remote for us to conveniently get to, but hopefully we can gather some information by being where Matthew had been just prior to the explosion."

"I hope it works for you," Kyle said. "Do me a favor and keep me posted. I would love to hear what you find out. I have to admit this whole thing still fascinates me."

"It fascinates me, too," Jenny confessed, "and I'm the one living with it."

She concluded her call with Kyle and focused on Zack. "Okay, my dear…here's your newest challenge. If you were living in Terryville, South Carolina in 1961, and you were catching a train on a rail line that is now defunct, at what station would you board said train?"

Zack took a deep breath. "This may not be an easy search."

"But that's why it's in your hands, dear. You're so *savvy*." Jenny fluttered her eyelashes at him repeatedly, emulating southern charm.

"Flattery will get you everywhere," Zack replied as he began typing. Jenny sat back in her chair as Zack conducted his research, her mind wandering. Without the distraction of the investigation to focus on, she realized just how hot she was. Using her hand as a fan, she contemplated joining the Moores in the indoor pool, but she quickly thought better of it. The room that housed the pool was about a thousand degrees and reeked of chlorine; she ultimately determined she was better off sweating it out in the lobby.

After what seemed like an eternity, Zack announced, "I think I finally have it." He tilted his laptop screen toward Jenny. "It looks like the nearest train station was about fifteen miles from Terryville in a small town called Sparta." Pointing at the image, he added, "If he was to catch the train anywhere, I would imagine it would have been from here."

"Okay, so how far are we from that station?"

"About an hour."

Jenny glanced at the clock. "I guess it's about time we get a jumpy little wet guy out of the pool."

The abandoned station had a giant pothole on the platform and boards with a *keep out* sign covering the front door. The windows were broken and graffiti tagged the cobweb-covered walkway. It looked nothing short of eerie—the kind of building that neighborhood kids would dare each other to enter. For a moment Jenny chuckled at the irony—perhaps the station really did have lingering spirits. She wondered how many kids would actually accept the dare if they knew that.

Jenny took Devon by the hand as they walked closer to the station. Sounds started to fill Jenny's ears—horrible sounds: screeching brakes, terrified women shrieking and men howling in pain. She turned to look at the little boy next to her, desperately hoping he was being spared from the horrific noises that swarmed around Jenny's brain.

"Do you hear that?" she whispered.

Devon looked up at her innocently. "You mean the birds?"

Relief washed over Jenny. "Yes, honey. I mean the birds." Whoever this Matthew was, he seemed to have mercy on his five-year-old conduit. Jenny's respect for Matthew Ingram grew at that moment, making her all the more determined to figure out the message he was trying to send.

The screams were distracting to the point of being debilitating. Jenny closed her eyes, trying to calm herself enough to get some kind of message. It appeared Matthew's spirit may have been stuck in the throes of the accident; was there something specific from that moment in time he wanted her to know? Or was he just unable to get past the horror of it?

In a second, the screams all stopped, exiting Jenny's head in a sudden and dizzying swirl. For the brief moment that followed, she saw the station the way it had looked in its prime—the windows intact, the building free of spray paint and the overgrown weeds replaced with neat landscaping. People bustled on the platform in every direction, although Jenny's attention was drawn to one face in particular. A pretty, dirty-blond woman stood near her, dressed style reminiscent of Jackie Kennedy. The mystery woman glanced in Jenny's direction and flashed a subtle smile before dissolving out of sight.

Jenny kept her eyes closed for an additional second, committing the contours of the woman's face to memory, before turning to the young boy holding her hand. "What are you seeing?"

"I see an old building," Devon said, pointing to the station itself. "Somebody broke the window."

Was it possible that Jenny was the only one receiving a vision? "Do you see anything else? Is Matthew visiting you?"

Devon shook his head. "No, but he's been here." He raised his free hand to point down the abandoned tracks. "The bad place is that way."

Jenny squatted down to look at the young boy at eye level. "Do you know what I want to do, sweetie? I want to draw. Do you like to draw?"

With wide, adorable eyes, Devon nodded silently.

"So, what do you say we find a store that sells paints and crayons, and we sit down somewhere and make some pictures?"

Jenny tried to ignore the fact that she was sweltering as she sat at a picnic table next to Devon. The sun was beginning to set, so she was optimistic that the temperature would only get lower as the evening progressed.

Devon busied himself with his own drawings as Jenny reproduced the image of the woman at the train station. For fun, Zack and Kayla drew their own pictures, too.

"I think I am the worst artist that ever lived," Zack said flatly, holding up his picture and regarding it with a furrowed brow.

"No, I'm pretty sure that honor belongs to me," Kayla replied with a smile, showing Zack her paper. "I'm not even sure what this is supposed to be."

"I'm good at drawing," Devon announced in typical kindergartener style.

Kayla smiled. "Yes, honey, you are very good at drawing." She looked over at his picture. "What are you making?"

"Fire," he said innocently as his feet swung under the picnic table.

"Is the train on fire?" Zack asked.

Looking a little confused, Devon replied, "It's a school bus, but some of the seats are sideways."

"He's never seen the inside of a train," Kayla explained. "I guess a school bus is the only point of reference he has."

"I can fix that," Zack said, pulling out his phone. He called up an image of the inside of a train from the 1960s, turning the picture toward Devon. "Is this what you're talking about?"

After a quick glance and a nod, Devon simply said, "Uh-huh."

Jenny leaned back as her colored pencil made its last sweeps across her paper. "Hey, Devon," she called, turning her drawing so the boy could see the finished product. "Do you know who this woman is?"

He looked at the image for only a second before his eyes rose to meet Jenny's. "That's Julia."

"Julia," Jenny repeated. "Who is Julia?"

With an expression more serious than any Jenny had ever seen him wear, Devon replied, "She's my wife."

Jenny exchanged worried glances with the other adults at the table. "She's your wife?"

With a subtle nod Devon added, "Have you seen her? I've been looking all over for her."

Chapter 4

The fact that he spoke in first person was worrisome to Jenny, but she decided to respond in kind. "Was she on the train with you?"

Confusion set in to Devon's little eyes. He stuck out his lip, shrugged his shoulders and returned to his drawing. His feet resumed their fidgety swing.

Zack discretely pulled his phone out of his pocket, pressing some buttons without saying a word. Jenny and Kayla both remained silent, the gravity of the moment taking a little time to sink in.

"There was no one by that name on the list of victims," Zack eventually stated in a soft but serious tone. "If she was on the train, then she was one of the survivors."

"She was definitely at the platform," Jenny said, "but that doesn't mean she got on the train with him. She may have been waiting with him so she could say goodbye when he boarded."

"The sad thing is she only meant to say *so long*," Zack noted. "I'm sure she had no idea it was going to be goodbye."

Jenny held up her hand to get him to stop talking. "Too sad to think about."

She meant it.

She got her own phone out of her purse and called Kyle. If anyone could determine Julia Ingram's whereabouts—then and now—it would be him. After putting in a request to track her down, Jenny ended her call and returned her attention to the people at the picnic table. Devon was still wrapped up in his drawing, so Jenny casually said to the adults, "I noticed the use of the word *I* in his last statement."

Kayla nodded. "He does that sometimes, and those are the moments that frighten me the most."

"But it's not always like that," Jenny observed.

Shaking her head, Kayla added, "No...he often describes the situation like he's an observer, but every once in a while he recounts it as if it's his own memory—like M-a-t-t-h-e-w is doing the talking *through* him."

Jenny respected Kayla's desire to keep Devon in the dark by spelling.

Looking very serious, Kayla added, "Even his demeanor changes. You know as well as I do that he constantly runs around like a wild man—but when uses the word *I,* he has a maturity about him that makes me feel like it's not even him in there."

Jenny glanced down at the little boy who was wiggling while he drew and wondered exactly what he experienced when he had a contact. Did Devon temporarily stop existing within his own body? Had Matthew taken over somehow? She didn't think Devon would be able to explain it, even if she asked. He would most likely need to mature quite a bit before he could describe what went on in that gifted little mind of his.

"Well, I'm hoping we're on the right track to getting M-a-t-t-h-e-w the answers he's looking for," Jenny announced. "It seems he may just want to know where his wife is. If Kyle can track her down, maybe M-a-t-t-h-e-w will be satisfied and cross over."

Kayla didn't look appeased. "But what about next time? If he really does have this gift like you say he does, won't this keep happening?"

Jenny considered the possibilities. Suppose Devon got contacted by somebody with more evil intentions? Considering he seemed to think—and even act—as if he was the spirit himself, would he have been susceptible to behaviors he otherwise wouldn't engage in? Could he have ultimately found himself in a lot of trouble carrying out deeds that weren't of his own doing?

Looking compassionately at Kayla, Jenny said, "I think you should get this little boy to a doctor...not for treatment, but rather for documentation…let someone know that sometimes he may not be acting under his own free will. If it makes you feel any better, I'd be willing to talk to his doctor and explain the situation. I have the names of a few law enforcement officers who can testify to the validity of my gift—hopefully that will give *me* credibility when I attest to Devon's psychic ability." She smiled before adding, "It's probably best to have this on record *before* anything becomes an issue. It'll be a much harder sell if you try to convince people of his ability afterward."

"After what?" Kayla asked with a look of concern.

Jenny didn't know how to answer that; suddenly she wished she hadn't said anything at all. "After anything that comes his way."

Mercifully, Zack interjected, "I've done a little math…if our deceased friend was thirty-nine in 1961, then he was born in 1922, give or take, depending on when his birthday fell. Now, if convention dictates, his wife was probably around the same age, so that would mean she's in her nineties now—if she's even still alive."

"If she's not," Jenny noted, "that might give M-a-t-t-h-e-w the incentive to cross over. If he wants to find her, he needs to look on the other side."

"Do you think the spirits have a sense of time?" Kayla asked. "Does M-a-t-t-h-e-w even know he's been gone for over 50 years? Or do you think it all feels like yesterday to him?"

Jenny reflected back to her other cases. "I'm pretty sure they do have a sense of time, or at least some of them do. My first case involved a man who knew his *teenage girlfriend*," she said with finger quotes, "was currently in her eighties in a nursing home. His spirit had hovered around her throughout her life, though, watching her grow old. While I'm not sure it felt like sixty years to him, I do believe he knew the time had passed."

Devon wordlessly scooted himself off the picnic bench and started to run around the grassy area nearby. Kayla reached over and lifted up his picture, turning it toward herself. She lowered her eyebrows and shook her head with a loud sigh. "It breaks my heart to think about what he sees in his mind."

She placed the picture down flat on the picnic table so Zack and Jenny could see it. While the details were difficult to discern, the flames were quite clear. Jenny didn't respond, simply because she didn't know what to say.

Zack seemed to remain in his own little world. "Do you think if we either introduced Devon to Julia—or else showed him her grave—Matthew would get the idea and move on?"

"Maybe," Jenny replied. She raised her eyes to meet Kayla's. "Is that something you'd be willing to do?"

She seemed to give the notion some thought. "I don't really want to bring my five-year-old to a cemetery, but if that's what it takes to get Matthew to be on his merry way, I am fully on board with the idea." Tears looked as if they were on their way to the surface. "I'm willing to do anything to help my son."

Unpacking their luggage for the second time in two days, Jenny and Zack made themselves comfortable in their new hotel room. This hotel was closer to the abandoned train station, the only place Jenny had been able to get an informative reading.

The sound of Jenny's cell phone interrupted the unpacking. "Hello, Kyle."

"Hello to you, Jenny."

"Were you able to track down Julia Ingram?"

"I was," Kyle announced, "but unfortunately you won't be able to talk to her."

Jenny had suspected this would be the answer she'd receive. "She passed away?"

"Back in 2005."

"Okay, then, we go with plan B. Do you have any idea where she's buried?"

"I do," Kyle said. "She's buried in Portland Cemetery in Harbor Falls, South Carolina."

Jenny pursed her lips. "Huh," she said as she contemplated the implications.

"What's the matter?" Kyle asked.

"You had said Matthew was buried in Ohio...I wonder if that's going to cause a problem."

"Because they're not together?"

"Exactly. Do you think maybe that's why he's been looking for her? He wants to be laid to rest next to her?"

"I don't know," Kyle said, "but he's in for a double-whammy if that's true. Not only *isn't* Julia buried next to Matthew, but she *is* buried next to her second husband."

Jenny grimaced. "Oh, dear."

"I did find out one other thing for you. Julia and Matthew had a child—a daughter named Mary—who is still very much alive, although her married name is now Mary Walker."

"How old is Mary?"

"Sixty-two. She's living in Mason, South Carolina now."

After a little math in her head, Jenny declared, "So she was about ten when the train accident happened?"

"Thereabouts."

"I'm guessing she should remember her father, then," Jenny deduced.

"Presumably."

The wheels in Jenny's mind were turning. "Do you happen to have her contact information?"

"Would I be the world's best private investigator if I didn't?"

Jenny couldn't sleep. Her brain kept running through the conversation she would inevitably have with Mary Walker. Of all the strange phone calls she'd had to make, this one would certainly top the list. *Hello, Ms. Walker...I have a five-year-old boy here who, at times, claims he is your deceased father.* Even though Kayla was okay with the idea of Devon meeting Mary, would *Mary* be okay with that? And if Mary wasn't going to agree to a meeting, what would Jenny do to convince Matthew to cross over? Bringing Devon to Portland Cemetery to see Julia's grave could have actually done more harm than good considering it wasn't next to Matthew. Would that have made him angry? If so, how would he react? Would that put Devon in danger?

Her thought process shifted gears to Julia's decision to be buried next to her second husband as opposed to her first. She had died in 2005, which meant she was most likely in her eighties when she passed. If she had been in her thirties when she lost Matthew, that meant she could have spent more than half her life with her second husband. Had he really been the man she considered to be her life partner? Is that why she chose to be laid to rest with him as opposed to the man she only got to spend a short time with?

Jenny thought about what a difficult decision that must have been for Julia. She imagined herself in the same situation. Being buried with her first husband, Greg, was not even a remote option, but considering that marriage ended in divorce, nobody would have expected that. She and Greg didn't even like each other, after all. But suppose—God forbid—she became widowed in the near future while her love for Zack was fully intact. Suppose she also met another man in a few years and spent four or five decades with him. Would she really go back and get buried next to Zack? Or would she stay next to the man with whom she'd grown old?

What a heartbreaking decision poor Julia had to make.

Returning to the matter at hand, Jenny forced her mind back to the issues concerning Matthew. What if he had gone to his grave assuming Julia would eventually be buried next to him? Was he still waiting for her? Was that why he said he was looking for her?

Was this why he lingered?

"None of this is doing any good," Jenny said to herself in a frustrated whisper. "You need sleep." She rolled clumsily onto her right side, bringing the pillow that rested between her legs with her. Soon after, she remembered her obstetrician's advice to always sleep on her left side, so she reversed the process and resumed the same position she had tried to get out of before. A heavy sigh escaped her.

For a moment, she contemplated how desperate she was to lie face-down; she had always been a stomach sleeper, and she hadn't been able to get in that position for several months now. She began to fantasize about finding a nice beach somewhere and digging a giant hole in the sand for her stomach to fit in; then she could lie face-down for hours and hours and hours...

Lovely thought, Jenny concluded, but not immediately helpful. She threw off the covers and put her feet on the floor, trudging across the room to the laptop that was charging on the dresser. Taking a seat in the only chair the hotel room had to offer, she opened the computer and began to do some research. If she wasn't sleeping anyway, she figured she could at least make some use of her time.

After a few minutes of searching, she sat back in the chair and whispered, "Holy shit."

Chapter 5

"Devon's not alone," Jenny told Zack over breakfast in the lobby. She was having a difficult time shaking her fatigue—a direct result of her inability to catch any decent sleep the night before. Nonetheless, she poked at her scrambled eggs and continued, "There are apparently other kids who have made similar claims. They have memories they simply shouldn't have—they know things that a child their age shouldn't know."

"What kind of things?" Zack began to attack his plate, which was piled high with free food.

"Well, one article featured a kid who was three years old and knew how to fix a car," Jenny began. "His father was changing his oil in the driveway, and the three-year-old came out and climbed up on the fender, pointing out to his father that the antifreeze was low. The father looked, and the antifreeze *was* low. The father asked how the child knew that, and the child replied that he had been stranded on the side of the road once because his car had overheated. He said that he'd let the antifreeze get low, and he vowed he'd never allow that to happen again. The father asked exactly when the three-year-old had been stranded on the side of the road with an overheated car, and the child said, *That happened when I was Keith.* Mind you, the child's name wasn't Keith."

"Freaky," Zack said.

"Indeed. The kid went on to describe a red Mustang convertible in vivid detail, using terms a child that age wouldn't understand. Even I didn't understand it when I read it last night…it was about horsepower and liters and rims and something that involved a V." Jenny pointed at Zack with her fork. "*And* he talked about the exact intersection where he had died in a car wreck. When the dad did some research, it turned out a fatal accident involving a nineteen-year-old named Keith *did* happen there a few years before the child was born…and Keith had been driving a red Mustang convertible when the accident happened. "

"You think this kid was possessed by Keith's sprit?"

Jenny took a sip of juice, wishing it had three coffees worth of caffeine. "They called it *reincarnated* in the article." She made finger quotes. "But it sounds a lot like what is going on with Devon."

"Maybe this kid had the gift but nobody knew it?"

With a shrug Jenny said, "Maybe. I honestly don't know enough about that case to make a guess. What I did learn was that there was a doctor who had researched this case and several more like it. He came to the conclusion that something supernatural had to be going on. Kids, by nature, have vivid imaginations, but these children could recall *facts*—very specific facts about people's lives…things they never should have known."

"Maybe you can put Kayla into contact with that kid's parents," Zack noted. "It might make her feel better to know she isn't alone."

"That's a good point. I was thinking I would actually try to contact the doctor who had studied these kids. I would feel a lot more comfortable if I talked with someone who was experienced with this before I did anything that involved Devon. We're dealing with a child here. I would hate to handle this improperly and do something that would ultimately end up hurting him in the long run."

"Smart move," Zack said as he put a huge forkful of pancake in his mouth.

Even after all this time, Jenny still marveled at just how much that man could eat and stay so skinny. Maybe he had a tapeworm. Pushing that thought aside, she added, "I've already contacted Kyle, asking him to find the doctor's information. It was the middle of the night, so I sent him an email instead of calling; at this point I'm just waiting for him to get back to me. I figured, in the meantime, I could contact Mary and drop this bomb on her...that can give her some time to get used to the idea before we introduce her to Devon—if, that is, she's even willing to meet him."

"I'd think she would be," Zack said. "I'd be curious if some little boy claimed to be a deceased relative of mine."

She cocked her eyebrow at him. "You'd be curious? I might be inclined to think that the person calling me was a loony making an outrageous—and completely fictitious—claim."

Zack shrugged. "That too."

"I guess there's only one way to find out how she'll react," Jenny said with a sigh. She reluctantly pulled her phone out of her purse, looking at it motionlessly for a while; at times like this, her innocent little phone looked so intimidating. "Here goes nothing."

"I'm not even sure how to tell you this," Jenny said apprehensively, "but there's a very young boy from North Carolina who keeps claiming his name is Matthew and he died in a fire. He led us to a desolate area in South Carolina, near Cumberland, stating that's where the fire had taken place." Jenny cleared her throat, hoping her message was being well received. "He was referring to the place where the train accident that claimed your father had occurred."

The silence on the other end of the phone was deafening.

Jenny continued, "When the little boy speaks as Matthew, he claims to be looking for his wife, Julia." Jenny paused one more time before noting, "I believe that was your mother's name."

"It was," Mary said softly. She added nothing more.

"I know this is strange," Jenny said quickly and professionally, "and I'm sorry to spring this phone call on you...but this child's mother actually contacted me to try to help her son. She was very concerned by her child's behavior, for obvious reasons, and she wants some answers. Now that I know this Matthew really existed and was presumably your father, I would like to get some answers for *you* as well."

Mary seemed confused. "And who are you again?"

"My name is Jenny Larrabee; I am a psychic from Tennessee."

"A psychic from Tennessee," she repeated with suspicion.

Jenny wanted to make sure she wasn't overwhelming this poor woman. "I'm so sorry about this; I know this can't be easy for you to hear. If you want I can call you back later once this has had a chance to sink in."

"No," Mary said, clearly still in shock. "I'm fine. I-I-I'd like to discuss this more, actually. You say it's a little boy from North Carolina who claims to be my father?"

"Yes, ma'am. He is a five-year-old child with a very rare gift. He has the ability to receive messages from the deceased, but in my experiences, the spirits only bother to make contact if they have an unresolved issue." Jenny cleared her throat again. "Like I said, Matthew has mentioned that he's looking for his wife."

"She passed away a few years ago," Mary said.

"I know that," Jenny replied, "but I don't think your father knows that."

Silence penetrated the phone.

"Mary, was your mother on the train that day?" Jenny asked. "It has occurred to me that he may be concerned for her safety on the day of the explosion."

"She was," Mary replied. "In fact, we both were, but we didn't sit near my father. The train was nearly full, so he let my mother and I sit together in the back of the car, and he took one of the empty seats in the front." Her tone became sad. "That's where the explosion happened. That's why he wasn't able to get out but my mother and I were."

A chill crept up Jenny's spine. She always marveled at how such trivial decisions could end up dictating who survived and who didn't. Simply by choosing a seat in the front of the train car, Matthew sealed his fate that day. Although, if someone in his family had to die, Jenny presumed Matthew would have wanted it to be him so his wife and child could survive.

"My other thought," Jenny continued compassionately, "was that your father might be waiting for your mother to be buried next to him, although I know that isn't going to happen."

"My mother got buried with my step-father," Mary said.

Jenny nodded slightly, although Mary couldn't see that. "I know."

"She figured my father had his entire extended family around him, and my step-father would have been buried alone."

"That sounds like a very fair solution," Jenny replied sincerely, "but if that's what your father is concerned about, we may have a tougher time appeasing him."

Once again Mary was silent.

"If it makes you feel any better, I do know something wonderful is on the other side," Jenny said quickly. "Including your mother. Your father can see her again if he crosses over, so that might be a comfort to him, even if they aren't physically buried together here on earth."

More silence. Jenny began to regret bringing up that whole topic.

"On a different note," Jenny stated matter-of-factly, "there have been reports of other children who have made similar claims about being contacted by the deceased, and a doctor by the name of Albert Wilson has made a career out of studying those kids. I have started the process of trying to contact him. Ideally, I want him to come out and meet this young boy; I'm hoping he can advise me as to what is the best course of action. We are talking about a child here, so I don't want to do anything that will cause him harm in any way."

"I don't either," Mary stated emphatically.

"But if it comes down to it, I'm wondering if you'd be willing to meet the child."

"I-I-I suppose I could," Mary said, "if you think that's the right thing to do."

Relief washed over Jenny. "I'm not sure if it's the right thing to do or not," she confessed with a laugh. "That's for Dr. Wilson to decide."

Dr. Albert Wilson caught the first plane into Columbia, arriving at the hotel shortly after dinner. He appeared to be in his late forties, with what was left of his hair kept in a very short buzz-cut. He reminded Jenny of a college professor in his blazer, jeans and gold-rimmed glasses. While she had to acknowledge he was a strikingly handsome man in a distinguished sort of way, she personally felt no attraction to him.

She only felt pregnant.

In order for Jenny and Kayla to be able to talk freely with the doctor, Zack had agreed to bring Devon to a place called *The Jump Zone* that featured a series of indoor trampolines. Deep down inside, Jenny worried about Zack's ability to remain in charge of an overactive child in such a large and unstructured area, although she figured the one-to-one ratio would work in Zack's favor. Kayla, on the other hand, expressed concern for the welfare of the trampolines, wondering just how much money she was going to owe *The Jump Zone* for repairs by the time Devon left the place.

Nonetheless, the adults dove right into the business at hand, taking up shop in the hotel restaurant. "When did you say the accident happened?" Doctor Wilson asked.

"1961," Kayla replied.

The doctor took notes. "Are you aware of any living relatives of the deceased?"

"I spoke to his daughter earlier today," Jenny said.

Dr. Wilson looked at Jenny over his glasses. "What was her reaction?"

"She was shocked by the call, of course, but she seemed like she was supportive. She even agreed to meet with Devon if need be."

"That's good to know, but I'd rather hold off on that for a little while," the doctor explained. "First, I want to show the child some photographs from various points in Matthew's life and gauge his reaction. I want to see just what we're dealing with before we go any further."

"Do you think Devon is in any danger?" Kayla asked.

"Danger? No." Doctor Wilson shook his head. "Most of the children I've worked with haven't experienced any problems, aside from the occasional nightmare."

Jenny leaned forward onto her elbows. "Dr. Wilson, I have read about your work, obviously, and I find it fascinating. The one thing the articles didn't tell me, however, is how these cases got resolved. For instance, the boy who said he used to be a man named Keith who died when he crashed his Mustang...whatever happened to that child? Does he still make those claims?"

"He doesn't. In fact, as he progressed through the primary grades, the talk of Keith slowed and eventually ground to a halt. Now that boy is a teenager and has no recollection of ever speaking of anyone named Keith."

"What do you think happened to make it stop?" Kayla asked.

"I honestly can't say. All I know is that these spirits generally attach to very young host children. As the children progress through the early grades, the talk of past lives stops."

"Well, as you know," Jenny began, "I have the ability to receive messages from the deceased as well. I'm not sure if we're dealing with the same thing, though, considering I'm an adult. But when I get contacts, the spirits usually stick around until their issues get resolved. Once the spirits are satisfied, they cross over and I don't hear from them again. Is it possible that the same thing is happening with these children you study?"

"I'm inclined to believe it's not," Dr. Wilson explained. "These kids all seem to outgrow their talk of reincarnation right around age six or seven. It would be strangely coincidental if all of these spirits happened to get their issues resolved when the host children reached that particular age."

Jenny tapped her finger on the table, deep in thought. "We may be dealing with two different things, then. When I met Devon, I was instantly able to tell he has the gift, which is something that—to the best of my knowledge—doesn't go away with age. Personally, I didn't even discover my own gift until recently." She looked intently at the doctor. "What do you think is going on that gives these kids the ability to receive spirits until only age six or seven?"

"My guess has been that it has something to do with the immaturity of some portions of the young brain. I've been researching the developmental stages of the different lobes, trying to determine which neurological changes would make these youngsters no longer susceptible to outside influences."

This was becoming a little more scientific than Jenny had wanted to be. "So, they outgrow it?" she said with a smirk.

The doctor didn't return the smile. "Yes, it appears they outgrow it. Although, I am doing some comparative studies to see if there's something different about the make-up of these kids' brains that makes them predisposed to receiving supernatural contact. Most kids, obviously, don't have this ability...I want to see what makes these children different."

"In my family, it's inherited," Jenny noted, "but it started with a near-death experience of one of my ancestors. Ever since then, some of her descendants have been born with the ability."

Kayla finished the sentiment on Jenny's behalf. "My son had a near-death experience at birth. He stopped breathing shortly after he was born—for quite a while, too. Jenny seems to think that's how he got this ability."

Dr. Wilson shifted his gaze back and forth between the two women until his eyes eventually landed on Jenny. "I would love to get a look at your brain," he said in a tone which, under other circumstances, could have been perceived as flirting. "Would you be willing to submit to an MRI?"

Jenny thought about lying flat on her back in a small tube while radiation surged through her body. "Can I give birth first?"

The doctor nodded stiffly. "That sounds reasonable. Would it be okay if I called you in a few months?"

"Absolutely." Jenny thought for a brief moment before adding, "Actually, can we make it a barter?"

"A barter? What would you like to trade?"

"I'm wondering if you can introduce me to the boy who once claimed to be Keith."

Dr. Wilson was on the phone with Mary when Zack and Devon returned. Devon came running into the hotel lobby, his smile wide, eager to tell his mother all about his adventure on the trampolines. Zack walked much more slowly behind him, looking a little worse for wear. Jenny bit her lip to keep from laughing.

After Devon's long-winded and passionate description of his 'twenty-foot-high' jumps, Kayla turned to Zack and asked, "How did it go? Did he behave okay?"

"He behaved fine," Zack replied. "He just never runs out of energy."

Kayla laughed. "Don't I know it?"

"I'm exhausted and I didn't even do anything; I just watched him do his thing," Zack said. "I don't know how he can still be running around."

"He has two speeds," Kayla explained, "go, and stop. Once he lies down, he'll be asleep in thirty seconds, but then when he wakes up in the morning he'll hit the ground running...and I do mean *running*."

Zack shook his head. "I don't know how you do it."

"Why do you think we stopped after one child?" Kayla looked down at Devon. "Did you thank Mr. Zack for taking you to *The Jump Zone*?"

"Thank you," Devon replied mechanically.

"No problem, buddy."

Dr. Wilson ended his phone call and headed back toward the table. "I assume this is Devon," he announced mechanically.

"The one and only," Kayla replied as Devon squirmed on her lap.

Dr. Wilson knelt down in front of Devon and said, "Hello, there, young man. I'm wondering if you can help me with something. I have someone sending me some pictures tomorrow, and I'd like you to look at them. Can you do that for me?"

Devon nodded silently in agreement.

Dr. Wilson shifted his eyes to the adults and said, "Hopefully, that will give us some of the answers we're looking for."

"Sorry it took me so long," the doctor said as he walked through the door of Devon and Kayla's hotel room, where everyone had congregated. "It was hard to find a place where I could print these out."

He carried a thick manila folder in his hand, setting it down on the desk along the closest wall. Jenny watched him nervously, curious about what was going to transpire. Dr. Wilson opened the folder and sorted through papers inside. Pulling a few out, he laid them out on the bed. Jenny noticed they were black and white photographs of houses.

"Hey Devon," the doctor said, "can you come here and look at these pictures for me?"

Devon scooted off the chair where he had been playing games on his tablet, handing the device to his mother. He walked over and climbed up onto the bed, briefly glancing at each picture. By the time he reached the fourth photograph, his brow furrowed and his gaze remained fixated on that one image.

"What do you see?" the doctor asked.

"That's my house," Devon replied.

"Which one?"

Devon reached out a little finger and touched the fourth picture. Jenny's eyes rose to look at the doctor, whose expression didn't change.

"Where is that house?" Doctor Wilson asked.

"Summerset."

Jenny remembered the name of the town where Matthew had lived to be Terryville, and she wondered if Devon's claim was legitimate or imagined.

Next, the doctor held up an image of a young girl, a photograph clearly taken several decades earlier. "Do you recognize this girl?"

Devon looked up at the picture and studied it, but he ultimately shook his head and confessed, "Nope."

Unfazed, Doctor Wilson flipped that picture to the back of his stack, revealing another photograph of a similarly-aged girl. "How about her?"

Devon didn't look at this picture quite as long before saying, "No."

The process repeated. "Do you know this girl?"

After only a second, Devon's wide eyes rose to meet Doctor Wilson's again. "That's Maribel."

"Who is Maribel?"

"She's my daughter."

Once again, Jenny felt like the details might have been off. The daughter's name had been Mary, not Maribel, and she wasn't sure if the picture Devon had chosen was of the correct child. The doctor's facial expression gave no indication, either, although Jenny suspected that was his intention.

Devon continued, "I haven't been able to find her. Have you seen her?"

"I haven't seen her," Dr. Wilson said, "but we can certainly try to find her for you."

The doctor spread several more photographs out on the bed; these were in color. "Do any of these pictures mean anything to you?"

Devon scoured the pictures, ultimately pointing at a picture of what appeared to be a manufacturing plant. He seemed only half interested in what he was doing.

"What is in that picture?" the doctor asked.

"It looks like my work, but it looks a little different."

"What looks different about it?"

"Those letters are different."

"Do you know what those letters say?"

"That's an E; that's an S; that's a T."

"Can you read the words?"

Devon only shook his head no.

"What work do you do?"

"I fix things."

"You fix things? What kind of things?"

"Machines." He held his little arms out wide. "Big machines."

At that moment, Devon turned away from the bed and approached Kayla. Jumping up and down, he informed his mother he wanted his tablet back. Jenny determined the session had just officially ended whether they wanted it to or not.

The adults exchanged glances, and Zack took the hint. "Hey Devon," he said, "do you want to go get an ice cream?"

Devon immediately put the tablet down on his chair and ran at full speed toward the door. With a smile, Zack said, "I'll take that as a *yes*."

Once Devon and Zack were gone, Kayla immediately asked Dr. Wilson, "Did any of his facts line up?"

"Some did and some didn't, or at least that's how it appears at first glance. He chose the correct house, but the location was Terryville, South Carolina, and he said Summerset. He also chose the right child but said the wrong name."

"What about the job?" Kayla asked.

"That one he did get correct. The building has changed names, so the writing on the wall was different. It used to be called Shatney Everson, and it was a textile plant; it has since been bought out. Matthew did work as a machinist there, so Devon was able to pick out the right building *and* he could recognize the work Matthew did, or at least he described it as well as a five-year-old can be expected to."

Jenny was admittedly a bit shaken by this information; the notion that Matthew had just resurrected himself inside that little boy was unnerving.

"I do want to call Mary and see if there may be an ounce of truth to Devon's other statements," Dr. Wilson continued. "I don't want to declare he was incorrect unless and until Mary can verify that the information was false."

Kayla looked uneasy while the doctor dialed Mary's number and put the phone on speaker. Mary also sounded apprehensive when she answered.

"Well," Dr. Wilson began, "we just put Devon to the test, and he did well with some aspects of it." He explained the notions Devon had gotten correct. "We do have a few questions, though, about some of the other information he had given us. Can you tell us if there is any significance to the name Summerset?"

"Oh my God," Mary said softly. "That was the name of the subdivision where I grew up."

"That's where he said his house was."

Mary sounded shaken. "Well, he was right."

"Let me ask you one other thing," Dr. Wilson said. "Did your father ever have any nicknames for you?"

"Just one," she replied nervously.

"And what name was that?"

"He always used to call me Maribel."

Chapter 6

A chill worked its way up Jenny's spine; Devon shouldn't have known that.

Unfazed, Dr. Wilson explained the situation to Mary. "That's the name he gave when he saw the picture of you as a young girl."

He paused, waiting for Mary to reply, but she didn't. Jenny could only imagine what was going through her head.

"The good news in all of this is that Devon's reactions to the photographs were quite benign," Dr. Wilson added. "He didn't get agitated at all upon seeing the pictures, which provides me with hope that this process will go smoothly."

Jenny briefly wondered what case was being used as a basis of comparison.

"So, then, what's the next step?" Kayla asked.

"Well, after hearing what Devon has said, wondering if we've seen Julia and Mary, I think the logical conclusion would be that he couldn't find them during the fire. If I put myself in his shoes, I would be positively desperate to make sure my wife and daughter were okay…but if the flames were too high or the smoke too thick, he wouldn't have been able to get to them."

"The smoke was horrible," Mary said through the phone. "It was amazing how quickly the whole car became filled with it. You couldn't see your hand in front of your face." She let out a shallow breath, indicating just how painful this memory was to recall. "People were screaming...it was pure chaos. I guarantee my father couldn't have found us, no matter how hard he tried."

Trying to put an end to Mary's pain, Jenny interjected, "I think it's reasonable to assume that's why he's lingering." She secretly hoped there wasn't a second motive which involved being buried next to his wife. "I guess now it's just a matter of letting him know that they survived?" She phrased it more like a question than a statement.

"That's definitely the plan," Dr. Wilson replied. "We just need to figure out the most delicate way to do that."

"Delicate?" Jenny asked before her filter had a chance to stop her. "Wouldn't this be good news for Matthew?"

"It would be good in the sense that they survived, yes. The only problem is that the young girl on the train is now in her sixties. She's led an entire life that Matthew didn't get to be a part of. That aspect of it might be difficult for him to hear."

Jenny thought back to her earlier conversation, where she had come to the conclusion that spirits did have a sense of passing time. "You don't think he realizes it's been that long?"

"Maybe not," Dr. Wilson said. "You said yourself that some spirits are aware of how long it's been because they have a point of reference, specifically if they watch a loved one grow up or grow old. But if Matthew has been spending this time around the crash site looking for his wife and daughter, he may not be aware it's been sixty years."

Kayla's voice was solemn when she noted, "It probably feels like longer."

"We have to get him out of that hell," Mary said with conviction. "If he's been frozen in time in that one terrible spot, we need to save him from that."

"Agreed," Dr. Wilson replied, "but like I said, we have to be delicate, not only for Matthew's sake, but for Devon's."

"Will he be in danger?" Kayla asked.

"No," Wilson replied impatiently. Jenny guessed his intolerance was because he had mentioned this before, although, to her, it seemed a bit rude. "I just don't want to overwhelm him."

"So what do we do?" Mary asked.

"Mary, I need you to send me some photographs of the milestones in your life...high school graduation, your wedding, the births of your children, if you have any. We can show those to Devon and let Matthew know you are no longer the nine-year-old girl who rode the train that day. Once he's had enough time to get used to that idea, we can introduce you to him."

"Should I bring my children along when I meet him?" Mary asked. "Or even my grandchildren?" Her tone became softer when she added, "I have to admit, one of my biggest regrets is that my father never got to see his grandchildren—and now his great-grandchildren."

An uncharacteristic smile graced Dr. Wilson's lips. "Let's see how this goes; hopefully that will be able to happen."

When Mary got off the phone to search her house for pertinent photographs, the others decided to get lunch. While the five of them sat in a booth waiting for their food to arrive, Jenny seized the opportunity to bring up the other source of her curiosity. "Dr. Wilson, I still have an interest in meeting Keith."

"I have no objection to that," Dr. Wilson replied, pausing to sip his water through a straw, "although your doctor might."

Jenny placed her hand on her belly. "Does he live far away?"

"Colorado, to be precise. I don't think you'd be allowed to fly out there, as pregnant as you are."

With slumping shoulders, Jenny couldn't mask her disappointment. "Well, do any of your other...clients...live within driving distance?"

Dr. Wilson stiffened, albeit slightly, causing Jenny to wonder what nerve she had just struck. "Only one."

He didn't elaborate.

"Which one is it?" Jenny's curiosity had multiplied when she saw his reaction, leading her to wonder which of the children from his article could have caused him to respond that way.

"No one you know of." Dr. Wilson shook his head almost imperceptibly. "I haven't written about her yet."

Once again, Jenny remained quiet, waiting for him to continue. This time, he spoke more on the subject. "About a hundred miles from here, there's a little girl who, not too long ago, dealt with a spirit that was…" He twisted his face as he searched for the appropriate word. Ultimately, he settled on, "more agitated than most."

"More *agitated*?" Kayla asked, the fear evident on her face.

Dr. Wilson nodded. "It was the first time I'd seen any hostility; the other spirits prior to hers had all been rather benevolent."

With a furrowed brow and a piqued curiosity, Jenny asked, "How did the spirit let you know it was angry?"

He sighed and lowered his shoulders. "It was the girl's behavior when she was being visited." He held up his hand in Kayla's direction and assured her, "She was never in any danger…she just acted in a way that was very uncharacteristic for a five-year-old girl."

Dr. Wilson seemed reluctant to divulge the specific behavior, which only made Jenny all the more curious to hear it. "What did she do?"

With defeat, he admitted, "Swearing. Spitting. Blatant disrespect." Dr. Wilson's eyes met Jenny's. "Adverse reactions every time she saw a police officer."

"Who was she?" Zack asked. "I mean, who had taken her over?"

Shaking his head, Dr. Wilson admitted, "We never did find out. Every time we tried to ask the questions that would lead us to determine who the spirit was, we were only greeted with vague replies. It was as if he—or she—was perfectly happy with us not discovering an identity."

Jenny sat up straighter. "Is this girl still being plagued by the spirit's presence?"

"No, she has since outgrown it. She's eight now."

Tapping her foot under the table, Jenny commented, "She may have outgrown it, but that doesn't mean the spirit is gone." She looked around the table at the others. "I would like to go there after we get Matthew his answers. I want to see what this is about."

Zack turned toward Jenny. "Do you really think that's a good idea? Going to visit an angry spirit when you're pregnant?"

"It can't hurt me," she replied. "I would just like to figure out what it wants in case it has plans to take over another child."

"What if it wants to kill people?" Zack asked. "And he wants to use you as a tool to carry it out?"

"I'm quite sure I'll be able to resist the urge."

Dr. Wilson looked intrigued. "Jenny, you said that you were able to instantly recognize that Devon had the gift when you met him. How were you able to do that?"

"There's an aura that surrounds people who have it," she explained. "I can't describe it with words very well, but it's almost like déjà vu...when I come in contact with a fellow psychic, I just know it."

He contemplated that information for a moment. "I would love to introduce you to this little girl," he eventually said. "It would be wonderful to know if one of these children would trigger that reaction in you. My current belief is that they are not actually psychic, because I would imagine they wouldn't outgrow that, but it would be great to know for sure." He leaned forward onto his elbows. "Since you have an interest in meeting her, I will contact the girl's mother and see if she's willing to let her daughter meet you. I know the mother was quite relieved when the spirit stopped coming around and that chapter of their lives seemed to be over. Considering her daughter's behavior during that time, she may be reluctant to revisit it."

"Well, if we can figure out what this spirit wants, he may cross over and never be a threat to anyone's child again." Jenny immediately regretted her word choice of *threat* in Kayla's presence. She hoped it would fly under the radar. Undeterred, she added, "Hopefully that will be incentive enough for the mother to agree."

"I imagine it would be."

At that point, the food arrived, temporarily diverting the conversation. Halfway through the meal, Dr. Wilson glanced at his phone. "It looks like I have a few photographs waiting for me." His eyes scanned the others. "Once we're done here, I'll go print these out. Then we can take Matthew on a little trip through time."

Worry was evident on Kayla's face as she glanced down at her son. She placed her hand lovingly on his back, a gesture that he didn't even seem to notice.

"Don't worry, Kayla," Jenny whispered sympathetically. "From what I can gather, Matthew is kind. He was a father, after all—I think he'll be sensitive to the fact that he's dealing with somebody's child."

Kayla nodded silently, looking distant. Ultimately, she focused her gaze on Jenny, simply adding, "I just hope we don't make him angry."

"I will take this as far as I can until Matthew disappears or Devon begins to seem agitated, which I sincerely doubt," Dr. Wilson explained as he straightened out the photographs in his hands. He sat on the edge of the bed in the hotel room, using his lap to help organize his pictures. "There is no hurry on this; we will take as long as we need to let Matthew know just how much time has passed."

Kayla stood with her arms folded tightly across her chest. As nervous as Jenny was, she knew Kayla had to be even more so.

Perhaps due to experience—or maybe the lack of a soul—Dr. Wilson seemed unfazed. "Does anyone have any questions before we get started?"

The others exchanged glances, their silence implying they had nothing to ask.

"Okay, then, I guess we can bring Devon in."

Jenny got up from her seat and went to the door, calling Zack and Devon inside from the hallway. Devon had a candy bar in his hand, giving away their whereabouts while the adults had conferred. "You guys can come on in, if you want."

The child came bounding in the room; Zack walked in a little more reluctantly. The tension in the room was palpable, making Jenny wonder whether or not Devon could sense it. His behavior, however, led her to believe he was oblivious to anything and everything that was going on around him.

"Hey, Devon," Dr. Wilson said with remarkable ease, "can you come here for a second?"

Devon didn't say a word as he jumped—literally jumped—over to Dr. Wilson and looked up at him with wide eyes.

Exposing a photograph, Dr. Wilson asked, "Do you know who this is, Devon?"

He studied the picture wordlessly for a moment. "That's Maribel."

"And how old is Maribel?"

"Nine."

"She's nine?"

"Yup."

The doctor removed that photograph from the stack, revealing the next one. "Devon, do you know who this is?"

He looked at the picture, and his wiggling suddenly stopped. His brow lowered, and he noted, "That looks like Maribel, but she's too old."

"That is Maribel, actually," Dr. Wilson said matter-of-factly. "She survived the fire, and here she is at her thirteenth birthday party."

Devon remained motionless, captivated by the image in front of him.

"What do you think about that?" Dr. Wilson asked.

For a long time, Devon said nothing. He looked as if he was studying every detail of the picture. Ultimately he asked, "Where is she?"

Wilson seemed confused by the question. "Do you mean, *where is she now?*"

With a slight nod, Devon added, "Is she with Julia?"

"Not right now," Dr. Wilson told him, "but Julia did survive the fire as well."

Still frozen, Devon seemed to be absorbing the information, although it looked like he was both overwhelmed and terribly confused. He pointed at the picture, remarking, "But if she's thirteen..."

He said nothing else.

Standing up straight, Devon giggled as he flopped his upper body onto the bed. He rolled over so the back of his head was on the bed and he faced the ceiling, his arms flailing loosely like a jellyfish.

The session was clearly over.

Jenny's eyes remained fixated on Dr. Wilson, who nonchalantly organized the pictures and put them back in his file. "At least we made some progress," he declared.

"How so?" Kayla asked, taking the words out of Jenny's mouth.

"It registered," he explained. "Confusion is to be expected." He put the file into his bag. "Imagine you were in a similar situation—you were just shown a picture of someone you know, but that person is visibly older in the photograph. Wouldn't that throw you for a bit of a loop?"

Jenny remained silent as she contemplated the situation.

Dr. Wilson continued, "If I am to guess, I would suspect that Matthew is trying to digest this information right about now. He's probably realizing that his last memory is the train fire, but time has obviously passed since then."

"Do you think he's just now realizing he's dead?" Kayla asked.

With a shrug, Dr. Wilson said, "It's possible." He looked at Kayla intently. "As you could imagine, that would be a difficult notion to accept."

She flashed a worried glance at her son, who had since busied himself with other things.

"If it makes you feel any better," Jenny began, "I don't think Matthew is around. I mean, speaking from my own personal experience, in between visions, I lead a perfectly normal life, seeing things only through my own eyes. If the spirits go through any…difficulty…I don't pick up on that unless I'm in the throes of a vision."

Kayla didn't say anything; she just looked helplessly at Jenny.

Zack watched Devon for a moment before declaring, "He seems okay to me."

At that moment, Devon walked up to his mother and asked for his tablet. She released a breath and said, "Sure, baby, I'll get it for you."

As Jenny watched this exchange, the baby in her own belly began to hiccup, reminding her of its presence. Sympathy surged through her veins, as did a small amount of fear. Seeing Kayla and Devon interacting, Jenny may have been looking at a glimpse of her own future—desperately trying to instill normalcy in the life of a child who was anything but.

Despite the fact that Jenny had found herself caught up in the moment, Zack clearly hadn't been. "So, what do we do now?" he asked the doctor.

Dr. Wilson responded matter-of-factly, "Now, we wait."

There they were—three of the words Jenny hated most. She felt the need to be doing something productive to make the time go faster; she certainly couldn't just sit there and watch the time tick by until Matthew made another appearance. "Dr. Wilson, now that it seems we have a little time to kill, can you tell us a little more about the girl who was visited by the not-so-friendly spirit?"

"In fact I can," he replied. "I called the mother while I was printing these pictures out, and she agreed to meet with you. She also gave me permission to discuss the specifics of the case."

Jenny briefly wondered if semantics had posed a problem for the slightly-too-intelligent doctor. She wasn't really asking if he *could* talk about the girl; she was wondering if he *would* discuss her. She waited for a moment, debating whether she should ask the question again using better phrasing, but she didn't need to.

"Her name is Addison Roth," Dr. Wilson began, "but she goes by Addy."

"Who?" Zack asked. "The mother or the daughter?"

"The daughter. The mother's name is Cheryl—she came to me after several months of hearing her daughter use dated—and derogatory—vernacular for the police and authority in general. At times, Addy was acting more like a belligerent teenager than a typical preschooler. Those moments were fleeting, though, causing Cheryl to wonder just what was causing them."

"What made her suspect it was a spirit?" Jenny asked.

"The terminology. Addy was using slang that hadn't been commonly used in decades, referring to cops as 'pigs' and such. Cheryl couldn't imagine that Addy had heard those terms during her short lifetime."

"Pigs," Zack repeated thoughtfully. "Isn't that a sixties term?"

"Thereabouts," Dr. Wilson confirmed. "She also spoke a lot about 'the man,' which is another indication that we're dealing with that time period."

Kayla looked concerned. "How do you know that Addy wasn't talking about an actual man?"

"Cheryl didn't, at first. As you can imagine, she was quite concerned when her three-year-old daughter started talking about 'the man,' especially in the context Addy used. She had mentioned that the man was out to get them all, and of course Cheryl's first thought was that there was an actual *man* threatening the family. When questioned about it, though, Addy clarified that she was talking about the government." Dr. Wilson looked at each of the faces around him. "How many three-year-olds know about the government, let alone are able to spew out theories that the government is spying on them and is out to sabotage them?"

Jenny rubbed her eyes. "Okay, so you say you have no indications about who this person may have been...but you said the spirit was agitated and made Addy act in inappropriate ways." She said it like a statement, although really it had been more of a question.

"That is correct," the doctor agreed.

"Exactly what kind of behavior did she exhibit?" Kayla asked.

"Well, it all began at the South Carolina State Fair, apparently. There were a few police officers standing in a row near the entrance, and Addy made some kind of comment about the pigs being there. Cheryl and her husband were mortified; they had never used such a term, and they couldn't imagine where she could have heard it. Not only that, but they had always taught Addy to trust the police. When they reminded her of that, she replied by telling her parents that by assuming that attitude, they were part of the problem. Then, when they walked by the officers, Addy spit at them."

"Like, spit at them, spit at them?" Zack asked. "Or just stuck out her tongue and went phhht."

"She shot saliva in their direction," the doctor said mechanically.

Jenny only shook her head, imagining how shocked the parents must have been by that behavior, hoping she would never know the feeling personally.

"That was just the first of many incidents," Dr. Wilson continued. "She seemed to always react that way when she saw law enforcement, to the point where her parents went to great lengths to never bring her to a place where officers might be. Although, as you can imagine, that is something you can't always predict."

"Was it just law enforcement that brought out that reaction?" Kayla asked.

"Police and politicians. She did routinely make comments about the man being out to get them, questioning the validity of taxes and talking about how the government wants to control everybody."

Zack's eyes grew wide. "A three-year-old was questioning the validity of *taxes?*"

Dr. Wilson smiled. "No…a three-year-old was saying the words, but someone else was clearly doing the talking."

The wheels in Jenny's head were turning. "You say this started at the state fair. Where was that?"

"Right here in Columbia."

"But you said they lived a hundred miles away, right?"

"They do, and they did then. They were here visiting family on a mini-vacation."

Jenny glanced at Zack and Kayla. "Do you think it's possible that they drove through an area where this spirit had been lingering? Kind of like what Devon did with Matthew?"

"It's certainly possible," Zack said. "Where do they live?"

"A small town in Georgia called Milldale, about halfway between Atlanta and Savannah."

Zack called up a map on his phone, eventually remarking, "It looks like they may have taken Route 1 to Highway 20 to get here." He glanced at the others. "Do you think we should bring Jenny down the same path to see if she can get anything?"

"It can't hurt," Jenny agreed. "Once we get some answers for Matthew, we can start working on that."

At that moment, as if on cue, Devon appeared from behind his mother's leg. He looked up at Dr. Wilson and sheepishly said, "Mister? I'd like to look at more pictures, if you have them."

Chapter 7

Dr. Wilson looked surprised, but only for a second. "Absolutely," he said professionally, once again opening his file.

Devon moved closer to the doctor, a look of curiosity on his face. "Do you have any pictures of Julia?"

"I do," Dr. Wilson replied as he flipped through some photographs. He eventually spun one around so Devon could see the image, which featured the same woman Jenny had seen in her vision from the train station but with shorter hair that was fashioned into a sixties-style bob. She was sitting on a bench, smiling genuinely at the camera.

Jenny directed her eyes toward Devon to gauge his reaction. Outwardly, he had none. He simply asked, "When was this taken?"

Wilson spoke without a trace of emotion in his voice. "This one was taken at a family reunion in 1965."

"1965," Devon repeated in a whisper. For Matthew, that would have been four years into the future. Jenny sucked in a breath and held it, waiting for an outburst from Devon that never came.

Instead, the little boy raised his brown eyes to Dr. Wilson and commented, "She looks happy."

"From what I understand, she was happy," Dr. Wilson confirmed. "Even though she went through a very difficult period after the train explosion, she did eventually go on to feel joy again."

Devon returned his gaze to the picture, which he studied for a long time. Eventually, he whispered in a much sadder tone, "She looks pretty."

Jenny released the breath she'd been holding forever, briefly hanging her head. She couldn't help but feel that she was witnessing a man coming to terms with his own death, realizing his wife and child had survived and lived a lifetime without him. Despite her urge to cry, she put her emotions in her back pocket, aware that any type of interruption could cause Matthew to disappear. The last thing she wanted to do was ruin the moment; there would always be time for tears later.

Devon's eyes hadn't left the photograph when Dr. Wilson asked, "Would you like to see more?"

The little boy only nodded.

The next picture Dr. Wilson revealed featured Mary in a cap and gown, wearing a huge smile and holding her diploma. A similar smile graced Devon's lips as pride beamed in his eyes. "Wow," he said with awe.

"She graduated with honors," Dr. Wilson told him.

Devon looked up at the doctor and added, "She always was smart." Then, with words that ripped Jenny's heart out, he added, "She's really that old?"

If only Matthew knew that photograph was taken forty-five years ago.

True to form, Dr. Wilson's actions remained mechanical. "Let me show you some more pictures." He sorted through the stack, ultimately landing on one that depicted Mary on her wedding day. She and her new husband were holding hands and looking exhilarated in the foreground with a crowd gathered behind them. He turned the photo around so Devon could see it.

This time, Devon reached out and took the picture into his own little hand. He brought it closer to him, studying every detail. "Wow," he said again. "Look at her."

Jenny remained frozen as Devon continued to examine the image. Eventually, he looked up and asked, "Is he a nice man?" He pointed to the groom.

"I've never met him," Dr. Wilson confessed, "but I'm sure he is."

Devon's eyes made their way back to the picture, and he continued to look at it lovingly for a long time. His brow eventually furrowed, though, and a look of confusion and hurt took over his face. He leaned in toward the picture, giving it a closer examination, posing, "Who is that with Julia?"

When Devon handed the photograph back to the doctor, Jenny was able to see that in the upper right corner, Julia stood off in the background, looking lovingly at her daughter. A man, who Jenny presumed to be Julia's second husband, was next to her with his arm around her shoulder.

Jenny's breathing became so shallow it almost stopped.

"His name is Davis Auerbach." An eternity seemed to pass before Dr. Wilson added, "He is the man Julia went on to remarry."

He might as well have said, *Devon, there is no Santa Claus.* The saddened expression on the boy's face was heartbreaking, but mercifully it only lasted a few moments. Devon then turned to his mother and announced, "I'm hungry. Can I have a snack?"

A pause indicated that Kayla was having a more difficult time with the transition than her son had. She quickly recovered and offered Devon some crackers, escorting him over to the corner of the room.

Jenny looked at Dr. Wilson with just her eyes, inviting an explanation, despite the fact that she was pretty sure she knew what she had just witnessed.

"He's retreated," Dr. Wilson announced. "He clearly will need some time to get used to the idea of Julia with another man."

"Did you do that on purpose?" Jenny asked. "Show him a picture that had Julia and her second husband together?"

Dr. Wilson turned to her and replied, "I wish I could say yes to that, but I can't. I was so focused on the image in the foreground that I didn't look closely enough to the people in the background. Ideally, I would have liked to have broken the news to Matthew a little more gently than that."

Jenny began to get worried. "Do you think it will pose a problem?"

"I don't think so. Matthew doesn't seem to have a score to settle; he just wants answers." Dr. Wilson's face looked slightly grim. "Although, I'm sure he would have preferred the answers to be presented a little more subtly."

Jenny felt overcome by sympathy as she glanced at Devon, although she knew the person she felt sorry for was not currently housed within his body. Her eyes circulated the empty space around her as she wondered if Matthew was there, watching them, licking the wounds of his broken heart. She briefly put herself in Matthew's shoes, imagining how it would have felt to be shown a picture of Zack looking quite happy with another woman…at the wedding of her child, who, last she knew, was only nine years old. She rubbed her eyes, ultimately running both hands through her hair; she wished she had the ability to provide solace to Matthew somehow, but, unfortunately, he had to go through this alone.

It didn't seem right.

"Do you think he'll take comfort in knowing that Julia has passed and he can see her again?" Jenny asked, pausing before adding, "And that all he has to do to see her is cross over?"

"I'm sure he will," Dr. Wilson said. "If he's been looking for her all this time, it will inevitably be gratifying to know that he can finally find her."

"Shouldn't we tell him that, then?" Jenny asked, eager to put Matthew out of his misery. "And soon?"

"In due time," Dr. Wilson replied. "I would like to get him together with Mary before we encourage him to cross. This is such a rare occurrence; we should let all aspects of it play out."

Jenny released an impatient sigh; she couldn't help but feel that this was less of a rare occurrence and more of a rare *opportunity* for Dr. Wilson to gather data. She genuinely wondered if Dr. Wilson's primary goal was to bring Matthew some answers or to bolster his own research.

Irritation and restlessness stirred within her, so she turned to her husband and posed, "Zack, do you want to take a trip?"

He looked at her with confusion. "To where?"

"Highway 20 to Route 1."

Zack's puzzled expression remained. "You want to go *now*?"

With a shrug, Jenny said, "Sure. Why not?"

"Um…because we don't have a car. We came down in Kayla's minivan, remember?"

"We can rent one." She looked at him with urgency that she hoped he could interpret. "Besides, maybe we can discover some answers about Addy while we wait for Matthew to come back." The reality was that Jenny found Matthew's discoveries to be painful to watch, and she preferred not to be around as they unfolded.

"I guess we could try," Zack replied with surprise still present in his voice. Fortunately, he seemed to understand her desire to leave, even if he didn't know the reason for it. "I'll get a couple of waters for the road."

"I'm not even sure what to research," Zack admitted as he sat in the passenger seat of the rental car, looking helplessly at his phone. "It's not like Matthew's case where there was a fire to investigate, or other situations where I had a name attached to a victim. Here we just have a person from the sixties who apparently doesn't like authority, which limits it to—oh, I don't know—an entire generation of people."

"I haven't gotten anything yet either," Jenny admitted, "and we're about halfway to Milldale, according to my calculations."

"Are we getting off the highway soon?" Zack asked.

Jenny nodded. "Another couple miles or so."

Her previous irritation regarding Matthew's situation had mostly subsided by then, making her feel like it was a topic she could discuss without too much emotion. "So, what's your take on what's happening with Devon?"

"My *take?*"

"Yeah. Do you think we're being fair to Matthew? Is it right to drag this thing out, exposing him to little bits at a time? Or do you think we should just let him know that Julia's on the other side and encourage him to cross over?"

Zack thought about it for a moment before saying, "I think if both Mary and Julia were dead, the humane thing would be to tell him to cross immediately. But since Mary's alive, he may want to see her first. At least, that's what I would want, if I were in his shoes." Jenny's phone squawked out a warning that the exit was approaching. Zack continued, "I imagine that would be a touchy subject that you would have to address slowly...if we just put Devon in a room with sixty-something-year-old Mary, that might be too much for him to handle all at once."

Jenny contemplated that thought as she turned on her blinker. "I guess you're right," she conceded. "I just can't help but feel that what we're doing to Matthew is mean. It's like we're ripping the band aid off way too slowly."

"Well, when you consider there's a possibility the guy didn't even know he was dead, slow is probably the way to go. To be honest, if anything, I feel like we're throwing things at him too fast."

"Really?" The car rounded the exit ramp.

Zack shrugged with one shoulder. "That's my impression, although it's only one person's opinion."

"You're probably right. It just may be that I'm a little extra sensitive these days. It's so hard to tell how much of my emotions are legitimate and how much are pregnancy-related." She let out a sigh as she merged into traffic on Route 1. "I guess part of what's bothering me is that we can't comfort him. Every time he hears news he doesn't like, he retreats back into his spirit world. It's not like all the times when I've delivered bad news to the living; I can at least console those people. Poor Matthew gets hit with some mind-bending piece of information, and then he's required to go digest it by himself."

"He's not required to," Zack pointed out, "he chooses to. Maybe that's just how he operates. Some people are like that, you know."

While she could see validity in what Zack was saying, Jenny replied, "I still wish there was some way we could comfort him a little bit."

He glanced at her out of the corner of his eye. "He's been wandering around aimlessly for sixty years...I think the fact that someone can finally hear him is probably comforting enough."

Perhaps Zack was right; Jenny decided to leave that conversation alone. "So," she began, "let's try to formulate some kind of theory about this new, authority-hating friend of ours."

"That's just it," Zack replied, holding up his phone helplessly, "I've been trying to. There is absolutely nothing to go on. I've looked for murders that happened along this stretch in the 1960s, but I haven't been able to find anything."

"Not every lingering spirit involves murder," Jenny noted. "Take a look at Matthew...he just wants to make sure his wife and daughter are okay."

"Exactly...and that just makes it even worse. If some guy died peacefully in his sleep and simply wants to send a message to a family member, how am I supposed to figure out who he is?"

"You're not," Jenny said with a smirk. "I am. You've got a ringer on your team, remember?"

"And how much information are you getting?"

Jenny giggled. "Precisely none."

Leaning back in the passenger seat, Zack said, "That's what I thought."

A few miles passed by before Jenny's mind went back to a familiar topic. "We're going to be parents in a couple of months, do you realize that?"

Zack kept a straight face as he said, "The thought has occurred to me, yes."

"Are you ready for this?" She paused before adding, "Am I ready for this?"

"We'd better be," Zack replied. "It's too late to turn back now."

Jenny was having one of her moments where the reality of the situation was nearly overwhelming. A baby. She was going to have a baby. She scrunched her face and said, "I guess we are committed, aren't we?"

Zack patted her leg and said, "I've told you a million times already that you're going to be a great mom."

Somehow Jenny's nerves didn't subside. Zack's vote of confidence was great, but how was she going to know what the baby needed when it cried? What if she made mistakes with the baby? What if she held it too much and spoiled it? What if she didn't hold it enough? Would the child grow up detached?

The responsibility was so great and the stakes so high, Jenny could feel herself drowning in the thought of it.

Her thought process quickly shifted, however, when she felt a wave wash over her. The moment was fleeting but powerful, leaving her to only say, "Whoa."

"What's the matter?" Zack asked.

Jenny shook her head as she tried to determine the best way to describe it. "I just felt something...something very strange. It felt like a bizarre mixture of serenity and anger."

He cocked an eyebrow in her direction. "Like something a hippie might feel if he was upset with authority?"

"Possibly." She said nothing else in an attempt to keep her mind open for more contact.

However, the minutes ticked by, and Jenny didn't feel anything else. She was beginning to wonder if she should turn around when a second, longer-lasting sensation occupied her body.

She felt enlightened. Sounds were sharper, smells stronger. Worry left her body as she developed an awareness of the clothing on her skin and the gas pedal under her foot. The steering wheel felt smooth in her hands. Words echoed inside her head, as if spoken in a cavern.

That's what the man would have you believe.

She felt a physical twinge with every syllable spoken, like the words themselves had crashed into her skin. Her soul felt free and light, contained only by the message that had just been uttered, dampening her spirit to the point of making her feel violated. If only the man would stop trying to control her...then she could experience total freedom, the way nature had intended.

Damn the man.

Jenny snapped back into the present with unnerving intensity. She blinked exaggeratedly several times before announcing, "I think I may have just been high."

"What?" Zack was clearly confused.

"I had a contact...and it was unlike any I've ever had before. Everything was so...much."

"So *much*?"

She knew that had been the wrong word, but she couldn't come up with anything better. Despite the fact that she had an expansive vocabulary, at the moment her mind was virtually blank. She shook her head and explained, "My senses were on overdrive. Everything was...heightened."

Heightened. That was the word she'd been searching for. She felt like she'd had a minor victory when it finally came out of her mouth.

"Heightened, huh?" Zack said with a sly smile. "That does sound like it may have a little outside influence involved with it."

A tug started to generate within Jenny, causing her to ease off the gas pedal as they headed down the road. She soon felt the need to turn right down a side street, weaving her way through expansive stretches of desolate farm land. After several left and right turns onto roads that became increasingly narrower, she found herself venturing down a path that appeared to be tall grass trampled by tires. Eventually, she pulled up to a huge lawn with an old house that looked like it hadn't been occupied in decades. A clothes line, complete with an abundance of laundry hanging from it, suggested otherwise.

"This is where I was drawn," Jenny proclaimed as she turned off her car.

"This is insane," Zack observed.

"Agreed."

"What are you feeling?" Zack asked. "Anything?"

Shaking her head, she replied, "Not at the moment."

He looked out the passenger window at the ramshackle house and equally run-down surrounding buildings. "This place looks like it's been here since the dawn of time. Does it even have indoor plumbing?"

"It doesn't look like it would." Jenny did notice a well and a windmill on the property, as well as vast expanses of gardens. Chickens and goats roamed around freely, and the clothing on the line blew in the breeze. The significance of the location, however, remained elusive as they quietly contemplated for a moment in the car.

"I want to pet one of those goats," Zack finally announced, out of the blue.

Jenny's attention became drawn to the little animals, who jumped and frolicked playfully, unaware that they had spectators. She had to admit that she would have liked to pet them, too, although she chose to stay focused on the matter at hand. "I want to figure out why we're here..." She looked around. "And I'd also like to figure out where *here* is."

Checking his phone, Zack informed her, "I don't have any bars."

"Well, that sucks," she replied as she searched in every direction for some clue about of where they were; all she could see were these buildings and the surrounding property. She didn't even see any telephone poles that would have been indicative of electricity.

"Why don't you drive back the way we came, and I'll look and see where we are once I get some bars."

Jenny wordlessly started the car and turned around, giving one last glance at the house over her shoulder as she drove down the barely-recognizable path her car had traveled on the way in. She was being given no indication of what role the house would play in the investigation, but she imagined it was significant if she had been drawn there.

Zack's eyes stayed glued to his phone as the car ventured back down the narrow strip of matted grass. Once they returned to the asphalt, Jenny asked, "Do you have anything yet?"

"Nope."

After a few minutes, however, he announced, "Hey...I've got a bar."

"Excellent. Need me to pull over?"

Zack grunted in a way that let Jenny know it wasn't necessary. He scrutinized his phone before declaring, "I believe we are officially in Bumfuck, Georgia."

"Bumfuck?"

"Not a real place," he clarified. "It's just a much-less-classy way to say we are in the middle of nowhere."

"Great. How is it this trip keeps leading us to places with no names?"

"Luck." Zack manipulated the screen with his finger. "Just plain old luck." He alternated between looking at his phone, Jenny's odometer and the scenery, trying to get a feel for exactly where they were. Once Jenny pulled up to an intersection, Zack announced, "Got it. We were about six miles past Marvin's Mill Road on Route 3236. That's about the best way I can describe it."

Jenny remained quiet as Zack continued to play with his phone. "What are you doing now?"

"Looking up the closest police station."

"Police station?"

"Yup," he declared. "I figure we can go there and ask if anything substantial happened there back in the sixties."

Remembering how much more useful people were than websites the last time, she said, "*That* is a great idea."

Zack told Jenny how to get to the station, which turned out to be a good twenty minutes from where they had been. By the time they arrived, Jenny was more than grateful to get out of the car; her backside had been getting numb. Pregnant bellies and long car rides didn't mix very well.

The police station was small, as expected, and the couple was able to walk in without having to pass through any security measures. Zack approached the desk first, addressing the older gentleman sitting behind it. "Hi," he began, "I was wondering if you could tell me if anything significant happened at a location six miles past Marvin's Mill Road on route 3236 back in the sixties."

The gray-haired officer looked suspiciously at Zack. "You ain't from around here, are you?"

"No, sir."

Leaning back in his chair and interlacing his fingers across his chest, the officer continued to speak slowly. "That place you're talking about...that's Eden."

Jenny felt her face scrunch up. "Eden?"

With a vigorous nod, he said, "Yes, ma'am. That's the place where all them hippies committed suicide back in 1968."

Chapter 8

"Suicide?" Jenny demanded. Anger tore through her body as she raised her finger to point at the officer's face. Awareness soon came over her, however, and she lowered her hand, hoping she had done so before the policeman had a chance to notice.

"Yes, ma'am," he continued. "There was a good lot of them, too. They all took a bunch of sleeping pills. They were directed to by that crazy leader of theirs..." He snapped his fingers several times in an attempt to remember. "What was that asinine name he called himself?"

Jove. Jenny knew the name, but she was not inclined to tell it to that asshole sitting in front of her. It took everything she had not to jump across the desk and punch him in his arrogant face.

The officer gave up trying to recall the name, waving the notion away with his hand. "Makes no difference. Anyway, the whole town was glad to be rid of them, to tell you the truth. They were nothing but trouble. They stole stuff, ran around naked all the time...between you and me, it was a relief when they offed themselves."

Jenny felt her whole body shake with anger, although she maintained the ability to repress it.

Zack remained unaffected. "So, you remember this?"

"I was a kid back then," the policeman explained, "but I do remember my father talking about what a nuisance them hippies were. He was as happy to see them go as anybody. He was the sheriff, and he knew he finally wouldn't be getting any more calls about them. His job got made a million times easier when they all took those pills."

"There weren't any pills," Jenny spewed, her ability to keep quiet temporarily overshadowed by her anger. Resuming control, she closed her mouth, sealing her lips tightly, but hate shot out of her eyes like flames.

Both Zack and the officer looked at her, awaiting an explanation.

She offered none.

Zack put his arm around Jenny's shoulder and thanked the policeman for his time, leading his wife quickly out the door to the safety of the car. "What was that about?" he asked as soon as they crossed the parking lot.

Feeling the fury leave her body, Jenny was finally able to calm down. "It wasn't suicide," she declared emphatically. "Jove did not have anybody take any pills."

"Jove?"

Jenny climbed inside the car as Zack did the same. "Yes, Jove. That was the spiritual leader's name." She closed the door behind her. "And he never would have done such a thing."

Zack cocked his eyebrow and looked at Jenny. "Do you think it was murder, then?"

"I absolutely do," she declared, "and I'll bet anything that guy's pig of a father was behind it."

Zack looked at Jenny with wide eyes. "Did you just call him a pig?"

She had. She knew she had. Although, she also knew that word would have never come out of her mouth if she had been in control of her actions. The notion of what may have just happened to her terrified her to the point where she said nothing in response to Zack's comment.

"Jenny, are you okay?"

This time she nodded. "Yeah, I'm okay. I was just really, really angry for a moment there." She swallowed before adding, "Frighteningly so."

"You know, that wasn't smart of me at all," he stated, shaking his head. "I shouldn't have taken you to a police station considering we're dealing with a spirit who doesn't do well around cops. That could have been a disaster."

"If I had done what I was inclined to do, it would have been," Jenny declared. "I felt the urge to yell at him and slap him across the face. I think I was able to resist simply because I'm an adult and I know it's wrong to do that to an officer. If I were a child, though, I may not have been able to stop myself."

"Which is probably what happened to Addy," Zack declared.

Jenny's tone reduced to a whisper. "Which is probably what happened to Addy."

"What was it like for you, being in there?"

She released a breath and shook her head as she pulled the car out of the parking lot. "Frustrating. And strange. Somehow, I just knew that the cop was lying about everything. I knew the spiritual leader's name was Jove, first of all, which is something I shouldn't have been aware of, and I was *positive* that he had never told us to take pills. We didn't steal from the people around us, either, and we were *not* the nuisance he made us out to be. It was very hard to just stand there and listen to him talk about us so badly."

"You're saying *us*," Zack pointed out warily. "You are Jenny in there, right?"

With a nod and a slight laugh, Jenny said, "Yeah, it's me. But during the conversation with the officer, I felt like I had been a one of those people living at Eden—and he had been telling lies about me and the people I considered family."

"Well, it sounds like there are definitely two sides to this story," Zack concluded, "and we need to figure out which one is correct."

"Probably the third one," Jenny replied, glancing at Zack out of the corner of her eye. "Isn't the truth usually somewhere in the middle?"

He began to look at his phone again. "That it is."

As Jenny followed the directions from her GPS to get her back to the highway, Zack busied himself with the Internet. After a while, he announced, "Go figure. Once again, now that I know what I'm looking for, I am able to find a good deal of information about it."

"What does it say?"

"This says…" He changed his tone to indicate he was reading directly from the article. "*The Family at Eden took up residence near*

Bedford, Georgia in the early 1960s. With an emphasis on communal living and oneness with nature, the group of forty-five young adults lived largely off the land, foregoing many modern conveniences such as electricity and running water. They lived a vegetarian lifestyle, eating the food grown on the property and eggs laid by the chickens who freely roamed their land.

"At times, members of The Family would venture into town, bartering or even selling their crops and firewood with members of the community. According to longtime residents of Bedford, however, the bartering was not always consensual. 'Sometimes we would wake up to find our garden tools had been replaced with a dozen eggs, or our clothes had been taken off the line and a pile of firewood would be there instead,' complains Sherman Abbot, who was in his thirties when the Family at Eden took up residence near Bedford. 'We had always been able to leave our doors unlocked at night, but once those hippies came around, all of that changed.'

"Most of Bedford's residents shared in Abbot's sentiments, although a select few sympathized with The Family's plight. 'They did need to stop taking things that didn't belong to them,' admits Thelma Morton, another longtime resident of Bedford , 'but I never felt like we were in danger of meeting any harm because they lived close by. I even tried to help them out sometimes by buying some of their produce or hiring them for some household tasks. I realized they had very little means to make money, and they were just trying to get by. Unfortunately for them, it wasn't possible to live solely off the land. They did need a little help once in a while.'

"In addition to the complaints about theft, many of the town's residents also took exception with the frequent drug use and flagrant nudity exhibited by members of The Family. 'We certainly didn't need our kids seeing them parading around with no clothes on,' Abbot said with disgust, 'and they did it all the time. It just wasn't right.'

"Although she represents the minority, Thelma Morton has a different take on the situation. 'It wasn't like they walked around town naked…they kept the nudity on their own property. It seemed to me that people would drive out there just to catch them with no clothes on, and then they would turn around and complain about it. Eden was in a very secluded spot...if the townspeople didn't want to see them naked, they didn't have to. I think people just looked for excuses to complain about them.'

"On June 17, 1968, all forty-five members of The Family were found dead at Eden, the cause of death being an apparent mass suicide by overdose. For the members who had autopsies, toxicology screens revealed fatal levels of the barbiturate Nembutal in their systems, which was commonly prescribed as a sleeping pill and often abused in the 1960s."

Zack looked up from his phone. "Hey, it says here that Nembutal was one of the drugs in Marilyn Monroe's system when she overdosed."

"I guess it's potent," Jenny replied.

"Apparently."

"So, what do you make of this?" she asked. "It appears our little spirit friend believes this was a murder, but everyone else seems to think it was suicide...even the author of that article, who obviously went to great lengths to represent both sides of the story."

"I'm kind of leaning to the murder theory, myself," Zack concluded. "I imagine the spirit would remember if he had taken pills. Besides, if he's pissed off enough about his death to stick around for fifty years, I have to think that he didn't do it on purpose."

Jenny silently digested the information. Zack's point was valid; suicide didn't appear to be likely. Perhaps the spirit's version of events was correct. But had the sheriff really murdered everyone in The Family so he could be rid of them? This, too, seemed like implausible behavior from a man who had sworn to serve and protect. Although, Jenny had learned in previous cases that nobody can be above suspicion. Considering how strongly the spirit felt that the sheriff was guilty, she certainly couldn't ignore the possibility that it was true.

But how to find out?

She let out a sigh as she posed, "What do you think the chances are that we will be able to find out exactly who this spirit is? I get that he—or she—was a member of The Family, but maybe if we can get a name we can find some people who may have known him." Jenny scrunched her face. "Or her."

"You're going to have to tell me that, chief," Zack replied. "Do *you* think you can figure out who it is?"

Jenny stayed quiet for a moment. "Maybe." Although, she didn't have any idea how.

"You know what I think we should do?" Zack began. "I think we should contact your private investigator friend to see if he can track down the whereabouts of this..." He referred back to his screen. "...Thelma Morton. It seems she didn't have a problem with the people at Eden, so she might be able to give us their side of the story or, at the very least, an account that isn't heavily biased in the other direction. It seems like most people in the town would side with law enforcement on this one."

Jenny waved her finger at Zack. "You know, that's not a bad idea. It said in the article that she had interactions with them, buying their stuff and hiring them. Maybe she knew some of them personally."

"That's what I'm thinking. The only problem is...what are the odds she's still alive?"

After some quick mental math, she said, "Well, it's been fifty years, give or take. How old was she back then?"

"The article doesn't say," Zack observed, "but her name is Thelma. That sounds to me like she'd be old."

With a laugh, Jenny noted, "You do realize that every old lady named Thelma was once a little girl named Thelma."

"Yes, but they were little girls named Thelma back when Thelma was a popular name, which was probably in the twenties or thirties."

"If she was born in 1920, she'd be..." Jenny stopped while she calculated the number.

"Old." Zack finished her sentence. "Probably too old to give us any helpful information."

She made a face to express her defeat, but she quickly regained her optimism. "Does that article say the names of anyone who died at Eden? Maybe we can contact a living relative of one of the victims themselves. They'd probably be able to give us The Family's side of the story."

"This one doesn't give names," he clarified, "but that's not to say another wouldn't."

"Can you look up some other websites?"

"One step ahead of you." Zack's finger was already busy pressing and swiping the screen.

Jenny silently contemplated the obvious hole in the theory. If the spiritual leader had called himself Jove, the other members of The Family may have gone by assumed names as well. Even if they were able to find out that *John Doe* had died at Eden, that doesn't mean Jenny would have been able to determine which member of The Family that had been. Perhaps this time the identity of her contact would always remain anonymous, and she'd just have to settle for seeking justice for the entire group as a whole.

At that moment, a thought occurred to her. "Zack, do you remember what Dr. Wilson told us...that they were never able to get the name of the person who spoke through Addy? That she was always just vague when they asked what her name was?"

His attention remained focused on his phone. "Yeah."

"You don't suppose it's possible that they actually did get the name but didn't realize it?"

With that, he glanced in her direction. "You're going to have to clarify what you mean by that."

"The spiritual leader went by Jove. Maybe this particular person went by the name Tree or something, and when Dr. Wilson asked for the spirit's name, he didn't realize Tree was actually a legitimate response as opposed to a defiant sarcastic remark."

Zack shrugged and frowned as he considered the notion. "True. Or perhaps when they asked for the spirit's name, Addy replied with, 'fuck you, asshole.'"

"I guess we'll have to find out," Jenny said as her phone rang from inside her purse. As she fished her hand around her bag, she added, "Remind me to ask him about that." She found her phone, putting it to her ear. "Hello?"

"Hi, Jenny, it's Kayla."

"Oh, hey...how's it going?"

"Okay. I was just wondering how things were progressing for you and when you planned to come back."

"We're on our way back now, actually." Somehow Jenny got the impression that the question had been loaded. "Did something happen that we should be aware of?"

After a sigh, Kayla admitted, "Matthew made another appearance, wanting to know exactly how old Julia and Mary were."

Jenny cringed outwardly as she braced for the rest. "Did you tell him?"

"The doctor did, yes."

"And how did he react to that?"

"He didn't say anything when we told him that Julia was dead, but when he found out Mary was still alive and in her sixties, he demanded to see her." She paused before adding, "And soon."

Chapter 9

"I knew it," Jenny said, banging on the steering wheel as soon as she hung up with Kayla. "I knew Matthew would want to speed things up." Suddenly, she was upset with herself for not making a bigger case on his behalf.

"What happened?" Zack asked.

"It seems Matthew made another appearance while we were gone, and Dr. Wilson followed his old routine of showing pictures that made Mary grow up slowly. After a couple of photos, Devon looked at him and asked, 'where are they now?' According to Kayla, Dr. Wilson hemmed and hawed a little bit, but Devon insisted he answer. Long story short, he now knows that Julia is dead and that Mary is a grandmother…and he insisted on seeing Mary as soon as possible. I guess he doesn't want to waste another minute."

"I can't say I blame him for that. Fifty-some years is a long time to be in limbo."

"Agreed," Jenny said with frustration evident in her tone. "I knew that before, and I yet didn't do anything about it."

"You can't possibly be beating yourself up over this," Zack replied with conviction. "You're the reason Matthew is getting any answers at all."

"No, I'm not," she protested. "That honor belongs to Devon."

"Devon drew pictures of trains on fire. You took it from there."

She strummed her fingers but said no more on the subject. Dwelling on what she should or should not have done—or who deserved credit—wasn't going to get her anywhere. At this point, she needed to focus on where things were going, especially since the case seemed to be progressing in a hurry. "Kayla said Dr. Wilson is working on arranging a meeting with Mary."

"That ought to be interesting," Zack said as he returned his attention to his phone.

"Interesting, indeed," Jenny muttered. Her mind began contemplating all of the different scenarios that could possibly unfold during the meeting, some good, some bad. She wondered what Devon's demeanor had been like when he insisted on seeing Mary. Had he been angry? Was he pleading? Or was he simply matter-of-fact? Jenny wished she had asked Kayla that question.

After many miles in silence, Zack finally spoke. "I found a website that has a record of the people who died at Eden that day."

The morbid nature of that list was not lost on Jenny. She wondered whether those were the names of people who had willingly committed suicide or if they were the victims of one of the largest—and most subtle—mass murders in history. "Oh, yeah?"

"I'm finding one of these names to be especially interesting."

Jenny became instantly curious. "What name is that?"

"Robert Morton." Zack seemed proud of himself.

Jenny, on the other hand, was only confused. "Why is that name interesting?"

"Do you remember the article I read to you? That lady named Thelma was sympathetic to the cause?" She remained silent, so Zack continued. "Thelma *Morton?*"

After it had been spelled out for her, she was finally able to make the connection. "Oh...A relative, maybe?"

"It's possible. It says here that Robert was only nineteen; maybe Thelma had been his mother?"

Jenny mulled it over. "That depends on how old Thelma was."

"I think that might be a good question for the world's greatest private investigator."

"That's what I'm thinking, too," Jenny said as she handed Zack her phone. "Can you dial Kyle Buchanan for me? He's a contact."

"We're slated to meet up with Mary tomorrow afternoon," Dr. Wilson announced as he took a seat in the hotel's restaurant, joining Jenny, Zack and the Moores at a table. "She will bring her children and grandchildren with her, but we will hold off on having them come into the room until after we see how things go with Mary."

"How do you expect they will go?" Kayla asked quickly and nervously.

"Fine," Dr. Wilson said emotionlessly. He sipped the water that the others had ordered for him. "He's given us no reason to expect otherwise."

Kayla didn't look appeased.

"Even though I presented the offer for us to come to her, she decided to make the journey herself. She said it would give her something to do rather than sit around and wait for us to arrive," Dr. Wilson continued.

"Where is she coming from?" Jenny asked.

"Montgomery, Alabama."

"But that's far," Jenny protested, "and she's older. Won't that make for an uncomfortable trip?"

"Ummm…" Zack said. "Are you implying the drive would be more comfortable for you?"

Jenny thought about her numb backside after the relatively short journey to Georgia and simply giggled at her own suggestion.

"She said her son would drive her," Dr. Wilson explained, "so she should at least be more comfortable as a passenger. Besides, I made the offer more than once, and she insisted."

With a shrug, Jenny decided to drop it. "Okay, so how will this unfold?"

"Well, I've arranged to use one of the meeting rooms in the hotel lobby, although the goal is to keep it casual. I just wanted us to have some privacy and a little more space than the guest rooms provide."

"Will I be able to stay with him?" Kayla asked, her nerves apparent on her face.

"Absolutely. We want this to be as comfortable and natural for Devon as possible."

With that statement, Kayla's expression relaxed a notch.

"But how do we know Matthew will even be there when Mary arrives?" Zack asked. "He seems to come and go as he pleases...what if he's not making an appearance at that moment?"

The doctor shrugged. "It's always possible, but I whole-heartedly believe that Matthew will come around when Mary enters the room."

Zack remained confused. "How will he know it's Mary? Last he knew she was nine. Now she's a grandmother. It's not like he'll necessarily be able to recognize her."

Dr. Wilson cracked a rare smile. "You'd be surprised; the parental bond runs deep."

Jenny placed her hand on her belly.

"How do we act when she comes in?" Kayla asked.

"It's largely hands-off," Dr. Wilson explained. "We sit back and watch how it unfolds."

"But what if it gets..." Kayla couldn't seem to find the word she was looking for.

Holding up his hand, Dr. Wilson said, "If things start to become tense, we can have Mary step out of the room, although I don't see that happening."

Kayla covered her mouth with her hand as she shot a worried glance at her son. The parental bond did indeed run deep.

Having much more experience and substantially less invested in the matter, Dr. Wilson remained scientific. "I'd like to record the encounter." He turned to Kayla before adding, "With your permission, of course. The camera will be off in the corner; it should be rather inconspicuous."

Kayla silently nodded her approval. Jenny imagined that was the least of her concerns.

"I guess it all really comes down to show time," Zack noted.

Dr. Wilson's gaze met everyone else's at the table. "It all really comes down to show time."

Kayla wrung her hands as Dr. Wilson set up the camera in the corner of the meeting room. Devon sat innocently at one of the tables, his attention focused on his tablet. He was blissfully unaware of what was about to transpire.

"Are you okay?" Jenny whispered to Kayla.

She nodded in return, releasing a deep exhale. "I just want this whole thing to be over. The whole thing. I want the meeting to be done, and I want Matthew to go away and leave Devon alone."

Jenny's first thought was that if Devon had the gift, Matthew may have just been the first of many encounters for him. However, she didn't want to bring that up at the moment. She simply rubbed Kayla's back and said, "Hopefully, it will be over soon."

Kayla seemed to appreciate the support.

Jenny continued to talk so she could keep Kayla's mind occupied. "Mary seemed nice when we spoke to her in the lobby."

"Yes, she did," Kayla agreed. "She looked scared to death, the poor thing."

"This can't be easy on her, either."

"No, it certainly can't."

"She's got her family here, though," Jenny said. "That has to be comforting."

Kayla nodded. "It does."

"Okay," Dr. Wilson said as he walked away from the camera. "I've got the video recording, so at this point I think it's time to let it happen."

Jenny could see Kayla's hands trembling as Dr. Wilson walked toward the door. He turned around to survey the room as he posed, "Is everybody ready?"

Kayla released another deep breath and said, "Let's do this."

Dr. Wilson excused himself out the door, returning with a very nervous Mary, who took tiny steps into the room as her eyes fixated on Devon. The tension was palpable.

At first, Devon didn't look up from his tablet, completely unaware that anyone had entered the room. After a subtle gesture of encouragement from Dr. Wilson, Mary cleared her throat and softly said, "Hello."

Devon's eyes immediately raised, his face remaining expressionless for quite some time. Hours seemed to tick by as he studied Mary's face without saying a word. The silence was eventually interrupted by Devon's tiny, awe-filled voice announcing, "You look like Nora."

Jenny immediately shifted her gaze to Mary. Although Jenny had never heard the name Nora before, Mary seemed to know exactly who Devon was talking about. Tears pooled in her eyes as she let out a nervous laugh and said, "So I've been told."

Rising from his seat, Devon walked slowly toward Mary, who sat down in a nearby chair so she could look at him at eye level. The two stared at each other as Mary clearly fought her urge to cry. Jenny felt unable to breathe, and she could only imagine the feeling was a million times worse for Kayla. She slipped her arm around Kayla's shoulder, pulling her in tighter for support.

"Your eyes look the same," Devon noted in a hushed tone.

The apprehension that had filled Jenny's body was quickly replaced by sadness. She imagined very little else about Mary resembled the little girl Matthew once knew. Her smooth, unblemished skin was now wrinkled; her brown hair had turned gray. But eyes don't age, and Matthew was able to find that one trace of the child he had loved more than life itself and spent more than a half-century trying to find.

It took every ounce of energy for Jenny to maintain her composure.

Mary was unable to refrain from crying. "There's so much to tell you," she blurted through sobs.

Devon reached out his little hand and placed it on Mary's shoulder. She rested her hand on top of his, closing her eyes and allowing the tears to fall freely. "I didn't know you were still here," she said.

"I couldn't find you," Devon replied. "I looked everywhere."

Mary nodded. "I know you did."

"I'm sorry I couldn't help you."

She let out a little laugh that appeared to be a mixture of anguish and dismay. "There's nothing to be sorry for. I'm just sorry you didn't escape the accident."

Jenny could see the sudden change in Devon's expression; he looked like he was having trouble understanding what Mary had just said. "The accident?" he asked.

Mary's demeanor also switched, but from sad to nervous. She glanced quickly at Dr. Wilson before returning her focus to Devon, explaining, "Yes…the accident." She swallowed before adding, "The train explosion."

In an instant, Devon's face went blank. Before anyone had the chance to act, his eyes rolled into the back of his head and his little body went limp.

Chapter 10

Kayla shrieked as Mary grabbed hold of Devon's arm before he hit the floor. She held his seemingly lifeless body upright while every adult in the room rushed to his side. Within seconds, he opened his eyes and blinked repeatedly, looking around him to try to get his bearings. He noticed Mary supporting him, and his face immediately changed to show his displeasure that she had her hands on him.

Kayla scooped Devon up and spun him around, sitting him on her hip as she looked him in the eye. "Are you okay, baby?" she asked, clearly wearing a mask of bravery so she wouldn't scare her son.

He nodded slowly, raising a finger and pointing at Mary. "Who is that?"

"That's Miss Mary," Kayla explained. "She's a very nice lady. You don't remember talking to her?"

Devon shook his head before leaning in and wrapping his arms around his mother's neck. She squeezed him tightly, the look on her face indicating that she would have given anything to make this whole situation go away. They remained in that embrace for several moments before Dr. Wilson's voice permeated the room, stating the obvious. "I think maybe it's time we take a break."

A break. Jenny wondered if Kayla was going to allow this to continue at all. Considering everything that had just happened, she wouldn't have faulted Kayla for putting an end to this meeting and heading straight back home.

Jenny's eyes caught a glimpse of Mary, who remained motionless in the chair, looking white as a sheet. Feeling bad for her, Jenny approached and squatted next to her, placing her hand on Mary's shoulder. She could feel the trembling. "Are *you* okay?"

Mary lifted her gaze to meet Jenny's, helplessness apparent in her eyes. Her voice was little more than a whisper when she said, "I just don't want to do anything that will hurt that little boy."

"I know you don't." Glancing back over her shoulder, Jenny noticed that Devon had since let go of the death grip he'd had on Kayla's neck and was playing with her earring—a notion which provided Jenny with a good deal of encouragement that he was unharmed by the ordeal. Turning her attention back to Mary, she lightened her tone and stated, "He looks like he's doing better already." To get Mary's mind off the topic, she added, "So, who is this Nora that you look so much like?"

Mary smiled and looked at her lap. "My grandmother, on my mother's side. I have always favored her. When you look at pictures of us at the same age, the likeness is uncanny." Her tone grew more solemn as she noted, "I guess I'm about the age that my grandmother was the last time my father saw her."

Commotion from behind Jenny caused her to turn around. Devon had climbed down from his mother's arms and was running in circles around a table. Jenny smiled, focusing her attention back on Mary. "I guess that means he's doing okay."

Mary looked beyond Jenny to the hyper little boy, hanging her head and closing her eyes in relief. After taking a moment to regain her composure, she softly noted, "You know, my father was not a hurtful man at all. He'd never do anything to harm anybody, let alone a child. I don't know what caused that little episode, but I can assure you it's nothing my father did deliberately."

Jenny nodded and smiled compassionately. "I know. I have already gotten that impression about him."

Confusion clouded Mary's expression. "I wonder what made Devon faint, then."

"I don't know," Jenny confessed, "but I can try to find out."

Dr. Wilson had busied himself with his camera, a notion which Jenny found to be a bit cold considering what had just happened to Devon. Although, the behavior didn't surprise her considering she had concluded a long time ago that Dr. Wilson's bedside manor was virtually non-existent. Marching over to him with purpose, Jenny asked, "Any idea what happened over there?" The irritation in her voice was a little more pronounced than she had intended it to be.

Apparently pleased with the status of his camera, Dr. Wilson took several steps away from it and said, "My guess would be a rapid retreat."

"Rapid retreat?"

"We've witnessed it before," Wilson added, "although with less consequence."

Jenny didn't say anything; the doctor took the hint and continued. "When Matthew hears something he doesn't like, he tends to withdraw. It appears this time he withdrew so rapidly it caught Devon off guard. In the previous instances, Matthew has left slowly enough that Devon has been able to recover in what appears to be a seamless transition. This time, Matthew's departure was rapid—so rapid that, for a moment, neither Matthew nor Devon was in charge. I believe what you witnessed was a momentary lapse between the time Matthew left and Devon returned."

Jenny closed her eyes as she considered that Devon's body was essentially unoccupied for a moment—temporarily void of a soul. "That's frightening."

"Not really," the doctor said without emotion. "It's not the first time I've seen it."

Jenny's jaw dropped. Had she really just heard him correctly? "Then why didn't you warn Kayla that it might happen?"

"If she feared that her son might faint, she may not have given her permission for this meeting, which, I believe, is essential to complete Matthew's journey."

A million thoughts swirled around Jenny's head, none of them good. She contemplated calling him out, suggesting that he was less concerned about Matthew's journey and more concerned with his own. She wanted to express her disgust that he had misled Kayla into thinking this was going to be perfectly harmless, noting that doctor's licenses can be revoked when sketchy practices are put into play. After giving brief consideration to all of her arguments, however, she decided to say nothing, fully realizing that her hormone levels were running high these days. She could always voice her disgust later when she was more rational; shooting off her mouth in a moment of high emotion might have ended up being regrettable.

Although, it certainly was tempting.

Opting for the civil approach, Jenny said, "So Devon isn't in any danger?"

"None at all," the doctor said. "If my previous cases are any indication, he won't even remember that he fainted."

"It seems like he didn't even know who Mary was, even though he had just talked to her."

"He didn't talk to her," Dr. Wilson replied, looking Jenny in the eye. "Matthew did."

The words sent a chill down Jenny's spine. Even though she had intellectually come to terms with what was happening to Devon, she still found the notion to be quite eerie.

Jenny heard a distinct, "Hi-YA!" from behind her, and she was delighted to see that Devon had apparently made a full recovery and was showing his karate skills to Mary, who in turn smiled from ear to ear. Jenny couldn't help but laugh at the determined look on Devon's face; he was clearly very serious about his martial arts.

The laughter faded quickly, however, and Jenny hung her head when she came to a realization…her burst of laughter had made her wet herself—not completely, but enough to be noticeable. Grateful for her long maternity shirt that covered her bottom, she discretely walked over and told Zack she needed to head back to their hotel room for a moment. She was glad when he didn't ask why.

The ride in the elevator seemed to take forever, and she prayed that no one would join her in there. Fortunately, nobody did. She eventually made it to the room, pulling some clean underwear and shorts out of her suitcase, wondering how she was going to explain the outfit change when she got back downstairs. Perhaps she should linger for a while and claim she spilled something on herself while eating a snack.

Ooh, she thought, *a snack*. That sounded really good.

Once she got herself cleaned up and munched on some carrots and crackers, she decided to check her phone for messages. Her heart began to pound when she noticed she had a voicemail from Kyle Buchanan, hopefully with information about Eden. Pressing the phone to her ear, she listened to his message.

"Hey, Jenny, it's Kyle. I found out some information for you. It seems that Thelma Morton was indeed Robert Morton's mother, which would explain the sympathy she had for the group. However, Thelma passed away years ago. We obviously won't be able to get any information from her...*but*, she had a daughter who was a few years younger than Robert, and she's still alive. Her name is Dawn Sigle, and I put in a phone call to her. She says she does have a little bit information about The Family, although she admits it might be limited. She suggested that there was a couple that had lived at Eden but left the family shortly before the tragedy, and if we can find them, we can probably get some answers about what life was like there. Maybe they'd be able to tell us if this Jove character was likely to have orchestrated a mass suicide or if something else might have gone on.

"Anyway, I have Dawn Sigle's phone number for you. I'll keep working on trying to find out who the couple is that left Eden. I'll let you know if I get anywhere with that." He left the phone number and ended his message.

Sitting on the edge of the bed, she digested this information. While the sister may have known some things, that couple would have surely been able to provide much more information. She hoped that Kyle would be able to work his magic and find them—an inside source would have been invaluable.

Deciding that she'd taken enough time to explain the new clothes, she headed back downstairs to the meeting room. Devon was still entertaining Mary with his antics, clearly delighted to have a new—and extremely attentive—audience member. Kayla stood off by herself watching the show, the relief on her face obvious. Jenny slipped in next to her, whispering, "I take it he's doing better?"

Kayla shrugged, the awe obvious on her face. "It's like he never fainted at all."

"That's fantastic news." Jenny smiled genuinely. "I talked to Dr. Wilson before, and he said that he thinks Matthew retreated too quickly, and that's why Devon blacked out."

With a nod, Kayla said, "Yeah, I spoke to him about it, too."

Jenny balled her hands nervously into fists as she posed, "So, are you willing to let this go on?"

"I know I probably appear to be a bad mother when I say this, but, yes, I am. We haven't come this far only to turn around and go back home with Matthew still in our lives." She shook her head. "I just want him gone, and I'm hoping this is what it takes to make that happen."

"You don't sound like a bad mother."

With a smile, Kayla said, "Thanks. I appreciate that. I think the fact that Devon is a boy is actually helping me take this in stride. I swear that child is a set of stitches waiting to happen. He's constantly jumping off this and bumping into that and falling off things and face-planting...I think this fainting episode has startled me less than it should because I'm used to it by now. It's like nothing fazes me anymore." Kayla glanced at Jenny knowingly. "Speaking of which, I see you've changed your clothes."

Jenny felt herself blush. "I spilled something on myself."

"No, you didn't," Kayla retorted, biting her lip to keep from giggling. "I saw what happened. I recognize the look. But don't worry; we've all been there. In fact, I have a name for what happened to you—I call that the laugh-n-pee."

Jenny laughed out loud as Kayla continued, "I still do it sometimes, even though my son is five." She placed her hand on Jenny's shoulder and added, "There's also the cough-n-pee, the sneeze-n-pee...there's even the stand-up-too-fast-n-pee."

"You mean this wasn't an isolated incident?"

"Oh, heavens, no. You'll be doing this for the rest of your life. There's nothing at all glamorous about motherhood, let me tell you. In fact, I remember the 'three strikes' rule I used to have when Devon was a baby.

He was a puker...he spit up on me all the time. And when I say all the time, I mean *all the time.* If I changed my clothes every time he spit up on me, I would have worn twenty outfits a day. I certainly wasn't about to do that much laundry, so I developed my three strikes rule. Once he'd thrown up on me for the third time, then—and only then—would I change my clothes."

Jenny crinkled her nose, thinking about walking around with vomit on her.

Kayla continued, unfazed. "I'm telling you, I went to *the store* with puke on my shirt, I went to *friends' houses* with puke on my shirt...as long as there were two stains or less, I was going with it." She shook her head and giggled. "It was amazing just how low I had stooped. I used to take so much pride in my appearance, but then after Devon was born, I was like, 'who cares?' I came dangerously close to losing my baby during childbirth...after going through something like that, a little hurl on your shirt is nothing. Besides, when you have a new baby, you're just too damn tired to care about anything anyway."

Standing motionlessly as she digested the information, Jenny asked, "Why hasn't anybody ever told me this?"

"It's a conspiracy," Kayla replied quickly. "When I first had Devon, I was *shocked* by some of the things I encountered. I turned to my mother and my friends who had kids and was like, 'how come you never told me it would be like this?' They had all told me that I was just going to *love* motherhood and that they were so *excited* that I was having a baby. They never once mentioned the constant puke or the incessant crying or the fact that I would wet my pants every time I did a jumping jack."

"What did they say when you confronted them?"

"They told me they just didn't want to scare me. They figured they'd just let me find out on my own what it was all about. In the meantime, I felt like a freak because I thought I was the only person in the world who found parenting to be so difficult." She shook her head, the memory obviously still a little painful. "At that point, I decided I wasn't going to sugarcoat it with expectant moms. The truth is, having a baby is *hard.* Not only that, but you also have to come to the realization that your body is never going to be what it used to be. You wet yourself, your stomach is all stretch-marky and flabby, and your breasts fall to the floor. It's a lot to swallow all at once—and with the hormone changes that accompany it, it's almost unbearable at times."

Jenny smiled politely, although she felt deep down inside that Kayla was just being negative. Perhaps the other mothers didn't tell her it was going to be like that because, for them, it wasn't. Kayla's experience was probably unique because Devon had issues stemming from that incident where he had stopped breathing as a newborn. For most mothers, Jenny decided, it wasn't all that bad.

Devon's martial arts display came to an abrupt end. He froze for a moment, standing perfectly still, causing both Jenny and Kayla to direct their attention to him. He took several steps closer to Mary, whose face reflected her uncertainty, and simply asked, "Did you have a good life?"

"Did I have a good life?" Mary seemed unsure if she had heard him correctly. After taking a moment to let the question sink in, she smiled and softly said, "Yes, I had a very good life."

"Did your mom?"

Mary battled tears as she nodded. Gathering her composure, she was finally able to whisper, "She did."

"She got married again," Devon replied, more as a statement than a question.

Again, Mary nodded. "He was a very nice man. He was also a widower, so he understood what she was going through. He never asked her to forget you." She wiped a tear from her eye before adding, "We kept pictures of you on our wall."

Devon remained motionless, causing Jenny to wonder if there was going to be another fainting episode. She slipped her arm through Kayla's, positive that the nervous mother must have been thinking the same thing. Kayla placed her hand on Jenny's, silently expressing her gratitude for the reassurance.

Jenny's worry, however, was for nothing. Devon took another step forward, asking, "He treated her good?"

"Very." Mary smiled compassionately, love apparent in her eyes. "And he was good to me, too. I hope you're not upset by this, but he treated me like I was his own daughter. I never forgot you were my father, but I never felt like I got cheated out of having a dad, either. I just had a different dad."

Jenny felt Kayla's grip tighten, making her aware of her own body and the fact that she hadn't breathed in quite some time. She released a slow exhale, waiting for Devon to fall to the floor, but again, it didn't happen. Instead, he looked at Mary and simply said, "I heard you had kids."

Mary went into detail about her three children, who eventually came into the room and introduced themselves to Devon. The meeting remained productive until the grandchildren made their appearance; at that point, Devon recognized he had young playmates, and the overactive child returned to chase them around.

As the little ones played, the adults gathered around Mary, whose eyes reflected her exhaustion. Dr. Wilson began the conversation. "I believe this went well, no?"

Kayla wrapped her arms around herself as if warding off a chill. "For the most part. Aside from that one incident, everything seemed okay." She looked intently at Dr. Wilson. "Do you think Matthew will be gone for good now?"

"That hasn't been my experience in the past. From what I've always seen, the children just outgrow their ability to receive contacts."

"Well, for me," Jenny began in a voice louder than Dr. Wilson's, "the spirits usually cross over when their issue gets resolved. This case is a little bit unusual because Matthew's concern is different than most." Worry graced her face as she added, "Unlike the murder victims I've dealt with, there's no definitive end to what Matthew wants."

Zack spoke up for the first time in a while. "At no point did anyone discuss the fact that Julia has crossed over. Maybe if we let him know that's where he can find his wife, he will be eager to go there."

"But he knows she's remarried," Mary countered. "Do you think that will prevent him from wanting to cross? I mean, yes, his wife is on the other side, but so is her new husband."

"The new husband who took excellent care of her and allowed pictures of Matthew to remain on the walls," Jenny said compassionately. "It sounds to me like it shouldn't be an issue."

Kayla put her head in her hands. "I just want this to be over." She suddenly raised her head, seemingly aware of her potential mistake, and said to Mary, "No offense."

Mary stood, looking Kayla in the eye. "Believe me, none taken. I can't even imagine how this has been for you. As parents, all we want is what's best for our children, and you've had this crazy, unbelievable event to deal with. I'm sorry that your son had to be the person my father clung to, although at the same time I want to thank both you and him for helping my dad. I had no idea my father wasn't resting peacefully." She shook her head rapidly, clearly disturbed by the notion. "I want him to cross over as soon as possible, too…for everybody's sake. I hate the thought that he's been in limbo this long, and I hate knowing he's been haunting your son."

"Well, hopefully by tonight he won't be," Jenny remarked. "Matthew seems pretty adamant about making appearances today." She looked intently at Dr. Wilson and loudly said, "Maybe by tonight he'll know he should cross over, and he can be on his way."

Hint, hint.

"I hate to even mention this," Mary began apologetically, "but as long as we're taking a break, I could really use a bite to eat. I know it seems trivial in the scheme of things, but I get the jitters when I get too hungry, and I feel myself becoming shaky."

"By all means," Dr. Wilson replied, "let's go get something to eat." He glanced over his shoulder at the children running in circles around the tables. "It seems Devon is occupied for the moment anyway."

While the crowd filed out into the lobby of the hotel, Jenny approached Zack, who remained behind in the meeting room. "Hey," she whispered as she approached, "you've been quiet. Is everything okay?"

Zack squinted and shook his head slightly. "Just a headache, that's all."

"Do you want to get something to eat? Food seems to help when Mary gets jittery. Maybe a burger will help your head." She nudged him with a smile.

"Believe it or not, no. I think I want to go upstairs and lay down for a little bit."

Zack had just turned down food; he must have not felt well at all. "I've got some acetaminophen in my purse…it's one of the few drugs I'm allowed to take. You want a couple?"

He nodded without saying a word.

"Come on," Jenny said, gently taking his arm and leading him out of the room. "I just had a snack a little bit ago, so I don't need to eat, either. Let's go upstairs; I'll get you some meds and tuck you in for a nap."

"See?" Zack said warily, "I told you you'll make a great mom."

Zack took little time to fall asleep. Opting to avoid the crowd downstairs and take advantage of some quiet, Jenny slipped out onto the balcony that overlooked nothing and pulled out her phone, studying her contact list before pressing any buttons. She hated making these unexpected calls, although in this case Kyle Buchanan had paved the way for her. This call wasn't completely out of the blue. With a sigh, Jenny pressed a few buttons and, upon hearing a woman's voice, said, "I'd like to speak to Dawn Sigle, please."

Chapter 11

"I believe you've already spoken with Kyle Buchanan about this," Jenny began, "but I would like to talk to you about your association with The Family at Eden, if you're willing."

"I'm willing," Dawn replied in an apologetic tone. "I just don't know how helpful I'll be. I was a child back then, and it was fifty years ago."

"Well, any information you can give me will be more information than I have. Truthfully, I know very little about it." She scrunched her face tightly before adding, "I'm not sure how much Kyle told you…about how I came to be involved with this investigation."

"He didn't mention anything. Honestly, I was wondering why this came up all of a sudden. I haven't heard anything about it in ages."

Although the word *psychic* was rolling off Jenny's tongue more freely these days, she still dreaded saying the word to complete strangers. Since she had the ability to take another route this time, she took advantage of it. "You have probably never heard of Dr. Albert Wilson, but he works with children who appear to be visited by spirits, or even, at times, possessed by them."

The silence on the other end of the phone gave Jenny no indication of how this was being received.

"Recently, a young girl named Addy was contacted by a spirit that, we believe, has ties to The Family. This spirit seems to be under the impression that what happened at Eden was not a mass suicide, but rather a mass murder."

Jenny paused, waiting for Dawn to react; taking the cue, Dawn eventually said, "Okay...a child who is possessed by a spirit with ties to Eden believes they were all murdered? That's what you're telling me?"

"I know," Jenny assured her, "it's absurd, but I assure you that's what's happened."

"I-I-I...I don't even know what to say."

"I can imagine," she replied sympathetically. "It's a lot to swallow. I'm used to it by now..." She braced herself and added, "I'm a psychic, so I receive this type of contact on a fairly regular basis, but the first time it happens to you, I know it can be rather overwhelming."

"That's an understatement."

Jenny let out a little giggle. "I guess I should explain this whole situation from the beginning. The child, Addy, had driven with her parents along Route 1 on her way to a family vacation, and it appears the spirit latched on to her as she drove by Eden. Her parents didn't know exactly what had happened at that point; they only knew that Addy became insolent after that car ride, referring to cops as *pigs* and talking about her hatred of *the man*. Considering she was just a small child, they didn't think she would have ever heard such terms, especially in this day and age, so they were pretty sure she wasn't simply repeating something that someone else had said."

Dawn remained silent, inviting Jenny to continue.

"For several years, her parents suspected that she'd been overtaken by a spirit from the sixties, but they didn't know who it was. Actually, they still don't know who it is. That's why I ended up retracing their steps from that family vacation, hoping I could get an indication of who this person may have been. As I drove by Bedford, I felt a tug that led me to Eden. I can only assume the spirit belongs to somebody who resided there at some point."

"So, what makes you believe it was a murder?"

"My husband and I didn't know anything about the property when I got led there, so we went to the local police station to ask what had happened at that location. It was then that we learned about the..." Jenny paused to choose her words carefully; Dawn had lost her brother at Eden. "...the tragedy. But while we were at the police station, I couldn't help but feel like the former sheriff had something to do with the deaths all those years ago. The spirit contacting me was quite adamant that there were no sleeping pills and that The Family's mass overdose had not been self-inflicted."

Dawn spoke slowly, as if trying to absorb her own words as she said them. "You think the sheriff *poisoned* them?"

"I don't think that, necessarily," Jenny replied, "but somebody certainly does."

Jenny heard a sigh on the other end of the phone, which she could only imagine was the sound of a woman who was rethinking everything she had once known to be true. She continued, trying to put Dawn out of her misery. "I would like to get to the bottom of it, if at all possible. I know the sheriff is long since dead by now, so justice can't be served in that respect, but if I can determine what actually happened back at Eden, perhaps this spirit will find solace and be able to cross over. Unfortunately, this person has been hanging out in limbo for fifty years, trying to find someone who will listen to his side of the story—or hers."

"And you don't know who it is?" Dawn asked.

"No," Jenny replied, "sadly, I don't. I'm under the impression that the members of the family went by assumed names, so it may be hard for me to find out who it actually is in this case."

"That's true. My brother was called *Music Maker* when he lived there."

"Music Maker?"

Dawn made a sound that implied affirmation. "The Family believed that people shouldn't be labeled by what their parents had dubbed them before they even had a personality. That type of branding was just part of the government's way to control people, according to them. They believed that people should be allowed to choose their own names, and they didn't have to take the form of a first and last name like convention dictated…it should have been more personal—more indicative of their character."

"Did everybody feel that way?" Jenny asked. "Is it possible that some of the people kept their given names?"

"I don't believe so," Dawn replied. "I am pretty sure it was required that they leave their old name behind."

"It was *required*?"

Bitterness rose in Dawn's voice. "Yeah. There were a lot of *requirements* involved with becoming a member of The Family."

"Can you remember what they were?"

"Some of them," Dawn replied. "One of them was that they had to cut all ties with their families...their real families."

The inconsistency struck Jenny immediately. "If the members had to cut ties with their families, how do you know about what went on there?"

"We bent the rules a little." She let out a sigh, suggesting she was having trouble formulating the words. "Robert was rebellious, yes. He wanted to change the world and stick it to the man and all that, but he had a good relationship with me and my mom. He wasn't willing to cut ties with us altogether, so we pretended that we didn't know him. We acted like we were just a local family who sympathized with their cause, and we hired them to do odd jobs from time to time. Sometimes Robert did the work for us; other times it was someone else, but it enabled us to stay in touch with him and at least see how he was doing.

"We even managed to sneak in a little alone time with him," Dawn continued. "A few times, he stayed over for dinner under the guise that he was doing work at our house. My mother had to pay him for his time, of course, to make it look like he had actually done some work. How sad is that? Having to pay to have dinner with your own child?"

"I'm sure it was worth every penny to her," Jenny concluded.

"Oh, absolutely. It was for me, too. I remember being delighted on the days I could see him. I was, what, twelve or thirteen? And he was my cool big brother, you know?" Her voice became softer. "He was my idol."

Jenny bowed her head. It seemed that time didn't heal all wounds; it simply made them more bearable to live with. A deceased sibling would always leave a void, no matter how long it had been. Putting renewed vigor in her tone, Jenny asked, "Okay, so what was the reasoning behind isolating these people from their families? Was it an attempt to make sure members of The Family stayed at Eden and didn't return home?"

"Oh, I'm sure of it. It was part of the brainwashing. Jove, the *spiritual leader* of the group, claimed that he was all about choice. You get to choose your own name. You get to choose if you wear clothes. You get to choose when you sleep...and the theory was you get to choose your own family. Apparently, though, if you wanted to be part of Eden, you needed to leave your real family behind. I'm sure you can see the irony; Jove claimed to be all about choice, but then he had a rule that said the members weren't allowed to see their relatives. Where's the freedom in that?"

"Well, for your sake, I'm glad that Robert found a way to make it work."

Dawn's voice grew soft again. "I am, too. I just wish that he never got caught up with those lunatics to begin with. He might still be here today if he hadn't."

"I hope you don't mind me asking," Jenny began, "but how *did* he get involved with The Family?"

"Of course I don't mind," Dawn replied before adding another sigh, her tone returning to its troubled nature. "My mother always blamed herself for it; she was only sixteen when he was born. She was unmarried—hardly in a position to raise a child. She was a child herself, for goodness sake. Needless to say, she made mistakes. I mean, all new mothers make mistakes, but she probably had more than her share due to her age and her circumstances. Throughout my childhood, she always told me she hadn't been strict enough with Robert—that maybe she was a little too concerned with her own social life to provide him with the structure that he needed growing up. As a result, he lost interest in school and fell into drugs at a relatively young age. He officially dropped out of high school on his sixteenth birthday, which was the earliest the law would allow, but he had stopped going long before that. He had become a member of that counter-culture of the sixties...you know, free love and all that. When he caught wind of the fact that The Family had moved into town, he was all too eager to join them. They didn't work; they lived off the land; they did drugs freely—it seemed like the perfect fit for him. He was a bit upset that they required he write off his family, but he and my mother figured out how to get around that. My mother had since gotten married to my father and had a different last name than Robert, so they could pretend they didn't know each other." She let out a cynical laugh. "Not that it mattered anyway; to them he was Music Maker, after all. He could have been anybody's child."

Jenny made a face. "I thought your mother and Robert both had the last name Morton."

"They did—after a while. My father ran off with another woman, so my mother changed her name back to Morton. She didn't want to have my father's last name after the way things ended."

Had Jenny not gotten remarried so quickly, she would have probably gone back to her maiden name as well after divorcing Greg. Becoming a Watkins had been a mistake—something she symbolically would have wanted to undo. "I get that," she said, "and good for her...no offense."

"None taken. I love my dad and all, but that was a bad move on his part. There are much better ways to end a marriage. I completely understand my mother's animosity, even if I don't necessarily share it."

A million thoughts were running through Jenny's head; she had to focus on just one aspect to ask about. "Okay," she began, gathering her bearings, "when you had these visits with your brother, did you see any indication that he was contemplating suicide?"

"None," Dawn replied definitively. "And neither did my mother, which is something she agonized over for the rest of her life. I felt so bad for her...I know she thought this stint at Eden was just a phase Robert was going through, and that eventually he'd come to his senses and leave the group. That's why she was willing to help them so much—she figured that while he was going through this little identity crisis, she could at least make sure he had enough to eat and had clothes on his back. But when it ended like it did, she was heartbroken. Honestly, she was never the same after that."

"I imagine she wasn't." Jenny placed her hand on her belly again, saying a quick, silent prayer that she didn't outlive this child. She wasn't sure she could handle it. Pushing that thought aside, she asked the million dollar question. "So, Dawn...do you think it was suicide? Or do you think it may have been murder?"

Silence ensued, which Jenny respected. This was not an easy question to answer. Eventually, Dawn said, "I don't know. I might be inclined to say it's both. I mean, their spiritual leader had them brainwashed pretty well; if he had told them all to take a bunch of pills, I imagine they would have. What would you call that...murder? Suicide? I don't know."

"So you think Jove was responsible, and it wasn't the sheriff?"

"Do you really think the sheriff would have killed people?"

"I don't know," Jenny replied. "I've learned in my last cases that nobody is above suspicion. Just because the man wears a badge, that doesn't mean he's of sound character. And the spirit was very adamant that the sheriff had something to do with it when I went to the station. In fact," she added, "the current sheriff is the old sheriff's son, and he specifically talked about how pleased his father was when The Family disappeared."

"He was *pleased*?"

Jenny realized her word choice may have been insensitive. Taking a moment to figure out how to rephrase it best, she said, "*Pleased* may be too strong of a word, but he did say that The Family gave his father a lot of trouble. His father was *relieved* when the incident happened."

More silence caused Jenny to wonder if she had offended Dawn. The answer became apparent when Dawn simply replied, "I could see that. They did break a lot of laws at Eden."

"I know of drugs, theft and public nudity," Jenny said with relief. "Was there anything else?"

Dawn giggled. "I think you could add public fornication to the list. They took the term *free love* to the fullest extent of its definition, but as far as I know, they left that on the property. The nudity, too. They always had clothes on when you'd see them in town."

"How did they get their drugs, do you know?"

"I don't," Dawn confessed. "Well, they grew their own marijuana, but I'm not sure how they got their other, harder drugs. I wouldn't think they'd have enough money for that. Nobody at Eden was gainfully employed...they got everything they owned from working odd jobs or stealing. I can't imagine they could afford a habit for four dozen people."

"Where there's a will, there's a way, I suppose," Jenny replied.

"I guess so."

"Now, how was the relationship between The Family and the police? Was there a lot of animosity there?"

"There was certainly no love lost, but I'm not sure the extent of it. My mother used to complain that Sheriff Babson was unnecessarily hard on them, but she didn't give me details. I was a kid, after all. But I'm also sure my mother had a biased opinion. To be fair, the sheriff probably had some legitimate complaints about the group. The Family was part of that authority-hating counter culture, and I have to believe that they did their fair share of things to make the police department genuinely upset."

Jenny thought back to young Addy spitting on an officer who was doing little more than standing at the entrance of the State Fair. "You're probably right."

"Not to speak ill of the dead or anything," Dawn continued. "I'm just being honest."

"Well, honest is what I need if I'm going to figure out what really happened back then."

"Unfortunately, I don't think I'll be able to tell you much about the relationship between The Family and the police. The one thing I can tell you is that it's very reasonable to think that Jove directed everyone to take pills. I know my brother wasn't acting suicidal, but that doesn't mean he wouldn't have done it if Jove told him to. Their allegiance to him was blind; I think they would have done anything if that lunatic said it was a good idea."

"It sounds like Eden was more of a cult than a commune."

"I've never called it a commune," Dawn confessed. "It was absolutely a cult, in every sense of the word."

Chapter 12

As Zack continued his nap, Jenny joined the others in the hotel restaurant. Strategically pulling her chair up next to Dr. Wilson, she took advantage of a break in the conversation to direct her statement quietly at him. "I just got off the phone with a relative of one of the members of The Family at Eden. She believes that the spiritual leader would have been capable of orchestrating the suicide." Jenny held up her hand, correcting herself. "At least, he would have been *able* to coordinate it. He seemed to have the members wrapped pretty tightly around his finger, so if he gave the command, it would have happened. Whether he had it in him or not remains to be seen."

"That's useful information," Dr. Wilson replied flatly.

"I'm hoping that Kyle will be able to track down a couple who apparently left The Family right before the tragedy; it would be great if we could have the inside scoop about what actually went on in there. I'd also like to send Zack back to the police station when he feels better—he's sleeping off a headache right now. Hopefully, he can get a good idea of the relationship between the sheriff and the folks at Eden. I'd love to find out more, but I certainly don't want to go there myself, all things considered."

"The arrest records should be telling," Dr. Wilson replied, "and they are available to the public, if you know where to look."

"Of course!" Jenny proclaimed. "I don't know why I didn't think of that sooner." She stood up excitedly and patted Dr. Wilson on the shoulder. "Excuse me for a second."

Walking over to the bar, she called Kyle to ask him to look into the criminal records from Bedford throughout the sixties—particularly people who got arrested multiple times before the tragedy but never after. He agreed before adding, "I found the names of the people who had left Eden. It wasn't easy, but I finally made the connections. They were Troy Bauer and Sabrina Devereaux. I found Troy, alive and well in Minnesota, but Sabrina passed away about a decade ago."

Jenny pumped her fist in triumph. "Do you have Troy's contact information?"

"Sure do," he replied. "I'll text it to you."

"Thanks. Have I told you lately that you're the world's greatest private investigator?"

"I'm pretty sure you have."

"Good," Jenny said. "I wouldn't want you to forget it."

The camera was once again situated in the corner of the room; Mary had resumed her place in her chair, the look of worry apparent on her face. The other members of Mary's family had returned to their hotel rooms so they wouldn't be a distraction as she tried to convince Matthew to cross over. Even Jenny sat way off to the side.

"You know what you have to say, correct?" Dr. Wilson said to Mary.

She responded with a slight nod, looking as if she was mentally preparing herself for the task ahead. Closing her eyes, she appeared to be drawing every ounce of strength and focus she could muster from somewhere deep within.

"Are you ready to get started?" Dr. Wilson asked.

After a pause and a deep exhale, Mary spoke with conviction. "Yes, I'm ready."

Just as he had done before, Dr. Wilson went into the hall and retrieved Devon, who entered the room as if he hadn't a care in the world, followed by his mother, who looked as if that very same world was situated squarely on her shoulders. Devon galloped eagerly over to a table and sat down, kicking his feet in and out from underneath the chair. The deafening silence seemed to have no impact on the oblivious little boy.

"Mom?" he said loudly. "Can I have my tablet?"

"Not now, sweetie."

"Why not?"

"Now is not a good time."

"Well, what can I do, then?"

"You can talk to Miss Mary."

"But I don't *want* to talk to Miss Mary. I want to play with my tablet."

"Don't be rude, honey. Miss Mary is a very nice woman."

Jenny watched the exchange, wondering if this was going to be an exercise in futility. She allowed her eyes to shift to Dr. Wilson, who gave a subtle nod in Mary's direction. That had been her cue.

"Devon," Mary said timidly, "I'd love to talk to Matthew."

He glanced in her direction with wide eyes at first, followed quickly by the familiar furrowed brow. "Matthew isn't here."

Jenny's heart skipped a beat. Was it possible that Matthew had already crossed?

Mary clearly wondered the same thing; her helpless glance in Dr. Wilson's direction indicated she didn't know what to do with that statement. Dr. Wilson flashed a stern expression back at Mary, as if to say, *we rehearsed this.*

Returning her focus to Devon, Mary said, "I'd like to talk about my mother, Julia."

Devon froze for a moment, his face blank. "What about her?"

Jenny didn't know if Matthew or Devon had been the one asking.

"I want to let Matthew know how he can see her again."

The child remained still; his intensity made the room feel as if all the air had been sucked out. "How?"

Mary cleared her throat. "He needs to cross over. Julia is on the other side, and he can see her again if he crosses."

Devon looked confused. "How do *you* know that's where she is?"

"Well," Mary began sweetly, "that's where people are supposed to go after they pass away."

"I know that," Devon said matter-of-factly.

Mary still spoke in a tone reserved for small children, even though it wasn't obvious which person was communicating with her. "You do?"

Devon simply nodded before walking over to Mary, leaning his little body against her legs. "But how do *you* know that?" He tapped her gently with his pointer finger.

Mary put her arm around Devon, rubbing his back with the care of a loving grandmother. "Miss Jenny told me."

Seemingly satisfied with that answer, Devon lowered his gaze to the floor, looking as if he was deliberately avoiding eye contact with Mary. "You have to go there, too. Not now, but later." He paused before adding, "After."

Mary battled tears as she whispered, "I will. I promise."

"Good," Devon declared, "because I want to see you again."

Jenny's breath caught at the use of first person; apparently Matthew had been the one communicating all this time.

A surge of emotion seemed to hit Mary; she hung her head and bit her lip, managing only a nod as a response. Jenny watched as Devon stood motionlessly for several seconds, then quickly changed his demeanor and began to run aimlessly throughout the room. It was easy to tell the exact moment Devon returned to his natural state of being.

Jenny stood up and approached Mary, who was holding strong despite an obvious desire to cry. Her tone was sympathetic. "You did great, Mary."

With a childlike expression, Mary looked up and asked, "Do you think it was enough?"

"I hope so," she replied. "Only time will tell, I guess, but you seemed to get the message across."

Mary closed her eyes and spoke with determination. "I just want everyone to be at peace...my father, Devon, Kayla. I think that will only happen when my dad crosses."

"Well, now that he knows you are safe—and plan to join him one day—I would think he'd like to be with your mother on the other side. I don't know what exactly goes on there, but I am under the impression that it's amazing." Jenny shrugged her shoulders and widened her eyes. "It's got to be better than the last fifty years of fruitlessly searching around here."

Mary didn't look up when she muttered, "I think anything would be better than that."

Jenny contemplated what the past few decades must have been like for Matthew, deciding it surely felt more like centuries to him. She shuddered and whispered, "I agree."

Dr. Wilson appeared at their side, and Mary immediately posed, "Do you think he will require more contacts?"

"I should think not," he said, irritating Jenny with his robotic tone. "He had the opportunity to say more if he wanted, but he seemed satisfied. This appearance was brief, and it had even to be coerced to some degree; my conclusion would be that he is at peace with how things have transpired here."

Despite Jenny's growing contempt for Dr. Wilson, he was still the most knowledgeable person in the room on the subject of possession, so she directed her question at him. "Do you think he will cross now?"

"That's my impression."

The expression on Mary's face looked like a mixture of relief and sadness; while that conclusion was what everybody had wanted, it meant she had just said goodbye to her father…again. It was as if she'd lost him twice. Jenny compassionately placed her hand on Mary's shoulder; the gesture seemed appreciated.

With what appeared to be a forced change in mood, Mary clasped her hands together and said, "So, are we done here? Can Devon finally go home and go back to being a regular little boy?"

Jenny looked over at Kayla, who was fishing Devon's tablet out of her bag but clearly focusing her attention on the conversation.

Dr. Wilson's tone remained mechanical. "I believe he can."

The silence that ensued spoke volumes. There was an element of triumph involved with that statement, but jubilation was certainly inappropriate; the day's events had been much too somber for that.

The room was heavy, and everyone seemed afraid to speak…everyone, that is, except for Dr. Wilson, who turned to Kayla and emotionlessly asked her permission to write about Devon's story in his next publication. Jenny closed her eyes and shook her head; perhaps it was the pregnancy, but his emotionless personality was grating her last nerve. She wished she never spoke to him about visiting Addy Roth; then she could have made the visit without him. As it was, she had made him actively involved in that investigation.

As Kayla and Dr. Wilson talked logistics, Jenny focused her attention on Mary. "Are you going to head home after this, or are you going to stick around a while?"

Mary smiled pleasantly, which tugged at Jenny's heartstrings. She was a lovely woman, managing to keep her graces in the most horrible of circumstances. Everyone should be so amiable. "Well, my whole family is here; that doesn't happen often. We've all arranged to stay for a few days, so we're going to treat it like a mini-vacation."

Jenny smiled in return. "A little reunion, of sorts."

"Exactly." Mary's smile faded, but the agreeableness remained in her face. "What's next for you?"

"Me?" Jenny glanced over at Dr. Wilson quickly before replying, "I need to find out a little bit more about a place called Eden."

Everyone had cleared the meeting room except Jenny and Dr. Wilson. The camera had been disassembled and packed away, Jenny's swollen feet had found themselves stripped of shoes and propped on a chair. "So, Dr. Wilson, when you were dealing with Addy, you had mentioned that she wouldn't give you a name associated with the spirit."

"That is correct."

"Well, I have since found out that the people at Eden didn't go by their given names; they each chose their own, and they were unconventional. The two names I am aware of are Jove and Music Maker. Is it possible the spirit really did give you its name, but you just didn't know it was a name?"

With his eyes fixed on Jenny, he replied, "When asked her name, she told us she didn't have to give us...wait, what was it? Oh yes...us *corrupt prisoners of society* any information at all."

Jenny's expression deflated. "I suppose that wasn't the spirit's assumed name."

"No, I shouldn't think so."

Undeterred, Jenny continued, "I have the contact information of one of the people who left Eden. I can't remember his name off the top of my head, but he lives in Minnesota or someplace in that general vicinity. The woman he left with apparently died about a decade ago."

"Would you like me to call him?" Wilson asked.

Jenny stifled the snort that begged to come out; Dr. Wilson would have been the last person she'd want to make that call. "That's okay," she said politely instead. "You have a lot going on. I can give him a call. It would be great if you could call Addy's family, though, and try to arrange a meeting. Now that it appears we're done here, I'd like to go down and see her."

"I would like that, too," Dr. Wilson replied. "It would be great if you could tell me if she's a psychic or if there's just something about a child's brain that makes them susceptible to contact. That's been something I've been trying to find out for years."

"It shouldn't be too hard for me to tell," Jenny said. "All I'd have to do is meet her."

"Well, let's make that happen, then."

Yes, let's make that happen, Jenny thought, *so you can further your research.*

Then, she silently scolded herself for being nasty.

"I'd also like to make another trip to Eden," she added, "most likely getting a hotel nearby. I'm hoping a second visit to the compound will give me some insight about what went on there. I also want Zack talk to the Bedford police a little more—again, I don't want to go anywhere near the officers myself, for fear of how I might react." She smiled slyly and added, "I wouldn't want to slug anybody or anything."

No reaction from Dr. Wilson. What a surprise.

Jenny uncomfortably cleared her throat. "So, is that the plan, then? You arrange a meeting with Addy, and I'll do a little research about, and maybe pay a visit to, Eden?"

"That sounds like a good approach to me," he declared. "I have some writing to do about what happened here this week with Devon, but I can certainly squeeze in a phone call."

Jenny plastered on a smile, secretly wishing that she didn't need Dr. Wilson present to make any of this happen. Either that, or she wanted her hormone levels to go down a bit so she could better tolerate him. Sadly, she was confident that neither of those wishes was going to come true.

Troy Bauer's voice sounded deep and throaty on the phone, which Jenny assumed was due to a lifetime of cigarettes. Despite the gruff tone, however, he sounded like he had a jovial personality.

"I'd like to ask you about what life was like at Eden," Jenny concluded after getting him up to speed, "and, honestly, I'd like to find out why you left."

"That second part is easy," he declared with a chuckle in his voice. He reminded Jenny of a less wholesome version of Santa Claus. "We left because Sabrina was expecting a baby."

Jenny was pretty sure she was stating the obvious, and she wasn't certain about the tactfulness of the question, but she had learned over the past year never to take anything for granted. "Your baby, I assume?"

He let out another jolly laugh. "I certainly hope he was." He dragged out a lengthy and rough, "Naaahhh, I'm just kidding. It was my son. He came out looking just like me, for crying out loud—I couldn't have denied him if I tried."

Jenny smiled, loving the fact that her gift led her to people like Troy. She otherwise wouldn't have had the occasion to talk to an older gentleman from Minnesota, but his colorful character definitely brightened her day. Remaining professional, however, she simply said, "Did you leave because you didn't want the baby growing up on the..." Was the word *compound* offensive? "...at Eden?"

"We didn't want her *giving birth* at Eden. Jove had a rule against getting outside medical help—he called the whole health care profession *corruption at its finest*. He thought doctors were some of the most overpriced and over-valued people in the world; he felt they did little more than guess most of the time." Troy raised his voice an octave, which Jenny presumed was his imitation of Jove's take on doctors. *"You have a virus. Get some rest and eat some soup. Oh, no insurance? That'll be twenty dollars, please."* He returned his tone to its normal, gruff sound. "Keep in mind that twenty dollars back in 1960 was like a hundred dollars today. It certainly wasn't cheap, that's for sure. And you'd get nothing for it—at least, that's how Jove looked at it."

"But you and Sabrina wanted to have a doctor present when she had the baby," Jenny concluded, stating it more like a sentence than a question.

"We sure did, especially after what happened to that girl."

Jenny's nerves began to tingle. "What girl?"

A grunt signaled Troy's displeasure in telling the story. "She was a young thing—couldn't have been more than nineteen, I guess. She had some pretty, long blond hair—that's what I remember about her most. Golden One—that's what we called her, because of that hair."

Jenny listened politely, although she was eager for him to get to the point.

"She got pregnant while she was at Eden. I'm not sure who the father was—I can't rightly remember. I'm not even sure she knew, to tell you the truth. There was a lot of that...*free love* back then, although I guess I shouldn't be telling this to a young lady."

With a sincere smile, Jenny replied, "I can handle it. Besides, I'm not all that young."

"Oh, believe me, you are. I can hear it in your voice."

"Well, thank you." Trying to steer the topic back to Eden, Jenny said, "So, what happened to Golden One?"

Another grunt. "She died while trying to have that baby. Her water broke, but she didn't go into labor at first. Medicine Man kept her bedridden after that, but a couple of days went by before she actually started having labor pains. In the meantime, infection must have set in. So there she was, burning up with fever, trying to have a baby. I felt so bad for her. She looked as miserable as she could be."

Jenny put her hand on her own belly, trying to distance herself from the story.

"I told Jove she needed to see a doctor, but he said no. We had Medicine Man, who, according to him, knew just as much about healing people as any trained professional. Besides, he said anything they would have done to her would have been unnatural and unaffordable, and people had been giving birth without interference for thousands of years. He insisted she would be fine with just a little positive energy."

"Positive energy?"

"Yes." Troy sounded bitter. "Can you imagine? There was this poor girl, sick as hell, trying to give birth when she barely had enough strength to sit up—and there *we* were, the rest of us, dancing around and singing about shining the love light on her and crap. We were a bunch of high idiots, that's what we were. She was dying, for goodness sake, and all we did for her was *dance*."

No wonder Troy didn't like telling this story; he watched a young woman die when she didn't need to.

"If she could have just gotten a little bit of antibiotics, she'd have been fine, I bet," he went on, "but Jove didn't let that happen, and we all just sat back and allowed it."

Jenny's tone reflected the sympathy she felt for Troy. "How did the baby fare?"

"She lived a day; that was it."

Hanging her head, Jenny absorbed that notion. That baby should have had grown children by now. "I can't blame you for wanting to get out of there, then," Jenny said.

"I wasn't about to let something happen to Sabrina and the baby just because Jove didn't trust doctors. I may have been willing to do just about anything he told me, but I drew the line when it came to the woman I loved and my baby."

Jenny smiled. "What did Jove say when you told him you were leaving?"

The Santa-style laugh returned. "Oh, no...we couldn't tell him that. Are you kidding? There was no leaving Eden once you signed on. You had to take part in a commitment ceremony when you first joined, which made it against the rules to leave."

"You weren't *allowed* to leave?"

"Nope. We sure weren't."

Jenny thought back to Dawn's assessment of The Family as being a cult, determining she actually had it right. "Wow. What would be the consequence if you did?"

"Isn't it obvious?" Troy said with all joviality gone from his voice.

Jenny thought for a moment, but the 'obvious' punishment didn't come to her. "I'm sorry," she said, "but I'm afraid I don't know what it is."

"I'll give you a hint," Troy said flatly. "Forty-five people were dead two weeks after we left."

Chapter 12

Jenny's jaw hit the floor. "You really think the overdose was a result of you leaving Eden?"

His gruff voice made the words seem even more eerie. "It would be an awfully big coincidence if it wasn't, don't you think?"

She wiped her eyes with her free hand, trying to see how this latest piece of the puzzle fit in with the rest. Things weren't adding up in her head. "Mr. Bauer, I have a confession to make."

"A confession?" he asked. "What could you possibly have to confess about?"

Jenny giggled; Troy reminded her a little bit of Elanor, which may have explained why she liked him so much. "I guess *confession* is the wrong word. I have an *admission*; is that better?"

"Maybe. Depends what it is."

She released a sigh. "I'm a psychic, and I've been contacted by one of the members of Eden."

Met with the familiar silence, Jenny continued. "I'm not sure which person is speaking to me, but I got a very clear message that the members of The Family didn't voluntarily take pills. This wasn't an orchestrated suicide—it was a murder."

"I don't know about this psychic business, but I just told you it wasn't a suicide. Jove killed those people because we left; I never doubted that for a minute."

"But the spirit I'm dealing with doesn't believe it was Jove...he—or she—thinks it was the sheriff who committed the murder."

"The sheriff?" Troy remained quiet for a long time. "Sheriff Babson?"

"Yes, sir."

After more deliberation, he concluded, "Nah, I don't believe that."

"Can you tell me about your relationship with the sheriff? I've heard there was no love lost between you and him."

"You can say that again."

"Did you ever get arrested?"

"Often. Every one of us, but the charges would never really stick. We were like forty-seven thorns in the police's backside, but we weren't hardened criminals."

Jenny stifled a laugh. "Sorry if this is too direct, but what about the drug use? And the theft? Aren't those pretty substantial crimes?"

"*Theft* is a bit too strong of a word." He made a grunting sound, presumably as he put his thoughts together. "Look, I am the first to admit we did a lot of stuff we shouldn't have—sitting back and watching that girl die being the worst of them—but we weren't bad people. Yes, we did use things that didn't belong to us, but we always left some kind of payment in its place, and we returned most everything we could when we were done with it. We tried to be self-sufficient, but there are certain things you just can't make when you're living off the land. Like, how were we supposed to make a shovel?"

"You couldn't," Jenny said compassionately, hoping her empathy would invite Troy to continue.

"Exactly. So we would go into town, and if someone had left their shovel out, we would use it for a while. But we'd leave some tomatoes or cucumbers where the shovel had been, and we'd only use it until we could earn enough money to buy one for ourselves. Then we'd put it back."

"Did you ask if you could borrow the shovel?"

"We did at first," Troy admitted, "but everyone always told us no. That's why we had to resort to taking things."

"And this money you earned—was that from odd jobs?"

"Mostly. We did what we could. None of us had any regular income."

"Again, forgive me for saying this; I'm just trying to get an understanding of what life was like for you," Jenny began. "But wouldn't it have made sense for some of you to work regular jobs to support the rest of you?"

"We couldn't spare the manpower," Troy said. "I'm not sure if you have any idea of how difficult life was at Eden. We grew our own food, made most of our clothes, tended the animals...honestly, I never worked harder in my life, before or since. The thing was, we didn't work for money. We busted our humps all day long, but since we didn't get those green pieces of paper at the end of the day, people thought we were useless as tits on a bull." He paused. "Oh, sorry. Forgot who I was talking to for a second."

"I promise you, I'm not offended," Jenny said. Truth be told, she found him to be hilarious.

"The reality was, it took every single one of us to make that community work. If we started sending people out into the working world to bring home cash for The Family, we would have had to take short cuts to make up for it. Before you know it, we would have ended up just like everybody else, and that's exactly what we were trying to avoid. Unfortunately, though, in this modernized culture, people simply can't get by with no money at all. Every once in a while, we needed to send someone out to earn a few dollars."

"I heard Music Maker went into town from time to time."

Jenny didn't understand the exaggerated silence at first, until she heard Troy mutter, "Music Maker. I had forgotten about him." His tone made it sound like his memories of Robert were fond. "He was a good egg, that one."

"I've spoken to his sister," Jenny explained. "She spoke highly of him, too. They seem like a nice family."

"I'm sure they are," he replied softly.

Considering Troy believed himself to be the catalyst that triggered the deaths of everyone at Eden, Jenny imagined he harbored a lot of guilt when he thought of those people he once considered family. "I'm sorry," she said sincerely. "This whole thing must be very difficult for you to think about."

"It is," he assured her, "but it's not as hard as it used to be. I've spent a lot of time thinking about it over the years, and I realize it would have happened eventually anyway. Somebody, at some point, would have inevitably left The Family, and the rest of the members would have died anyway. If Sabrina and I hadn't left, we would have been among the body count, I'm sure. And Tristan—that's my son—he would have been, too." Jenny could envision him shaking his head over the phone, wishing away the disturbing notion that had crept inside his mind. "Nah, we needed to get out of there. I would have never forgiven myself if something had happened to my boy."

Realizing she'd allowed the conversation to steer off topic, she said, "You seem pretty certain that Jove had this in him...and that the sheriff didn't."

"Jove was a lunatic. I can see that now, even if I didn't recognize it back then. He could give a speech that would make anyone do anything, which made it seem like we were all acting voluntarily—but the truth is, he had a tight rein on all of us. Of course, that was helped along by the fact that we were high as kites a good deal of the time. It probably wouldn't have taken that much fancy talk for us to hop on board with whatever he was saying."

"How did you get these drugs?" Jenny asked. "If you didn't have money, how could you have afforded them?"

"We grew a good deal of it ourselves. The marijuana and the mushrooms were easy to come by. The fact that we had animals made the fields a perfect place for the mushrooms to grow. Those mushrooms love their shit, and God knows those sheep and goats shit a ton."

Jenny bit her lip to keep from laughing.

Troy continued, "We got the LSD from a guy who used to come by delivering it."

"But how did you afford it?"

"We bartered for it."

"You *bartered*?" Jenny asked. "With, like, cucumbers and eggs?"

"No, we used a much more powerful form of currency."

120

She thought for a moment before the realization hit. "Oh," she said, raising her naïve shoulders up by her ears. Then she considered it a little longer, and a second potential form of currency came to mind. "Oh, dear."

"Yep, it was the generation of sex, drugs and rock and roll, but the dealer wasn't all that interested in rock and roll. We just paid with weed, some shrooms and the company of women."

"Oh, my."

"See, I knew I shouldn't have been saying this stuff to a young lady."

"No, I'm not offended," Jenny assured him. "I'm just a little surprised, that's all. I have to admit this is all very foreign to me."

"As it should be."

With a smile, Jenny added, "But the sheriff couldn't arrest you for any of this?"

"Well, it ain't illegal to have shit in a field, and where there's shit, there's shrooms. We couldn't help that. We grew the marijuana off the property, so they couldn't directly tie it to us, and we kept the LSD well hidden. If the police wanted to catch us with it, they'd need a warrant to search the house. I think they tried like hell to get those warrants, but the judge never gave them any."

"Not enough probable cause, huh?"

"Chapping the sheriff's ass isn't probable cause."

This time Jenny laughed out loud. "Did they ever catch you with anything that had been stolen—I'm sorry—borrowed?"

"Sometimes they did, which is what led to our arrests, but those always got thrown out. The best they could do is hit us with possession of stolen property since nobody actually saw us take the stuff, but there were so many of us living there, the charges would end up getting dismissed. I mean, can you really arrest almost fifty people over a hoe? Taxpayers don't have that kind of money. So we'd agree to return the hoe to the rightful owner, pay a fine, and we'd be on our way."

She couldn't help but smile; somehow she was finding herself sympathetic to The Family's cause. "What about the public nudity? Did you ever get arrested for that?"

"A time or two. But walking around on our own property was hardly *public nudity*, especially if you consider how secluded that property was. The police had to come onto our land in order to catch us walking around naked, and then they tried to slap us with indecent exposure. The judge always threw it out, though, citing that the police had no reason to be on our land anyway. In fact," Troy added thoughtfully, "I think the police were starting to get in trouble for harassing us."

Jenny's pulse kicked up a few notches. "Do you think that would have infuriated the sheriff enough to want to take matters into his own hands?"

"And resort to murder? That seems a bit extreme, don't you think?"

"The spirit who spoke to me didn't think it was all that far-fetched."

Troy remained quiet on the other end of the phone. His silence was eventually disrupted by his declaration, "That type of action requires either a whole lot of hate or a whole lot of crazy. Truthfully, my money's on crazy."

Kayla rolled her suitcase behind her as she walked through the hotel lobby. "I can't thank you enough for all of your help. Are you sure you don't want to be paid for your time?"

Jenny smiled. "Your payment can be to call me in a few days and tell me that Matthew hasn't come back. That will be reward enough."

Closing her eyes, Kayla remarked, "If I can do that, I will be the happiest woman in the world."

Clatter caused Jenny to look over to the other side of the lobby; Devon was running around in small circles, touching everything his little hands could reach. Clearly, Matthew wasn't an issue at the moment.

"What's next for you?" Kayla asked.

"Well, Zack and I are heading down to Bedford to visit Eden again. I'm hoping we can get to the bottom of what happened to all of those people back then."

"If anyone can do it, you can," she replied with a smile.

"Thanks for the vote of confidence," Jenny said. "I only wish I was as optimistic as you are."

Loud shouts started to accompany Devon's hyperactivity. "Oh my God, I need to get out of here before he tears this place apart," Kayla said. "Devon, come on, honey. It's time to go." She turned her attention to Jenny, reaching in and giving her a hug. "You are a life-saver, do you know that?"

"I'm just glad I could help."

The women let go of their embrace. "Devon, give Miss Jenny a hug. I'm not sure you know how much she's done for you, but someday you will."

Jenny could see the impact coming, but there was little she could do to brace for it. Devon approached her at lightning speed, wrapping her legs into a hug that looked and felt more like a form tackle than a term of endearment. Although she stumbled a bit, she was able to maintain her balance.

"Devon, the woman is pregnant!" Kayla said emphatically. "Go easy on her, for goodness sake."

"It's okay," Jenny said with a smile. Remembering what her grandmother often said, she replied, *"Tough old bird* runs in my family."

Even though they had driven to Eden before, Jenny was glad she was being helped along by a guiding tug. The compound was so secluded, she wasn't sure she'd be able to find it again without a little spiritual intervention.

She pulled the car onto the flattened grass that served as a driveway until she reached the area that resembled a tended lawn. Zack remained quiet in the passenger seat, respecting her abilities as the car rolled to a stop.

A funny feeling washed over Jenny as she stepped outside, although she wasn't sure why she was experiencing it. She walked several paces across the grass, looking out over the vast expanse of garden before her. Even if Jenny hadn't seen the goats the last time she was there, the smell in the air left no doubt that there were animals on the premises. Jenny smiled, wondering if she could still find some of those magic mushrooms growing in the field as they had done decades before.

Although she felt funny, she wasn't getting any insight. She was just about to turn to Zack and tell him the trip might have been futile when a man and a woman walked into sight from around the corner of the house. "Perfect," she said, not taking her eyes from the couple. "Maybe we can ask them a few questions. It might be a longshot, but they may know something about what happened that day."

"Who are you talking about?" Zack asked.

She glanced back over her shoulder to look at her husband. "Those people," she replied, "by the house."

She returned her gaze toward the couple, only to discover that nobody was there.

Chapter 13

"I swear to God somebody was just there." She turned quickly back to Zack with wide eyes. "Two people, in fact—a man and a woman."

Zack remained motionless, appearing reluctant to say the words, "I never saw anybody."

Spooked from head to toe, Jenny whipped her head back toward the house. She looked at the garden again, noticing the plants appeared to be different than they had been a minute ago—there were fewer rows with more space in between. Her shoulders relaxed as she began to realize what was happening, noticing that the funny feeling she'd been experiencing was also gone. "It was a vision," she said calmly. "I think this place just looks so much like it did back then that I didn't realize what I was seeing was from the past."

"What did the people look like?" Zack asked.

"Hippies," she declared. "He had long, brown hair and a really long beard, and his clothes looked dirty. Her hair was long, too, and she wore a flowy dress that actually looked a little big on her. They were both barefoot."

"That sounds like it could have been from the sixties," Zack decided. "In fact, it sounds more like 1965 than today."

Jenny nodded in agreement. "I think I may have just gotten a first-hand glimpse at Eden."

"Cool," he replied. "Creepy, but cool."

"Creepy indeed," Jenny said. "Honestly, that was the craziest thing…those people were clear as day to me, and when I turned back around, they were gone. I felt like I was losing my mind until I noticed the garden looked different." She shook her head with awe. "This place looks almost *exactly* like it did back then. It's amazing."

"Maybe that will be helpful," Zack noted. "Seeing some things the way they looked when your spirit friend was alive may trigger something in him."

"Let's hope."

"Should we try to introduce ourselves to the new owners? They may not take too kindly to a couple of strangers hanging around their property."

Jenny flashed a glance in his direction, gesturing to her pregnant belly. "Do I *look* like I'm going to cause trouble? I don't think I could do anything bad and get away with it. A six year old could outrun me these days."

Zack raised a finger. "Ah, but you must remember that not all psychopaths look like psychopaths. In fact, you would make a spectacular front for a depraved killer. When a pregnant woman knocks on your door appearing to need help, you'd let her in, wouldn't you? And then, when you open the door, *bam*! I come in and kill everybody."

Looking at him strangely, Jenny admitted, "I don't think like you do."

"Well, some people do, so we need to go introduce ourselves before we upset these people." His eyes made their way around the premises. "Something tells me the owners have guns, and they may not like the sight of a couple of city slickers messing with their business."

"I'm hardly a city slicker."

"Compared to these people you are."

He had a point. "Well, I'm game if you are. I'd like to spend some time on the property, so I guess we should get the owner's permission to be here." Remembering what Zack had just said, she posed, "Should I be the one to ring the doorbell, or would I look like too much of a front?"

"Doorbells require electricity," Zack replied. "Somehow I think we'll be knocking."

They began their walk toward the front door, which was ironically situated around the side of the house. "I believe you have missed the point, my friend."

"Sorry. The old home-builder in me just popped out for a minute." He raised his eyes to the roof and said, "Although, I may have spoken too soon."

Jenny looked up as well, noticing a series of solar panels on the roof. "Is that evidence of electricity?"

"They've apparently got some, even if it's not a ton. Probably enough to run some basic appliances, at least."

The couple ventured up the porch steps that looked as if they had been there since the dawn of time. Jenny felt nervous as she knocked on the door, half expecting Billy Joe Jim Bob to come out with a big hunk of chew in his lip, a loaded rifle in his hand and a distinct look of hate in his eye. Her nerves remained elevated as the seconds ticked by, ultimately plummeting when enough time had passed and no one had responded to the knock. "I guess nobody's home," she concluded.

"It appears not," Zack replied.

They walked back down the rickety steps and started working their way back toward the entrance of the property. "Are you getting any funny feelings or anything?" Zack asked. "Any more visions?"

Jenny shook her head. "Unfortunately, no. I haven't been specifically trying, though. Maybe we can hang out by the car for a while and see if anything comes to me."

Zack shrugged. "That's as good of a plan as any."

Hearing a commotion from beyond the car, Jenny stopped for a moment and looked in the direction of the sound. Shortly after, the source of the noise made itself known; about fifteen people on bicycles rounded the corner, each with groceries in makeshift baskets tied to their handlebars. Their clothes all looked dirty and, in some cases, tattered. The men all had long beards and many of the women wore flowers in their hair.

Jenny didn't look at Zack as she posed, "You're seeing this too, right?"

"Yup," he replied, "this time I am."

The group of hippies grew larger as more people on bicycles rounded the corner. While they didn't look intimidating, Jenny felt uneasy, realizing full well that she and Zack were grossly outnumbered—and were trespassing on their property. She suddenly became aware that she must have looked like a deer in headlights; she plastered a smile on her face, hoping it appeared genuine.

The first person to reach them was a man who looked to be in his early-to-mid-twenties, although his ratty beard had made him look much older from far away. Despite being unkempt, his eyes appeared friendly, and, unlike Jenny's, his smile seemed to be sincere. "Hello, visitors," he said heartily. "What brings you here today?"

The rest of the group approached on their bikes. Some headed straight to the house, others flanked the speaker in what would have been an intimidating display had their bicycles been motorcycles. As it was, Jenny found the whole scene to be surreal to the point of almost being laughable.

She was grateful that Zack did the talking. "We're actually here because we're looking into what happened on this property back in the sixties."

The stranger's eyes quickly went from happy to genuinely sad. "Oh, the tragedy," he replied, lowering his head. "That was a horrible day."

Jenny found it odd that he was speaking of that fateful day as if he personally remembered it, but it had clearly happened decades before he was born. Deciding that she was being nitpicky, she simply said, "We'd like to speak to the property's owners so we can get permission to look around."

Some of the others lost interest in the conversation, riding their bikes closer to the house and emptying their baskets. Others remained, listening to what Jenny and Zack had to say.

The man in the front let out a laugh, gesturing his arms out in both directions. "You are looking for the person who owns this land?"

Jenny replied, "Ideally, yes."

"My friend, no one owns this land. How can anyone *own* the land? Do you put a fence around it, hand someone some money and say, 'now I own this? These trees are now my trees. This grass belongs to me. The flowers that bloom in the springtime—those are *my* flowers.'" He laughed again, shaking his head. "No, we don't own this land. We use it, but it is not possible for us to own it."

This had been much more of an answer than Jenny had bargained for. Unsure of how to reply, she simply scrunched her face and asked, "So, we can look around, then?"

"You may look around all you want," the man replied, his smile returning. "What, exactly, is it you're looking for? Maybe I can help you find something."

"We don't know for sure," Jenny replied. "We'll know it if we see it."

She felt a nudge on her elbow. "Tell him the truth," Zack said encouragingly. "I bet he'll believe you."

Taking a good look at the man in front of her, Jenny had to agree that he would probably be a believer. "I'm a psychic, and I've been contacted by the spirit of one of the people who died that day during the mass overdose."

The man's eyes grew wide. "You've been contacted by a spirit?" Awe remained in his voice. "Of someone who died that day?"

Jenny nodded, refraining from saying the usual 'yes sir' that would have popped out of her mouth had she been talking to anybody else. Somehow, she didn't find *sir* to be appropriate in this case.

"This is fascinating." He turned his attention to the bicyclists who remained around him. "Where's Delilah?"

With a point, one of the people said, "She went up to the house."

He looked back at Jenny and Zack. "You have to talk to Delilah." He gestured his arm toward the decrepit building. "And you absolutely must stay for dinner."

Jenny's curiosity was getting the best of her as they walked up the back steps in pursuit of this Delilah—why would she have been more interested in this than the others? Was she the 'resident psychic?'

A wave started to wash over her, causing her to slow her speed to a stop halfway up the stairs. She closed her eyes and hung her head, trying to tune out the noise of the large crowd bringing in groceries around her.

"Hey, Winding River."

She knew the comment was directed at her. She turned her head to see an incredibly tall and slim young man with long, greasy red hair and an unkempt beard. His arms were wrapped around a giant basket of vegetables; he seemed to struggle with the awkwardness of it. "Get the door, would ya?"

The wave seemed to leave, and Jenny opened her eyes, scanning the crowd for a lanky red-haired man among the people scurrying in front of her. Just as she had suspected, she didn't see one, confirming her suspicion that she had just had a flashback from the same spot decades earlier.

"Hey," Zack began. "You okay?"

Jenny nodded. "I think I just figured out what my name was—well, what the spirit's name was."

"Oh yeah? What was it?"

Looking beyond her husband, she saw the friendly hippie was glued to her every word as she announced, "I was called Winding River."

"Good to know," Zack said with a smile.

"The extra information can't hurt," Jenny replied, "but I'm not sure it will help, either, under the circumstances. Who knows what this person's name had really been?"

"At least we kind of know who we're dealing with...somewhat."

A strange moment of silence ensued, prompting Jenny to tell her guide, "Sorry—I'm good now. I'd love to meet Delilah, if you're still willing to introduce us."

He stood frozen with awe. "Did you just have a contact from the spirit?"

Jenny smiled; she had apparently just blown this man's mind. "Yes, a very short one."

He remained in place for so long Jenny began to grow uncomfortable. Finally he asked, "What was it like?"

"The contact?" She cleared her throat. "It was like a memory, I guess, except the memory wasn't mine." She described what she saw, which didn't take long considering how brief the vision had been.

Another freakishly long pause was interrupted by the man simply saying, "You have been sent here for a reason, you know. Delilah has been pleading with the universe to give her *something,* and you are exactly what she has been waiting for." He smiled and shook his head with wonder. "She's going to be so *happy.*" Without explaining further, he led Zack and Jenny into the house.

The door brought them immediately into the kitchen, where an overwhelming sense of familiarity hit Jenny like a cold wind in winter. She imagined the house looked largely like it had when Winding River had walked those very same halls. She didn't have much time to think about that, however; almost immediately, she found herself being introduced to the mysterious Delilah.

"I don't even know your names," the guide confessed, "but this is Delilah. Delilah, this young woman is a psychic who has contact with the spirits who lived among The Family."

Delilah was a natural looking woman with long, light brown hair and freckles covering her skin. Her face reflected awe similar to what the guide's had shown, and her hands dropped to her sides when she heard the words. She took several steps toward Jenny, looking her square in the eye. "You have contact with The Family?"

Jenny nodded modestly.

The woman looked both fascinated and confused. "But...how?"

"I have a gift," Jenny proclaimed, shrugging her shoulders. "I was born with it. And someone who lived here in the past is communicating with me—somebody named Winding River."

Delilah looked at the man who had introduced them and then back at Jenny. "By any chance, is he trying to tell you that Jove didn't kill those people?"

Chapter 14

Jenny wasn't sure what to say. "You know about Jove?" was what popped out first.

Delilah looked over her shoulder at all of the commotion resulting from a couple dozen people putting away groceries. "Can we go outside where things are a little quieter?"

Nothing would have made Jenny happier; the chaos was starting to get to her. "Absolutely."

They followed Delilah's lead through the house and out the front door on the other side. The sounds from inside instantly disappeared when the door closed behind them, and Jenny took a deep breath of fresh air. Feeling invigorated, she asked, "So, you are also under the impression that Jove didn't do it?"

"I couldn't be more positive."

"How do you even know about it?" Jenny asked.

Delilah walked slowly down the porch stairs with Zack and Jenny following suit. She tucked her hair behind her ear as she took several steps across the lawn. "Jove was my great-uncle…my grandfather's brother. Ever since I was a little girl, I've been told about what happened and how Jove got blamed for it. I've also been told that he didn't have it in him. He was about peace and love, not mass suicide."

"I guess if he was your great-uncle, that also means you know his real name," Jenny hinted.

"I do. It was Roger Hillerman," Delilah said with pride and fondness in her voice. "But he much preferred Jove."

"While I admit I don't know a whole lot about The Family," Jenny began, "I do know the people who lived here got to choose their own names; do you know why he chose to go by Jove?"

Delilah displayed an easygoing smile. "He loved to star gaze. He had a fascination with the universe—the sheer magnitude of it overwhelmed him. Each of those little stars you see in the night sky is actually a massive planet or a sun. It's humbling, if you think about it. We look like little more than a dot of light to other areas of the universe, and the beings who see that dot have no idea what life forms exist here on this wonderful planet. The trees, the birds, the people—no one would ever know about those things just from seeing our little dot in the night sky. He was convinced that there are millions of other creatures in thousands of worlds scattered all over the universe..." She twirled as she spoke, her arms outstretched to the side. "...and to us, it all just looks like sky."

Zack spoke plainly. "I don't get it."

The twirling stopped; Delilah looked at him with a smile. "Jove was the God of the sky in Roman mythology."

"Wow," Jenny said, "I'm impressed that you know all that."

She continued her slow-paced walk. "We talk about Jove in our family quite often. He's so misunderstood," Delilah said sadly. "We try to honor his spirit with light because so many other people associate him with darkness."

Zack asked, "You mean the families of the other forty-four people who died that day?"

"Them, the community, the media...everybody is convinced Jove orchestrated a mass suicide, but in my family we know better than that. I don't know who *did* do it, mind you, but I am quite certain that my Great-Uncle Jove *did not*."

"Well, the spirit who contacted me—Winding River, I guess his name was—seems to think it was Sheriff Babson." She decided against mentioning that Troy was equally convinced of Jove's guilt.

Delilah turned her head in Jenny's direction. "Sheriff Babson?"

"That was the impression I got, and it fits in with how this whole communication got started." Jenny summarized Addy's drive past Eden and her subsequent hatred of law enforcement, as well as Jenny's own adverse reaction at the local police station. "I couldn't help but feel like officers were somehow involved, and I was absolutely *positive* that I hadn't taken any pills—me being Winding River, of course."

Delilah stopped in her tracks. "You know that he didn't take any pills? How do you know that?"

Jenny spoke quietly. "I can't explain it, but somehow I just know that he didn't. It wasn't part of his memory. I can't help but think that he would have remembered deliberately committing suicide."

"Well then," Delilah said emphatically, "isn't that your proof that Jove didn't kill anybody?"

If nothing else, Jenny's experience has taught her to pursue every avenue. With an apologetic wince, she replied, "It shows that Jove didn't convince the others to commit suicide. It also provides evidence that someone spiked their food or water, making it a murder as opposed to a suicide." She cleared her throat uncomfortably. "Technically, though, it still could have been Jove." She held up her hand when she saw Delilah about to protest. "I said *technically*. I'm not suggesting he did it; I'm simply saying that we don't have enough evidence to prove otherwise at this point."

Delilah seemed pacified. "How do we get that proof?"

"Well, that's what we're here for. I was hoping I could spend a little time on the property so I could see if I could get any information."

"By *information* you mean contacts from the spirit world?"

Jenny nodded slightly. "I do."

Delilah's ensuing silence caused Jenny to look her way. An awe-filled smile graced Delilah's lips as she said, "You can spend as much time on the property as you need."

Zack chimed in. "Can I ask you a question?"

Delilah flashed a smile at Zack. "Of course."

"Is what you have going on here the same kind of community as Eden?"

"Yes and no," Delilah explained as she continued her leisurely walk to nowhere. "Back then, The Family was anti-government, but that's not how we operate. Yes, we do live communally, but we don't necessarily separate ourselves from the outside world the way The Family tried to. We're just trying to conserve as many resources as we can. The earth can't go on forever if people continue to live so wastefully. We've become a country of such excess...one bedroom per child has become the norm, people throw away perfectly good clothes because they've gone out of style, and fully-functioning furniture gets replaced because the homeowners are in the mood for something different." She shook her head as she walked. "That type of living is the path to disaster, environmentally speaking.

"Our goal here is to minimize our negative impact on this planet. We use only as much electricity as our solar panels will provide. We grow most of our own food, and when we do buy groceries, we make sure they come in recyclable containers. We also bike to the store most of the time."

"What do you do the other times?" Zack asked.

"We have two cars—hybrids—but we try to drive them as little as possible."

Zack seemed quite curious. "Where are they now?"

"Larry and Amanda have them. They both work outside the home; they bring in the income we need."

"They make enough money to support all these people?" Jenny asked with surprise.

"When you live like we do, it doesn't take a lot of money to get by. We're mostly self-sufficient."

Jenny thought about all of the items in her home that, when push came to shove, were truly optional. Suddenly, she felt a little bit guilty.

"Do you have, like, a TV and stuff?" Zack asked.

"A TV? No." Delilah twisted her hair, ultimately pulling it back into a bun without any type of clip to fasten it. Jenny made a face, completely baffled as to how she had done it. "We do have a computer, though. We're not anti-technology, like some people tend to believe. In fact, technology can be very helpful to the environment. We talk to our loved ones through email often—it's so much better than writing letters. That not only wastes paper, but it also uses a ton of gas to drive those mail cars along same route every single day." She shook her head. "I'm surprised that's still legal, to tell you the truth. We get receipts emailed to us instead of printed, we get the news without newspapers, we check the weather so we can bring the animals in if we need to...a television is largely for entertainment, so we don't have one. The computer, on the other hand, has a purpose." A sly smile appeared on her face. "So, can I ask a few questions about *you*, now?"

Jenny smiled. "Fire away."

"First of all, how pregnant are you?"

"Seven months. I'm due November eighteenth."

"Do you know if you are having a boy or a girl?"

"A boy," Zack replied assuredly.

"Don't let him fool you," Jenny said. "It's a girl."

As did everyone else who fell victim to this display, Delilah seemed confused. "So, is it a boy or a girl?"

"Let me put it this way," Zack said. "If it's a girl, Jenny is going to have some explaining to do. In my family, we only make boys."

Finally understanding, Delilah laughed. "You don't know for sure if it's a boy or a girl."

Jenny said, "It's a girl," at the exact same time Zack proclaimed, "It's a boy."

After another genuine laugh, Delilah said, "Okay, I see how it is. Let me change the subject, then. I guess the next obvious question is: how did you develop the ability to communicate with spirits?"

"I was born with it, although I didn't realize that until somewhat recently," Jenny began. "It apparently runs in my family on my father's side, but I didn't learn who my father was until a few months ago."

"Oh, I'm sorry," Delilah said sincerely.

"Don't be; it's all good," Jenny assured her. "But apparently, one of my ancestors on that side had a near-death experience, and ever since then, some members of the family have been born with the ability to receive messages from the dead, but only from spirits who linger instead of crossing over."

"Okay, so what you are telling me is that spirits can either linger or cross over?"

"That's right. People who are at peace cross over, but the ones who have some unresolved issue tend to linger. In this case, it seems Winding River wants to stick around so he can prove that Jove didn't orchestrate a mass suicide."

Delilah let out a grunting sound. "I've been trying to prove that for a decade."

"Well, now you have a ringer on your team," Zack proclaimed.

"I guess I do," Delilah agreed happily. "But let me ask you something…you say the ability to communicate with spirits runs in the family. Does that mean your baby might be born with it?"

Jenny placed her hand on her belly. "She might."

"I'm pretty sure he does have it," Zack added.

Delilah had already learned to ignore their debate. "How will you know if the baby has it? Do you just have to wait until the child has their first contact…or *doesn't* have one?"

"I'll be able to tell," Jenny said. "As soon as I hold her, I'll know if she has the ability."

"That's *fascinating*," Delilah declared sincerely. "I have never heard of anything like this in my life."

"I hadn't either," Jenny confessed. "Not until it happened to me."

Delilah returned into the house to give Jenny and Zack some privacy in hopes that the quiet would elicit a contact. As the couple strolled along the grounds, they collected their thoughts. "Delilah and Winding River seem to think Jove is innocent, but Troy is equally convinced he was guilty." Jenny stated. "I'm honestly not sure what to believe."

"Well, you have to consider the sources. Winding River died while he was still under Jove's spell, so to speak, and Delilah is related to the man. She's also basing her opinion on stories that have been passed down in her family, and you know how that goes. The story starts out with a guy who caught a two-pound trout, and after being told a few times by a few different people, it ends up being that he caught a forty-foot, man-eating shark with eight sets of teeth and fins the size of a small car."

Jenny giggled at his analogy.

"So all of that needs to be taken with a grain of salt," Zack concluded. "Honestly, I would imagine Troy's assessment is the most accurate—he's got no allegiance to Jove, and he was there."

Jenny nodded as she considered Zack's assessment. "Hopefully, Winding River will give me something to work with." She looked around, once again hoping the spirit was listening. "A little more information might do the trick."

"Well, after dinner, I can head down to the police station again and see what I can find out about Sheriff Babson. Once we get out of here and get cell phone service again, you can call Kyle Buchanan and ask him to find out everything he can about Jove, now that we know his real name. What was it again?"

"Roger Hillerman."

"Oh, yeah. Roger Hillerman. Is it just me, or does that sound more like a lawyer than a hippie?" Zack stuck out his lower jaw into an under bite and spoke pretentiously. "Hi, I'm Roger Hillerman, attorney at law, PhD, LLC, MD…"

"You are out of your mind."

The under bite remained. "Yes, but am I *wrong?*"

"Right or wrong, you're steering us off topic." Jenny said as she forced a fist into her belly. The baby had worked its way into an uncomfortable position, and she needed it to move. She felt the child wriggle, and with it came relief, so she continued. "I'm hoping that Dr. Wilson has called me to tell me he's arranged a meeting with Addy. Again, I won't be able to know that until we get back into civilization and I get some reception."

"Do you know what I hope?" Zack asked. "I hope this dinner we're about to eat isn't scary."

Jenny bit her lip. "I know; I've thought about that. The way I see it, though, is that they are most likely vegetarians, so it can't be *too* disgusting. It's not like we're going to be served…" She couldn't think of any animals that would have been especially gross to eat.

"Bat?" Zack suggested.

Somehow, Jenny knew he wouldn't disappoint. "Yes, bat. I doubt we'll be eating bat for dinner."

"But it could be alfalfa sprouts soaked in goat's milk with curds on the side."

Jenny closed her eyes. "I know, but I'm trying not to think about that."

Dinner proved to be spaghetti with marinara sauce and a delicious salad made from fresh greens from the garden. This was followed by a horrible case of heartburn for Jenny, which prompted her and Zack to excuse themselves shortly after the meal was over. Despite the fact that Jenny preferred to drive in case she became led somewhere, she handed the keys over to Zack and plopped into the passenger seat, wincing with pain. She had already gobbled a few pregnancy-approved antacids, but they hadn't worked their magic yet.

Zack tried to remain positive. "At least it wasn't bat…or curds."

"Dinner was great," she agreed. "I just think I need to cross pasta sauce off my list of acceptable foods for the next few months. Seriously, I'm dying over here." At that point she remembered what it had felt like when she vicariously experienced typhoid-like symptoms through a contact, and she realized her heartburn was minor in comparison. She also considered what she would be experiencing while giving birth, and she decided not to complain any more.

Slipping her phone out of her purse, she watched it until some bars appeared. The phone buzzed and vibrated, indicating several missed calls and texts during their stay in the middle of nowhere. With a silent wince from the heartburn, she worked her way through her messages, giving Zack the summary when she was done.

"Kayla let me know that they made it home safely, and Dr. Wilson did arrange a meeting with Addy's family for ten o'clock tomorrow morning. I guess he's eager to get his answers." She refrained from saying anything nasty about him. "I think I'll go ahead and call Kyle now…once we get a hotel I'm going to want to go straight to bed."

Zack patted her leg. "Hang in there, champ. Just remember, you're doing this for our son."

She didn't have the energy to argue about the gender, so as she dialed the phone, she simply said, "I've heard that heartburn means the baby will have hair. If tonight is any indication, I'm going to give birth to an ape."

Kyle picked up after the second ring. "Hey, Jenny. What's going on?"

"Lots and lots," she began. "First of all, thanks again for getting me in touch with Troy; he was very helpful."

"Well, that's my job."

"And you do it well...so well, in fact, that I have more for you."

"Okay, let me get something to write with." After some shuffling in the background, Kyle said, "Shoot."

"I was wondering what you can tell me about Roger Hillerman prior to, and during, his days here at Eden. He seemed to be the guy in charge of it all, and I am still trying to determine if he was capable of poisoning these people or not. I'd also like some information about the arrest records of the members of The Family; Zack can send you a link that has the names of all the people who died that day."

Kyle sounded like he was writing on the other end of the phone. "I think I can do that."

"And one other thing," Jenny said. "I want you to dig up as much dirt as you can on a sheriff named Babson."

Chapter 15

Jenny was admittedly nervous, but she realized her anxiety must have paled in comparison to that of Addy Roth's mother, Cheryl. Just as Kayla had expressed about Matthew, Cheryl must have been ecstatic when Winding River's spirit finally went away, and she was probably not all that happy about bringing the topic back into her life. In fact, Jenny wouldn't have blamed her if she had declined the meeting altogether, but instead she had graciously welcomed Dr. Wilson and two strangers into her home to discuss it. Jenny felt like that spoke volumes about her character.

The Roth's house was a shade of brownish-gray that would have been difficult to describe with a name. It was a nice house, average in just about every way, but definitely indicative that the people inside had reached the American Dream. That was, of course, until their world got rocked by a series of unwanted visits from a spirit with an ax to grind.

Jenny and Zack got out of their rental car as Dr. Wilson emerged from his own. He looked much more professional than either of the Larrabees did, sporting a blazer while Jenny wore a casual outfit she could have easily worn around her own house. Although, Wilson's personality was so stiff, Jenny wondered if blazers were his version of casual wear. She could even picture him sleeping in one.

They rang the doorbell, waiting only a short time before a tall woman with a blond ponytail greeted them with a smile. "Cheryl," Dr. Wilson stated. That was his only greeting.

"Dr. Wilson, please some in," she replied with a sweeping gesture of her arm. "And you must be the Larrabees."

"Hi, I'm Jenny," she stated with an outstretched hand.

Zack simply stated his name and shook her hand as well.

Three steps into the house, Jenny realized there was a problem. She could feel her lungs tighten and her eyes begin to water, and a tickle began somewhere inside her nose. "Uh-oh," she said apologetically, "I think I may be allergic to your house."

"Oh, dear," Cheryl replied. "Is it the cats?"

Cats. Plural. "Yes, I'm afraid so."

"Well, we can meet outside on the screen porch if you'd like. The cats never go out there, and it's a nice day."

"That would be great," Jenny said as Cheryl began to lead them through the house. "Sorry to be such a pain."

"It's no trouble. Besides, you have allergies; you certainly can't help that."

The tickle in Jenny's nose grew more noticeable, and she feared she might experience the sneeze-n-pee that Kayla had warned her about. She sniffed deeply and quickened her pace, trying to get out of the house before something embarrassing happened.

They arrived at the sliding door to the screen porch, which looked like it had once been a deck that was covered as an afterthought. It was still lovely, in Jenny's opinion, and she was more than happy to put her swollen feet up on the wicker ottoman in front of her chair. She felt like she could have fallen asleep there, although she knew she had other things to accomplish.

"I'm anxious for Jenny to meet Addy," Dr. Wilson began. "She claims that she will be able to tell if Addy has psychic ability, just by greeting the child."

"I'm eager to find that out, too," Cheryl confessed. "I have to say, I'm not sure whether I want her to have it or not."

"I completely understand that," Jenny said honestly. "I feel the same way about my own baby."

Cheryl smiled at Jenny. "There's a chance your baby can have it?"

"I'm not sure what the odds are, but yes, it is possible."

"I guess you feel my pain, then. Well, let me go get Addy; she's in her room, playing."

Uncomfortable silence ensued while Cheryl was gone, during which time Jenny interlaced her fingers over her belly and looked around. "This is a nice porch."

The men simply grunted in agreement; they certainly weren't helping Jenny's attempt to curb the awkwardness. She racked her brain for something else to say, but nothing came to mind.

Mercifully, Cheryl arrived from within the house, escorted by a girl who looked to be about nine or ten, but should have been younger according to Dr. Wilson's accounts. Maybe she was just tall like her mother. "Addy, you remember Dr. Wilson, right?" Cheryl began.

Addy nodded shyly.

"And this is Mr. and Mrs. Larrabee. Why don't you go shake their hands?"

Addy did as she was told, although she looked uncomfortable with the request. Jenny eagerly took the young girl's hand, giving it a delicate shake, immediately knowing the answer to everybody's question.

"Thank you, Addy," Cheryl said. "You can go back to playing if you'd like. I just wanted you to come out and say hi."

Without a word, the young girl turned around and went back into the house. Cheryl closed the door behind her and looked eagerly at Jenny. "Did you find anything out?"

"I did," Jenny replied. "That girl definitely does not have psychic ability."

"I knew it," Dr. Wilson declared triumphantly. "There is just something about a child's brain that makes them susceptible to contact."

Jenny looked over at Cheryl, who released a breath and lowered her shoulders. She imagined that reaction was one part disappointment, one part relief. "Well, the good news is that it looks like those days are behind her," Jenny noted.

With an emphatic nod, Cheryl said, "Yes, it does."

"That's good news for Addy," Jenny concluded, "but not necessarily for Winding River. His issue still isn't resolved."

Cheryl had obviously not been brought up to speed, based on the expression she wore. "Winding River is the name of the person who had been visiting Addy...well, Winding River is what he called himself. As for his real name, we may never know for sure." Jenny told Cheryl about everything she'd learned regarding Eden, mentioning that Kyle Buchanan was working on filling in some gaps. "I was wondering, though, if Addy may have said something at some point that will ultimately prove to be helpful— maybe something that may not have made sense at the time?"

"I kept a record, if you'd like to see it," Cheryl replied. "I documented everything unusual that she said or did, along with the date and the circumstance."

Jenny was shocked; she had no idea such a list existed. "I would *love* to see it."

"I've got to warn you," Cheryl declared as she stood up, "a lot of it doesn't make any sense." She had ventured into the house only a minute before returning with a spiral notebook, adding, "It's like reading Jim Morrison's diary on an exceptionally bizarre day." She handed the book over to Jenny.

Opening to the first page, Jenny read out loud. "September fourth, Addy spit at the police and said..." She didn't want to read the foul words that were written there. "We know about this one; this was the first sign of trouble, right?"

"Yeah," Cheryl said with a phony smile, "and it was a big one. She went straight for the gusto."

Deciding to skip the dates, Jenny just read the quotes. "This one says, *The man has it in for us. He's out to get us.*" Jenny winced. "That must have been scary before you figured out that *the man* meant authority."

"Horrifying is a good word, I think," Cheryl clarified.

Jenny continued to read. "*The pigs just won't leave us alone.*

"*The pigs were behind this, you know. I guarantee it.*

"*Golden one and innocence are waiting for me, I know, but I can't go to them without justice.*" Jenny looked up with wide eyes. "I understand that one."

"You do?" Cheryl was awestruck.

Jenny recounted the story of how Golden One died during childbirth, assuming that Innocence was the name given to the baby. "Winding River must know that they've crossed over and that he could, too, if he wanted, but this unresolved issue is causing him to linger."

"There were a few other references to Golden One," Cheryl said. "I never understood what she was talking about." Her voice softened. "I guess it makes sense now. My gosh, that's just terrible."

Jenny referred back to the notebook. "*Love and nature's betrayal has to have consequences.*" She thought for a moment. "I imagine Troy and Sabrina could have been Love and Nature, although I didn't ask when I talked to Troy." Shaking her head, she added, "I should have—I don't know what I was thinking. Why wouldn't I want to know what their names were while they were at Eden?" She mentally punched herself a few times.

"Troy and Sabrina?"

Jenny once again filled Cheryl in on what she knew, this time conveying the story of how the couple left just a few weeks before the tragedy. "Troy seems to think that the *consequence* of their exit was to kill the remaining members, just to make sure nobody else tried to leave."

"Wow, that's frightening," Cheryl noted.

"And now the story might be substantiated," Jenny added, although she continued to read further. "Okay, this one says, *the fucking pigs need to police themselves, man, and just leave us the hell alone.*"

Cheryl displayed another fake smile as the sarcasm rolled off her tongue. "That was one of my favorites."

"I can see why," Jenny replied in an equally biting tone. "How old was she when she said that?"

"Four or five."

"Oh," Jenny declared, "how lovely."

"I was proud."

Jenny was glad that Cheryl could at least have a sense of humor about this. Referring back to the notebook, Jenny said, "*The pigs would see golden one as proof that we are in the wrong, but it really demonstrates the flaws in society.*

"*The masses are slaves to the dollar.*

"*If you believe the man works in your best interest, then you are part of the problem.*"

Cheryl interjected, "That one was directed at me when I tried to tell her to trust the police."

Jenny nodded and continued to read. "*Even golden one and innocence couldn't protect us from the man.*

"*The predictor did not see this as our future. The man has fucked with the natural balance.*" Despite the lowercase first letter in print, Jenny assumed The Predictor was most likely a member of The Family.

"*The man has no regard for life. We appreciate all life, and the man hates us for it.*

"*Great seer knows the truth. The family will be revered.*

"*Joe couldn't go there and kill all those people. That's why he had to disappear.*" Jenny looked up at the others, asking, "Who is Joe?"

Cheryl shook her head. "I don't know, but it's the only name she used."

"Actually, it is and it isn't," Jenny said. "She said plenty of names, but she used their Family names. This sounds like the only time she used a birth-name."

"I wonder who it is," Zack asked.

"I don't know, but I can ask Kyle to find out." Jenny returned to the list. "*Gentle giant bears the brunt of the man's wrath. The most loving pays the highest price. Fucking pigs.*" She winced again at the language coming from such a small child. However, she realized she had a means to help translate the cryptic messages. "I can call Troy back and see who The Predictor, Gentle Giant, and The Great Seer were...and maybe even Joe. If we know who they are, this stuff might make sense."

"That would be great," Cheryl said. "I know it's behind us, but I would love to know what Addy was saying."

"Addy wasn't saying anything," Dr. Wilson interjected. "The person who went by Winding River was doing the talking; Addy was simply a mechanism."

Jenny ignored him. "There are a few more comments here. *The man values the dollar above all else.*

"The great seer can differentiate between selfishness and selflessness. Our way will ultimately be rewarded.

"The pigs fear us, so they seek to destroy us.

"Jove values loyalty above all else; love and nature nearly broke his spirit with their betrayal.

"The pigs come in and ruin everything. They always have.

"Breaking man-made laws does not make a person evil; selfishness embodies evil.

"The man values conformity above honor."

Jenny flipped the page to read more quotes, but there was nothing else written. "This looks like the end of it."

"That's it for what she *said*," Cheryl explained. "The stuff she said tended to be mild in comparison to how she acted. If you flip to the back of the notebook, you will see everything she *did*."

Jenny looked at the last pages of the book, which chronicled swearing and spitting at the police and politicians, both in person and on television. There were a lot of incidents on the list.

"It seemed any time a man in a suit gave a speech about the state of the union or his political campaign, she got angry," Cheryl explained. "I had never seen anything like it. And that was just on television...the worst was when we'd see a police officer in *person*—then she'd *really* go ballistic. It was frightening and mortifying all at the same time."

Jenny glossed over some of the things Addy had shouted at the police; that small child could have made a sailor blush. "Oh, my," was all she said.

"I know," Cheryl replied. "I am so glad that phase of our lives is behind us. The funny thing is, Addy doesn't even remember doing it." She held up her hand in Dr. Wilson's direction as he opened his mouth to speak. "I know...it wasn't her saying it. There's no way a kindergartener would have known even half those crazy words she spit out. But it still came out of her mouth, and it was..." She shook her head and sucked in a deep breath. "...dreadful."

"I can imagine," Jenny said sincerely. "The only thing I can say that might make it a little bit better for you is that I can call up Troy and try to decipher some of these more cryptic messages. As for trying to solve the mystery about who killed all those people, Winding River talked about the man being out to get them, but he also talked about the devastated feeling Jove had when Troy and Sabrina left. It's like he provided evidence against both suspects."

Cheryl made a guilty face. "Sorry about that."

"You have nothing to be sorry for," Jenny said. "This has been very informative." A residual sneeze from that pass through the house crept up on Jenny. She managed to pull it off without wetting herself, which made her want to stand up and throw her arms in the air in triumph. However, she remained silent in her chair, keeping her minor victory to herself. "Oh, excuse me," she said. "That came out of nowhere."

Cheryl and Zack simultaneously said, "Bless you."

"Thanks. As I was saying, any information is good information. I may not know where these puzzle pieces go, but the more pieces I have, the more likely I am to see the whole picture."

"But here's my question," Cheryl asked. "If the sheriff is dead, and this Jove character is dead, what will Winding River have to gain by figuring out the truth? It's not like anybody can serve time for this."

"Solace," Jenny said with sympathy. "If we can figure out who really killed all those people, Winding River's spirit can finally enjoy some solace."

Chapter 16

Zack tiptoed into the hotel room, closing the door quietly behind him. Jenny could feel his presence appear from around the corner.

"Don't worry," she called from the bed, "I'm awake."

With that, Zack tossed his keys noisily onto the dresser. "Okay. I just wasn't sure if you were napping or not."

"Nope. Just resting. How did it go?" Jenny drew in a deep breath and relished in how comfortable she was, surrounded by pillows on a soft mattress. She almost felt like she wasn't even pregnant.

Almost.

Zack walked around the bed and plopped down into a lying position in one not-so-graceful motion. "Well, I didn't find out a whole lot by talking to the police; the only thing I learned was that a Babson has been sheriff in Bedford for seventy-two years straight. First, it was the great-uncle or something, then this guy's father, and now this guy. But afterward, I headed to the local library. It turns out the head librarian, Edna, has lived here her whole life, and she prides herself on knowing the history of the entire county—and *boy* does she like to talk."

Jenny giggled. "What did she say?"

"Well, her son, Todd, just moved with his family to Missouri since he got promoted and all, and her sister, Betty, has won first place in the pie contest at the county fair for ten years running. She uses fresh blueberries, you know, never the canned stuff."

She gave Zack a stiff elbow to the ribs. "What did she have to say about *Eden*?"

"Oh, you want to know about *Eden*." He slid his arm around Jenny and pulled her in closer. "Why didn't you say so?"

Jenny smiled and playfully rolled her eyes. "You're such a goof."

"You flatter me. Okay, so apparently Eden used to be an old farm, owned by the Hillerman family. When I say old, I mean old...we're talking 1800s. But by the time the 1940s and 50s rolled around, the economy had changed, and the Hillermans stopped running the farm and got more industrialized jobs. From what Edna remembered, the farm sat empty for quite some time.

"In the early sixties, Roger and a handful of friends moved in, living that counter-culture lifestyle. It was a bit of a shock for the longtime residents in Bedford; they had been a God-fearing, conservative community, and then all of a sudden these flower children invaded. You can imagine the reaction."

"Betty and Edna must have been none too pleased."

"Exactly. Apparently, word got out about this little community, in an underground sort of way, and it became a destination for both hippies and draft dodgers. People would show up there, asking to join The Family, and they would essentially vanish from the real world."

"Draft dodgers," Jenny repeated. "I hadn't considered that."

"It makes sense, and I thought about it on the way home...didn't Addy mention something about Joe not being able to kill people so he had to disappear?"

Jenny gasped with realization. "She sure did. Is it possible that this Joe is Winding River...or used to be Winding River...or is the person Winding River used to be?" She shook her head. "I don't know how to say it right, but maybe Joe got drafted, so he headed to Eden and became Winding River."

"That sounds reasonable to me."

"I need to call Kyle again."

"I think so. But there's more to this story...as Eden grew bigger and the hippies became more of a nuisance, the people of Bedford started demanding some change. They were tired of having their stuff taken, even though it usually got put back. They were fully aware of the drug usage and the indiscriminant sex, and they felt like their town had been infiltrated by a bunch of sinners. They wanted Sheriff Babson—the father, that is—to do something about it, but his hands were tied. Like Troy told you, the charges against The Family would never stick, and the judge even started to get upset with the sheriff for harassing The Family."

"It must have been a progressive-thinking judge."

"Agreed. But as you can imagine, the people were becoming more and more upset that they weren't seeing any results, and the blame was falling squarely on Sheriff Babson's shoulders. Word was getting around that maybe it was time for a new sheriff—one with a different last name, who would actually be able to do something about The Family. And wouldn't you know, 1968—the year the murder took place—was an election year."

"Get out."

"Uh-huh. Quite a nice little motive, don't you think?"

"Wow, it sure is," Jenny said. "Maybe there's some merit to Winding River's theory after all."

"I'm not sure how we would go about proving that, though—one way or the other."

"Hopefully Kyle's information will be helpful. He hasn't called me back, yet, though. Well, he *did* call me back, but it was to tell me that he had to spend the morning following a cheating husband around town. He said he'd try to get to our case as soon as he could."

"What about Troy? Did you have any luck with him?"

"I left a message, but I haven't heard from him. I did take some time to look up a little bit about the Roman God, Jove, though, and what I discovered was pretty interesting."

"Oh yeah? What did you find out?"

"Well, Jove was another name for Jupiter, the Roman equivalent of Zeus...you know, the God of all Gods. He ruled the universe and created all human laws, expressing his dissatisfaction with people's behavior by hurling lightning at them and whatnot."

"Wow. It's a bit...pretentious of him to call himself that, no?"

"He seems like he was a pretentious guy. From the sound of it, Roger Hillerman considered himself to be the man in charge. In his mind, he may have been the God of all Gods."

"Silly Roger," Zack said. "Everybody knows that title belongs to me."

The couple settled into a comfortable silence, after which Zack put his hand on Jenny's belly and said, "How's little Steve doing today?"

"You mean Ashley? She's fine. I think she's practicing her tap dancing routine in there. She's been really active today."

"It's football practice."

"Oh, okay, we'll just see about that." After another extended period of quiet, Jenny asked, "Will you be disappointed if the baby is a girl?"

"Disappointed? No. Terrified? Yes. If by some bizarre twist of fate this baby does come out a girl, I'm going to pray that she's a lesbian. That way she won't have to deal with boys. Boys are pigs—I know; I am one."

"But what if this baby is a heterosexual female? Then what?"

"Then I buy a gun. Or eight. And I start lifting weights. And maybe get tattoo sleeves."

Jenny patted his arm as she enjoyed the comfort of lying with him. Her mind began to wander a little bit, and she eventually posed, "Do you think Betty and Edna fought when they were kids?"

"It would be hard to picture, when you consider what Edna looks like now. And knowing that Betty bakes pies for the county fair—somehow I can't envision them throwing punches at each other."

"It doesn't have to involve punches. Do you think they got along?"

"I have no idea," Zack replied. "Where is this coming from?"

Jenny sighed. "I was just thinking about how many kids we should have. I grew up in a family of four, and we all got along pretty well, but when I consider how much you and your brother hated each other..."

"And still do."

"...and still do, it scares me. I would hate to have multiple children who couldn't stand each other. Having met your mother, I am under the impression that she did a good job raising you and Tim—I just think you guys are so opposite that there's nothing she could have done to make you like each other."

"It is true; my mother tried like hell to get us to get along, but it just wasn't happening."

"Exactly."

Zack pulled Jenny in even tighter. "You do realize that we don't have to decide on how many kids we want right at this moment. We can let little Steve come out and say hello first, and then we can see how it goes."

"But there's some pressure on my end. What if this baby doesn't have psychic ability? Knowing how rare the gift is, shouldn't I try again? And how many kids would I have to have before I give up on having a psychic child?"

"Why do you do this to yourself?"

Jenny drew in a deep breath and let it out in a slow exhale. "I think it comes from that second X chromosome."

"All the more reason this baby needs to come out with a penis."

At that moment, Jenny's cell phone rang from across the room. "Let me get that," Zack said. "You stay put."

She smiled as he climbed out of bed; he was a good man, and she knew it. Somehow, that simple gesture calmed her fears, even though the two topics were completely unrelated.

"It's Troy," he informed her, holding out the phone.

"Ooh." Jenny sat up quickly, eagerly placing the phone to her ear. "Hello?"

"Hi, Jenny, it's Troy Bauer. I got your message...you wanted me to call you?"

"Yes, in fact I did. How are you doing today?"

"Can't complain. How about yourself?"

"I can't complain either." She got out of bed and walked over to the desk, taking a piece of paper from the notepad the hotel had provided and fishing a pen from her purse. "I do have a couple of questions for you, if you don't mind answering them."

"For you, darling? Of course I don't mind."

"I have dug up some names, and I'm wondering if you could tell me if they mean anything to you."

"Okay, fire away."

"Well, first of all, I assume that you and Sabrina were Love and Nature."

He remained quiet on the other end for quite some time before quietly saying, "Yeah...she was Love; I was Nature."

"I'm sorry," Jenny replied. "Is this making you sad? I don't want to upset you." She hadn't considered that discussing Sabrina, who was deceased, may have been difficult.

"Sad?" Troy asked. "No, sad isn't the word. Nostalgic, maybe, but not sad."

"It's not too hard to talk about Sabrina?"

"Nah. Sabrina and I didn't last but a few years after we left Eden. It's one thing to be young and high and running around having fun together—it's something entirely different to have a job and a kid to take care of. We grew up real fast after Tristan came along, and we found that we didn't do well together as adults. We got along well enough over the years—we had to...we had a son together—but she and I didn't last that long as a couple."

"I'm sorry to hear that," Jenny said.

Troy's gruff voice and likable personality came through loud and clear as he said, "Aaahhhh. Nothing to be sorry for."

Jenny smiled, adding, "Well, in that case, do you happen to remember anybody named Winding River?"

"Winding River...yeah, he was a piece of work, that one. He was very high strung...his moods were all over the place."

"When did he join The Family, do you know?"

"It was after I did, and I joined in 1965. I can't tell you exactly when it was, though."

"Well," Jenny replied, "maybe I can find that out myself. So you say Winding River was moody—can you give me some examples?"

"I don't know if I can think of anything specific off the top of my head, but I just remember he was very unpredictable. He'd get angry sometimes and it seemed like it came out of nowhere."

"Do you think the drugs had anything to do with his mood swings?"

"I'm sure they didn't help," Troy said, "but none of the rest of us was as batshit crazy as he was, and we were all doing the same drugs."

"Why did he call himself Winding River, do you know?"

"Because he flowed in whatever direction he felt like. He carved his own path; it didn't get chosen for him."

Jenny silently marveled at just how deep the meanings behind these names were. "I realize I'm probably grasping at straws here, but are you aware if his birth name was Joe?"

"I don't know anybody's birth name but Sabrina's."

"Fair enough," Jenny replied. Her phone beeped, signaling another call. A quick glance showed her it was Kayla on the other line; she figured she would just return the call once she was done talking to Troy. "Okay, how about Gentle Giant? Do you remember that name?"

"Gentle Giant...yeah, I remember that guy. He was one tall drink of water. He had to be six-five or six-six, and just as skinny as they come. Long red hair and a beard to match. He was kind of an ugly and gangly thing, but like his name suggests, he wouldn't have hurt a flea. He'd have given you the shirt off his back if you needed it."

Jenny thought back to her vision at Eden, and the man carrying the basket of vegetables fit Gentle Giant's description perfectly. Her heart grew heavy for a moment, knowing that kind man had met such a horrible fate at a shamefully young age. Suddenly, her quest to find the truth became much more personal. With renewed vigor, she continued, "If I say that Gentle Giant bore the brunt of the man's wrath, would that mean anything to you?"

Troy remained quiet, presumably as he thought, and then he said, "He *was* facing charges there at the end. Him, specifically, not just us as a whole like it usually was."

"Do you remember what the charges were for?"

"Theft." Troy actually let out a chuckle. "He was charged with stealing someone's wheelbarrow. He had gone into town in the middle of the night on his bike, looking to find a wheelbarrow he could borrow for a few days. He found one, but he hadn't thought the whole thing through very well. How was he supposed to bike home with a wheelbarrow? So he rode his bike home, then he walked back out to get the wheelbarrow. By the time he was heading home, the sun was up, and apparently some people had seen him with it. I mean, you don't rightly forget seeing a six-and-a-half-foot-tall redhead walking around pushing a wheelbarrow at seven in the morning. And since he was the only one at Eden who even remotely fit the description, the police knew it was him. We weren't being charged with possession of stolen property this time—Gentle Giant was being hit with actual theft."

"Oh, dear," Jenny said.

"Yeah, he was pretty scared about it. He was afraid of going to jail. His court date was coming up, but I think he never actually had it. He died before it was scheduled to happen."

Jenny closed her eyes for a moment, warding off the sadness that threatened to compromise her ability to think clearly. *Find his killer,* she thought. *It's the best thing you can do to honor his memory.* "Okay, so next on my list is The Predictor...do you know anything about him?"

"You mean *her*? She claimed to be able to see the future, but she was full of shit if you ask me."

"What kinds of things did she predict?"

"The same things you and I could predict. Rain, for instance. It would start to cloud up, and she'd predict that the weather was about to turn bad—but we were high a good deal of the time, so when she proved to be right, we were impressed. Now that I look back on it, though, I realize it was nothing but crap."

"I get the impression she had predicted a different fate for Eden than what actually happened."

"Of course she did," Troy said. "If she could have predicted they'd all end up dead, they would have gotten the hell out of there."

Jenny had to laugh at the stupidity of her own statement. "Very true," she said with a giggle. "Okay, this is a sad one, but I'm just looking for confirmation. Did you all call Golden One's baby Innocence?"

His voice lowered an octave. "Yeah, we did."

"Good enough," Jenny said quickly, trying to change the subject as fast as she could. "Who is The Great Seer?"

"The Great Seer...I'd almost forgotten about that. It was our own version of God. We couldn't believe in the traditional God, mind you, because we couldn't do *anything* traditional, so we created our own version of Him. He was The Great Seer, and He loved us and hated cops. Convenient, isn't it?"

"I suppose so," Jenny said with a smile.

"He was going to equalize everything; He saw that we were good, honest, hard-working people, and He saw that the police were just a bunch of assholes."

"When you say He was going to equalize everything...you mean, after you died? Like a Heaven-and-Hell kind of thing?"

"Something like that."

Jenny nodded with approval when she looked at her list. "Well, I think that just about covers it. Troy, I can't thank you enough. You have been very helpful."

"My pleasure, young lady. Just do me a favor..."

"What is it?"

"When you finally prove that Jove is the one who killed those people, give me a call and let me know."

Jenny decided not to bring up the other side of the coin. "Will do." She concluded her call, remembering that Kayla had beeped in while she was talking. Glancing at her phone, she saw there was a new voicemail.

"That went well," Jenny said to Zack as she punched in her passcode.

"Glad to hear it."

Jenny held the phone to her ear in time to hear Kayla's frantic voicemail.

"Matthew's not gone."

Chapter 17

Jenny stood frozen as she heard Kayla continue. "Devon just got through telling me that we needed to find the lady with the yellow hair. I asked him what lady he was talking about, and he said the one from the fire. I'm so sorry, Jenny, but is there any way you can come back?" Her voice cracked, indicative of tears. "I swear, I can't do this anymore. I thought he was gone."

Feeling sick to her stomach, Jenny hung up her phone. Turning to Zack, she asked, "Do you mind if we head back to South Carolina after this? It seems Matthew hasn't left yet."

Zack's face reflected what Jenny felt. "What?"

She sat on the edge of the bed and reiterated what Kayla had said. "That poor woman," she added with a shake of her head. "What a nightmare."

"Of course we can go back. When do you want to leave?"

Jenny closed her eyes and sighed. "I'd like to get answers about The Family first, since we're already here. But as soon as we can, I'd like to head back to help Devon."

"That sounds okay to me."

Jenny returned Kayla's call, letting her know they'd meet her in South Carolina once they wrapped up in Georgia. Kayla expressed gratitude, although she couldn't win the battle against tears. Jenny found herself fighting the battle as well. If sheer will could have made Matthew cross over, Jenny's alone would have been enough. At the moment, there was nothing she wanted more.

She hung up with Kayla, her previous good mood deflated. There was a tangible pit in the bottom of her stomach. "Wow," she said to Zack. "That certainly wasn't what I expected to hear."

Zack looked at her with a crooked smile. "Are you going to tell Dr. Wilson about this, or are you going to head back without him? I get the feeling he's not your favorite character."

Jenny grimaced. "Is it that obvious?"

"It is to me, but only because I know you so well. I don't think the others would necessarily notice it."

Relaxing her shoulders, she replied, "I don't know what it is about him that bugs me so much. He's just like fingernails down a chalkboard to me." She placed her hand on her belly. "I'm blaming Ashley for this. She's the reason I can't tolerate him. It's estrogen overload."

"Does estrogen make you horny?"

Jenny laughed. "No...testosterone makes you horny, and estrogen eats testosterone."

"That's a shame."

"Yeah, it kind of sucks to be you these days." Scratching her head, Jenny asked, "Do you remember the website that listed all of the people who died at Eden?"

"In fact, I do. You need me to find it again?"

"Yes, please. Hopefully there's only one Joe on that list, and maybe we can use it to figure out who this Winding River character was."

Zack's fingers tapped and swiped his phone screen. "I found the site," he said slowly as he concentrated. "Now let me just look for the names..." He read silently for a moment, eventually looking up at Jenny with a big smile. "There is only one Joe; his name is Joe Forte. Do you think that may be our Winding River?"

The mention of the name *Joe Forte* caused a wave within Jenny. She closed her eyes, allowing an image of a teenage girl to fill her mind. The girl sat on a hay bale, smiling, with the sun reflecting off her blond hair. Her expression showed just how enamored she was as she said, "I love you, Joe Forte." Her southern accent was thick.

The words echoed around Jenny's head, swirling, sounding as if they were coming from a million different directions. Warmth filled her body; she was clearly experiencing one of the best memories of Joe's life. The moment disappeared quickly—too quickly. Jenny found herself wishing she could have it back and hold on to it for just a little longer.

With the image—and the feeling that accompanied it—gone, Jenny opened her eyes and announced, "I most certainly do think we have ourselves a Winding River. Now maybe Kyle can tell us exactly what his story is."

"Kyle," Jenny said, "I'm so glad you called."

"Yeah, sorry it took me so long. I've had one hell of a morning."

"No problem," she replied. "It's okay if you haven't been able to come up with anything for us yet."

"No, I was able to. I just had to keep tabs on a very slippery husband all morning long. Damn near wrecked my car tailing him, too. Anyway, you asked me for arrest records, and I'm not sure you know what you were getting yourself into. It looks like the people at Eden got arrested every time they turned around. Although, the charges never seemed to stick, and I think I know why."

"Because they were unfounded?"

"I'm not sure about how *unfounded* they were, but I was curious enough to look into it. It just seemed odd to me that with so many arrests, nobody was serving any time. Well, it turned out this small town had only one judge—a man by the name of Thomas Cyr. After a little digging, I discovered he was the uncle of one of the young women at Eden, although she had a different last name than he did. I don't imagine anybody made the connection, but that explains why very little was done in terms of punishment to the members of The Family."

Jenny bit her lip. "It appears The Family had a very important ringer on their team. I guess Sheriff Babson had no idea that his arrests would always be futile."

"That man was fighting a battle he would never, ever win."

"That kind of makes me laugh," Jenny admitted. With lowered shoulders, she added, "Although, that inability to pursue charges may have inspired him to ultimately do the unthinkable."

"That would be awful if it did," Kyle agreed. "But on a happier note, I did get some information on those people you asked me about—Roger Hillerman and Sheriff Louis Babson. Which one would you like to hear about first?"

"Either. They are both my prime suspects."

"I'll start with Roger Hillerman; he appears to be clean as a whistle. The only blemish on his record is a divorce, but when you look at how young he was when he got married, it's understandable."

"I certainly can't hold that against him; I'd be a hypocrite if I did."

"Aside from that, the only remarkable thing about him was his intelligence. He had an IQ in the genius range."

With a grunt, Jenny gave that notion some thought. "It makes sense. He clearly had the ability to manipulate people and make them believe he was God-like. In fact," she continued, "I remember back when I was a teacher, one of my coworkers used to say, 'there's nothing more dangerous than an intelligent delinquent.' This coworker taught high school, and he said the regular troublemakers just did stupid things, but the smart ones had the potential to be calculating about it and make sure they wouldn't be caught."

"Well, there's no doubt that our friend Roger was one of the smart ones, but I'm not sure how much of a delinquent he was. Honestly, the man had no criminal record prior to his time at Eden."

"And none of the charges he faced with The Family involved violence," Jenny added. "It would be quite a leap to go from petty theft to mass murder, wouldn't it?"

"I don't want to speculate on that," Kyle said. "I just want to tell you what the facts say."

Jenny smiled. "Understood."

"Now, when I looked into the background of your other prime suspect, I find it to be equally as squeaky clean." She could hear papers shuffle in the background. "It seems Louis Babson was the model citizen. He was a boy scout, played little league, helped little old ladies cross the street and kissed babies. It's like he was campaigning to be sheriff from the time he could walk."

"Strangely enough," Jenny said, "that's part of what leads me to believe he might have done it. In Bedford, Babsons are supposed to be sheriffs. Actually, sheriffs are supposed to be Babsons. Either way, when he discovered his family's reign might be threatened by the folks at Eden, he may have gotten desperate. When the traditional means for getting rid of undesirable residents failed, he may have had to up the ante a little bit."

"I guess anything's possible."

"Yes," Jenny said with a sigh, "anything is possible."

"Well, before I let you go, I wanted to let you know that I found something else interesting for you, even though I have to admit I don't understand it."

Jenny's ears perked up. "Oh, yeah?"

"On multiple occasions, it appears the police did a sweep, arresting everybody on the property. I repeatedly see forty-seven arrests, forty-seven arrests, forty-seven arrests. However, in one instance, I see forty-eight."

"Forty-eight? Who else was there?"

"It was a man by the name of Paul Thomas, but I have no idea how he fits into all of this. All I do know is that he went on to have a substantial arrest record long after June of 1968, so he wasn't among those who died at Eden."

Jenny mulled that over for a while. "What did he get arrested for? After Eden, I mean."

"Drugs. Assault. Robbery. Weapons. The list goes on."

"They had a supplier," Jenny said as the wheels began to turn in her mind. "He would come to Eden every once in a while and trade his LSD for mushrooms and marijuana." She decided to leave out the part about bartering for sex. "Maybe he was there one day when the police raided."

"That sounds plausible."

"I bet I can find out for sure," Jenny replied. "Is there any way you can send me a picture of him from his arrest with The Family? Maybe Troy will be able recognize him and tell us who he is, or at least how he fits into all of this. And if it does turn out he is the supplier—and he is still alive—

maybe he can tell us if he gave Jove enough Nembutal to kill forty-five people shortly before the tragedy."

"I'm sure I'll be able to dig up a picture."

"Thank you. Again. And while I have you on the phone, can I ask one more favor?"

"Only one?" Kyle was clearly grinning as he spoke.

"Only one right now." Jenny returned the smile. "Can you please look into Joe Forte a little more? I get the impression that Joe might be the one contacting me."

"Is he on the list from those who died at Eden?"

"Yup, he sure is."

"Got it. I'll see what I can do for you. If you have nothing else for me, I guess it's time for me to meet with a woman and let her know that she's married to a scumbag."

"Yes, that's the supplier," Troy said over the phone. Jenny had forwarded the picture of Paul Thomas to him after she'd received it from Kyle. "We called him Bringer of Happiness, although I'm sure the women would disagree with that name. I forgot what an ugly bastard he was. I feel bad that we made the women sleep with him for his drugs."

"Well, did they *have to* sleep with him?" Jenny posed. "Couldn't they have said no if they wanted to?"

"I don't think so. We all did unpleasant things for the good of the group. This was among the job descriptions for the women."

Jenny winced but remained professional. "According to a private investigator I work with, Bringer of Happiness got arrested with you one day."

"I'm sure he did. He was there on a regular basis, so chances are he would have been there during one of the raids."

"Do you remember him getting arrested with you?"

"No, but we got arrested so damn many times it's hard to keep them straight."

"Do you think this guy can give me some insight about Jove's character?"

"Maybe," Troy said. "I have no idea how much he remembers. Probably not a ton, considering all the drugs he did. That is, if he's even still alive. I wouldn't be surprised if he ended up face down in a ditch somewhere after an overdose of his own."

"Actually, he's still alive. When the investigator sent me the picture, he also sent me an update. It seems Bringer of Happiness is fifteen years into a twenty-year sentence at a prison near Atlanta."

"That sounds about right," Troy said in his gruff voice, causing Jenny to giggle.

"Well, I guess my next step is that I should go about trying to set up a visit with him. Thanks again for all of your help."

"I didn't help you."

"Sure you did," Jenny replied with a smile. "You told me who this guy was."

"Eh," he said dismissively. "I'm sure you could have figured that out on your own."

Jenny sat across from Zack in a colorful booth in a Mexican restaurant. The table was decorated with a festive scene covered in glass; she was looking at the image when a glob of salsa fell off her tortilla chip, landing on the very spot she had been admiring. She let out a simple, "Dammit!" before wiping the mess with her napkin.

"Are you sure you should be eating that?" Zack asked. "You remember how you felt after the spaghetti."

"Ashley wants it," she replied, taking an emphatic bite of her chip. She chewed a few times before adding, "And she can be very demanding."

"Suit yourself, but don't say I didn't warn you."

The couple remained quiet for a short while before Jenny stated, "I hate this part. It's hurry-up-and-wait. Visiting hours aren't until tomorrow afternoon at the prison, and Kyle needs some time to do his research about Joe Forte."

"Well, let's think about what we *can* do. We can go back to Eden after dinner, provided you're not overcome by heartburn."

She stuck her tongue out at him.

Zack continued, "Or we can start looking into that yellow-haired woman from the train explosion."

"Ooh, I like that idea." Jenny flashed him a smile. "Although, I think we can call her *blond*."

"Okay, if you insist on being grown-up about it, we can look into the *blond* woman from the train explosion." He said the word exaggeratedly, causing Jenny to laugh.

When he pulled out his phone, Jenny announced, "Hang on...I want to see what you're doing." She scooched sideways in small increments, trying to squeeze her way out of the booth. It was not an easy task. "Good gracious, my gut hardly fits in this seat." Finally managing to break free, she sat next to Zack on his side of the booth.

"You know, I could have moved. All you had to do was ask."

She dismissed the notion with her hand. "So, what are you looking up?"

"The same site I had before. It gave a list of the victims that day, which is how I knew Matthew was thirty-nine-year-old Matthew Ingram." He concentrated on his phone for a few moments, pressing, swiping and waiting for information to load. Eventually he said, "Here's the article." Scrolling down, he added, "It looks like there were only three women among the victims: Sally Marsh, Diane Collins and Jacqueline Crespi."

"That should make it easier," Jenny noted as she typed the names into her own phone for future reference. "Although, we will probably have to rely on Kyle to get us information about these women."

"Suppose more than one of them is yellow-haired?" Zack glanced at her with a crooked smile.

Ignoring the joke, Jenny simply said, "Ah, but remember how well Devon could point at the appropriate pictures? If we get photographs of all three women, hopefully he'll be able to identify the correct one, even if they're all *yellow-haired*."

"But suppose the woman Devon was talking about wasn't a victim?" At that moment their food arrived, prompting Zack to say, "I swear I don't know how they do it. Mexican food always comes out so fast. Anyway, Devon only said there was a yellow-haired woman from the train...he didn't mention whether she had died or not."

Jenny outwardly appeared to be ignoring Zack, unrolling her silverware and quickly digging in to dinner, but inside she was contemplating what he had just said. "How will we find out her identity if she wasn't one of those three women?"

"That's exactly my point," Zack replied. "I don't know. I'm not sure if we can find out the names of the people who survived."

"Maybe Kyle can."

"Maybe." Zack took a bite of his dinner, pausing a moment before asking, "Do you think Matthew knew someone else on the train?"

"Mary didn't mention anyone else; she said it was just her and her parents."

"Maybe Matthew knew this other woman, but his wife and daughter didn't." He looked at her with raised eyebrows.

"Are you suggesting that he was having an affair?"

"It's possible."

Jenny shook her head. "I doubt it. Well, maybe he *was* having an affair, but I don't think he'd be stupid enough to put his mistress on the same train as Julia and Mary. Besides, if he loved his wife enough to linger this long trying to find her, I doubt he was cheating on her."

"I guess you're right," Zack conceded.

"I think our best bet is to try to get pictures of the three female victims, but that will have to be through Kyle. I'll shoot him a text now and ask him to look into those women for us. Maybe it is one of them and Devon will be able to recognize her. We could also talk to Mary and see if anyone else she knew was on the train."

"There's also a third thing we should do to help with this case."

Jenny raised her eyes to look at Zack. "What's that?"

"We should get you back to that train station and see if you can get another vision."

Chapter 18

Jenny refused to mention her heartburn for fear of the inevitable *I told you so.* Although she had taken some antacids while Zack wasn't looking, the pain was still trumping the medication.

The car made it down the trampled grass, coming to a rest next to the two hybrids that Delilah had described during their last visit to Eden. Jenny and Zack got out of the car and were greeted by several members of the communal group that currently lived in the house. Having been a guest at dinner earlier in the week, the couple was no stranger to the residents, who greeted them as if they had been life-long friends.

After some idle chit chat, Jenny asked for—and was granted—permission to wander the grounds. The residents didn't go back into the house, so Zack and Jenny walked a good distance away to the edge of the manicured portion of the property. They remained silent as they wandered so Jenny could try to get a reading, but secretly she wondered if the pain in her chest was enough to prevent one from happening.

Jenny saw some motion out of the corner of her eye, causing her to glance up in that direction. Three goats marched toward the couple, and Jenny's first instinct was to make sure they actually existed in the present day. "You see those?"

"I do. Maybe I get to pet one."

Jenny smiled, having forgotten Zack's previous desire to make friends with the goats. "Well, this looks like your golden opportunity; they're coming your way."

As soon as the words came out of Jenny's mouth, one of the goats broke into a trot and headed straight for the couple, lowering his head and butting Zack square in the thigh with his horns. "Ow, you little bastard!" he shouted. "What the hell was that about?"

Unable to contain her laughter, Jenny watched as the goat backed up and repeated the process, despite Zack's best efforts to prevent it. After that, the goat turned its focus to its mates, butting the other animals a few times before running in random zig zags back in the direction he had come.

The look of dismay on Zack's face caused Jenny to laugh even harder; her urine flowed freely, but because she was prepared, she didn't even care. The moment was just too funny for her to hold back.

"What the hell?" Zack said as the humor of the moment began to strike him. He rubbed his leg while a smile graced his face. "That's going to leave a mark."

"Do you still want to pet them? There are a couple more over there." Jenny asked through a bitten lip.

"No, I think I'm good. Who knew those things were so nasty?"

The other two goats expressed little interest in the couple, choosing instead to graze along the plants that surrounded the manicured portion of the property. As Jenny watched the animals and her laughter subsided, a wave started to come over her, causing her to close her eyes. The goats multiplied and chickens appeared; the contour of the landscape changed slightly. An authoritative voice echoed in between her ears. "Everybody, line up. No funny business."

Jenny could feel animosity and dread fill her body. It was happening again. She reluctantly faced the trees in her mind's eye, seeing others do the same. Soon she was flanked by a woman on her right and a man on her left.

The angry man continued. "You are all being charged with possession of stolen property."

A deep voice resonated within Jenny as she leaned over and whispered, "You hear that Music Maker?" Her masculine tone turned mocking. "Possession of stolen property."

Music Maker. Jenny's level of awareness increased a notch, but not enough to cause her to lose the vision. She glanced to her left, taking a look at Music Maker—the man who once was Robert Morton, beloved brother and son. She studied his face, noting the kindness behind his smile, feeling a desperate need to tell him to run away from this place. She knew the horrible things that awaited him here, and he had a family back home who loved him dearly. Anxiety began to brew within her, but she forced the feeling down, knowing it had the ability to compromise her vision.

"Hands behind your back, everybody. You're all going to jail."

Jenny heard a female voice come from down the line. "What's your bag, man?"

That seemed to anger the sheriff, who grabbed Jenny's arms with excessive force and placed handcuffs on her wrists. "My bag? What's *my bag*?"

While her arms hurt from the rough treatment, she didn't say anything. She simply listened as the cop worked his way to Music Maker and cuffed him as well.

"My *bag* is that the Lewis family has had to engrave their names into all of their lawn tools—thanks to you people—and what do you know? Their missing rake is here on your property. How *surprising*."

Jenny rolled her eyes. *All of this because we borrowed a fucking rake. The pigs will find any excuse to hassle us.*

The officer continued, "I don't see how you can get out of this one. The stolen goods are leaning against your *house*. You all need to get used to the idea of sleeping in a jail cell, because that's going to be your home for a while."

"Jenny!" Zack's voice penetrated the vision. Soon after, she felt a giant thrust against her backside, almost causing her to lose her balance. Zack grabbed her by her elbow and helped her stay upright.

She turned to look over her shoulder, seeing that same unruly goat disappearing into a retreat.

"My God, are you okay?" Zack seemed genuinely concerned.

Although she could foresee a butt bruise in her future, Jenny said, "Yeah, I'm okay."

"I didn't see him until the last second. Sorry I couldn't give you any more warning."

"That's okay." She rubbed the area that had been struck. "He's a strong little guy, isn't he?"

"Yeah, he's no joke."

Two of the people who lived at the house came rushing over; one came to check on Jenny, the other chased off the goat. "I'm so sorry," the unkempt young man who approached the couple said. "Are you alright?"

Jenny smiled politely. "Yeah, I'm fine."

"That's Butthead," the man explained. "I guess you can see how he earned the name."

Zack and Jenny both laughed. "Is he always like that?" Zack posed.

"Afraid so. I'm not sure, but I think something's wrong with him. We had him castrated a while ago so he doesn't reproduce; we would never have him put down, of course, but I certainly wouldn't want a whole field full of goats like him, either."

Bewildered, Jenny asked, "You can castrate a goat?"

"Sure. Happens all the time. It prevents inbreeding...kind of like fixing a dog."

Awe remained in her voice as she turned to Zack. "I guess you really do learn something new every day."

"So, I gather you were having a vision when you got bumped," Zack said. "What was it about?"

The man who lived at the house looked at her intently as she explained, "I saw myself getting arrested, and I could tell by my reaction that it was a routine occurrence. This time it was over a stolen rake...actually, a *borrowed* rake. I get the impression they only intended to use it for a while and then return it."

"You know, that seems like sound logic to me," the man said. "I would think that one rake could serve a whole community. It's rather wasteful for every home to own a separate one. Imagine all of the wonderful things you could do with the money you'd save by not buying your own."

Jenny thought about all of the things cluttering her home and her garage; that price tag would have inevitably added up. These people had a knack for making her feel guilty.

"I feel you," Zack said, "but there are lots of people who make their living at the rake-making factory. If everyone suddenly started sharing rakes, those people would be out of work."

The man looked at Zack for an uncomfortably long time. "A thinker," he eventually said. "I like that."

Jenny could see this conversation turning into a long and boring debate, so she said, "Unfortunately, I wasn't able to see the vision through. Butthead had other plans for me."

"Again, I'm so sorry about that."

"Don't be," Jenny said. "Believe it or not, I find the little guy to be endearing. He's kind of a think-outside-the-box goat. I had students like that in the past, and they always had a special place in my heart."

"I'd like to put him in a box," the man said. "That would keep him out of trouble."

"I used to want to put some of my students in a box, too, from time to time, but somehow I didn't think the principal would approve of that. But anyway," Jenny added, turning to Zack, "I was able to get a good look at Music Maker. It made me sad, knowing what was going to happen to him and how much his family loved him." She shook her head. "I wanted to warn him, but I guess the only thing I can do for him is figure out who did this. I hate that my role is always to avenge; I wish I could prevent."

"You do prevent," Zack told her. "Do you know how many people you've saved by putting Orlowski and Tate away?"

A defeated smile graced Jenny's face. She knew Zack was right, but she would probably always focus on the people who contacted her—the ones she was too late to protect.

"You put some people away?" the man asked.

"Well, I helped the police put some murderers away."

"Serial killers, to be precise," Zack said. "*Serial,* as in *would inevitably do it again if they didn't get stopped.*"

Jenny wanted the conversation to stop being about her; compliments were still difficult for her to accept. "Anyway, I'm not sure how insightful this visit was, but I am invigorated. I absolutely want to figure out what happened all those years ago—for Joe Forte and Robert Morton and all of those people." Her face grew sad as she looked up at Zack. "They weren't bad people, and they shouldn't have died."

Jenny looked fearfully at her breakfast plate. A plain bagel, some cantaloupe and a yogurt—those things couldn't possibly cause heartburn, could they? She gazed longingly at Zack's mound of fattening food, dripping with butter and syrup, knowing it wouldn't cause him any pain or a single extra pound. Life was certainly not fair at times.

Her phone rang from inside her purse; the number indicated it was Kyle. She picked up eagerly. "Hello, sir. How are you this morning?"

"Doing just fine, Mrs. Larrabee, and how are you?"

"Good," she replied. "Excited. Were you able to find anything?"

"I sure was. I'll start with Joe Forte, who was born and raised in Tyson's Bend, Alabama, a little dot on the map that nobody's ever heard of. He had a bit of a sad story, really. He lived in a house up until he was fourteen, when his father got arrested and they had to move."

"Uh-oh," Jenny said. "What did the father get arrested for?"

"Embezzlement. He ran the books for a local farm supply store, and it seemed he kept a chunk of the money for himself. The boss caught him and pressed charges. After that, things changed for the worse for Joe and his family. The mother, who had previously stayed home, had to go to work, and they had to sell their house and move into a trailer park, which is where Joe found his way into trouble."

With a wince, Jenny braced herself and asked, "What kind of trouble?"

"Drugs, mostly. Truancy from school. Victimless crimes, so to speak."

"So, he was not a violent person?"

"Violent? Not that I can tell. He did get in trouble at school, though, for outbursts against his teachers and principals. It seems he had a bit of a chip on his shoulder regarding authority after his father's arrest, but his episodes were always just verbal, never physical."

"Well, I can't honestly say that I blame him. Not that I'm excusing that behavior or anything—outbursts against your teachers are never acceptable—but I'm sure he was genuinely angry about what happened to his family. Granted, he was taking it out on the wrong people, but I think any hostility he had was understandable. He'd been dealt a pretty crappy hand, through no fault of his own, and that's tough for a fourteen-year-old to handle."

"No argument here," Kyle said assuredly. "I see a lot of kids dealing with bad situations in my line of work—they go through hardships that would be tough for an adult to handle. I wonder, sometimes, how they do it."

"Not always productively, unfortunately."

"Usually not. Anyway, our friend Joe Forte's number came up in the draft in early 1966, and after that, he disappeared from the radar. Nobody reported him missing or anything, but nobody knew where he was, either. It seems like his loved ones knew he was avoiding the military, but they didn't know exactly how."

"He stopped being Joe Forte, that's how," Jenny replied, "and he became Winding River."

"So there he is, in a nutshell," Kyle said. "Is there anything else you need to know about him?"

"No, that should do. I just wanted to get a feel for who this guy was; I always like to know a little about the people I'm dealing with."

"Well, let me know if you need any more information about him. As for your other request, I got some pictures and descriptions of the three female victims of the train explosion. I have that all saved in my computer; it might be easier if I just email them to you."

"Sounds good," Jenny replied. "I'll be looking for your message."

She finished up her call with Kyle, noticing Zack had eaten his entire plate of food during the short conversation. He was about to get up for seconds when he saw Jenny hang up; he aborted his mission and focused his attention on her instead. "I assume that was Kyle; what did he have to say?"

Jenny recounted the story about Joe Forte. "You know," she added, "that makes sense, if you think about it."

"What does?"

"The animosity toward the police. It may have started long before the harassment at Eden. I mean, you and I both know Joe's father created his own fate by stealing from the store he worked for, but it probably looked quite different from Joe's point of view. What he saw was the cops arrest his father, and then his life went downhill after that. He may have blamed the police for what happened to his family."

"Don't you think he'd eventually figure out that his father was the dumbass?"

"That type of thinking requires maturity. I'm not sure he was allowed to get old enough to do that."

Zack shrugged. "And what did Kyle have to say about the train victims?"

Jenny's phone chirped. "We're about to find out about that now."

Chapter 19

Zack refilled his plate while Jenny called up the email. Once he returned, she gave him the details.

"Okay, it looks like the first woman on the list is Diane Collins; she was forty-two years old and had what appears to be jet-black hair. Jacqueline Crespi was twenty-four, and look…" She held the phone out and showed Zack the picture. "Blond."

"And hot," Zack noted.

While Jenny did have to agree she was a beautiful young lady, that comment made her realize just how long it had been since Zack had said something similar about her. Acknowledging that now was not the time for such petty thoughts, she returned the phone to face herself and continued, "Last, we have Sally Marsh, who was thirty-seven and brunette as they come. So, if anything, it looks like Devon must have been talking about Jacqueline Crespi."

"Unless, like we said, the woman he was talking about didn't die that day. Then we're back at square one."

Closing her eyes, Jenny held up her hand, signifying her desire to stay off that path for now. "Let's get this picture off to Kayla and see what Devon has to say about it first. Then, we can worry about what to do after that."

With the touch of a few buttons, she forwarded the picture off to the Moore family with a brief explanation. Once that was done, she read more of Kyle's information about Jacqueline Crespi.

"It says here she was married and living in Severin, South Carolina, wherever that is."

Zack leaned to the side as he pulled his phone out of his back pocket. He held up a finger as he swallowed the food in his mouth, finally saying, "Give me just a sec, and I can tell you."

Jenny continued to read, "According to this, Jacqueline was on the train because she was going home to visit her parents in Pennsylvania." She sucked in a breath and looked up at Zack. "Imagine being her father…you're all excited to see her, keeping track of the time so you can get her from the station…but the train doesn't arrive. It caught on fire on the way. You hear that a handful of passengers died in the explosion, and you pray and pray that Jacqueline wasn't among them…but she was. She happened to be sitting in the wrong section of the wrong car in a long passenger train."

Zack shook his head as he continued to look at his phone. "Awful." He toyed with the screen a little more and announced, "The town of Severin is about fifteen miles north of Terryville, where Matthew was from. It was obviously a northbound train, so she must have gotten on a little after he did."

"And she took one of the few available seats, near the front of the car. It's almost like those people knew…the seats where the fatalities took place filled up last."

"Well, we don't know that. A buttload of people may have gotten off at the Severin station, and they happened to come from the front of the train, thereby creating empty seats." He looked proud of himself as he said the word *thereby*.

"It must have been weird for the people who got off at the Severin station, don't you think? The train exploded soon after they got off. That's like one of those too-close-for-comfort deals."

"Just think…if that person decided to light up their cigarette forty-five minutes earlier, the people who got off in Severin would have died, too. Or if the person with the oxygen tank had gotten off at the Severin station, there never would have been an explosion to begin with." Zack made a face, indicating he had just thought of something.

"What is it?" Jenny asked.

"Something's not right," he announced as he returned to his phone.

"What isn't right?"

He remained quiet as he looked up some information. "That's what I thought. In this article, it gives the names and ages of the people who died in the explosion. The oldest person to die was forty-four."

"That's so sad," Jenny noted.

"I know; it *is* sad, but that's not my point." He looked up at Jenny. "My point is: which one of those people would have been using an oxygen tank?"

"I hate visiting prisons," Jenny announced as they pulled into the parking lot of the facility that housed Paul Thomas. "They're such dismal and depressing places."

"At least you get to leave," Zack noted. "Those guys don't."

Jenny grunted in acknowledgement as she parked the car. She hoped her exploits never caused her to end up in a place like this; one of these days, though, she might run out of luck.

Having visited Brian Morris many times at Benning Penitentiary, she was familiar with the drill when she entered Axworth Prison. Metal detector, pat down, belonging search—at least it didn't faze her this time. She was led to the visitation room, taking her seat at what looked like a tiny cubicle with a glass partition in front and a phone on the side. She waited nervously, unsure what to expect from this Bringer of Happiness, who Troy had predicted would have already been found face-down in a ditch.

A man entered the room, looking older than Jenny had expected. She could tell by his disproportionately large nose that it was indeed Paul Thomas, the man Troy had described as 'an ugly bastard.' However, his pale and sunken face was littered with wrinkles, and his arms were frighteningly thin but flabby, indicating he had once weighed substantially more than he did at that moment. A distinct curve in his spine showed evidence of osteoporosis. His appearance was unnerving to Jenny, who felt as if she was about to start a conversation with a man who might not survive long enough to see it through.

Paul sat at the desk with some help from the guard, his whole arm shaking as he took the phone off the wall. He started to speak, inducing a phlegmy coughing fit which Jenny waited through patiently, although she had to fight not to grimace at the sight and sound of it. Once he regained his composure, he looked at Jenny with sagging eyes and said, "Who are you?"

She cleared her throat. "My name is Jenny Larrabee; I've been looking into what happened in Bedford back in June of 1968. I'm talking about a place called Eden, and I get the impression you were acquainted with those people."

He closed his eyes in a long blink, falling short of looking at her when he reopened them. "Yeah, I knew them. What is it you want to know?" His voice sounded raspy and sickly.

"Well, there's been a little bit of a debate lately about what really happened on the day they all passed away, and you may hold the key to clearing that up."

"Me? What, do you think I did it or something?"

"No," Jenny replied quickly, "I don't think..." Paul Thomas had the drugs. He had the access. But what would have been his motive? "...that you did it."

She was fully aware that she had paused mid-sentence; she only hoped that she'd been able to recover without giving away her sudden suspicion of the man sitting in front of her.

Based on the look on Paul's face, she hadn't.

She plugged on, pretending nothing out of the ordinary had happened. "I was just wondering if you had sold a large amount of Nembutal to Jove, or even Sheriff Babson for that matter, shortly before the tragedy."

Paul's short chuckle of disbelief turned into another disturbing coughing fit. After gathering himself, he posed, "You think I sold Nembutal to the sheriff?"

Suddenly embarrassed, Jenny said, "It was just a theory."

"Well, it's a bad one. That man had it out for us—if I was stupid enough to even *show* him a Nembutal, I would have been locked up faster than you can say dumbass."

"It wasn't an illegal drug," Jenny mentioned.

"It was if you didn't have a prescription for it."

She nodded with understanding. "Then how about Jove? I am under the impression that you supplied him with all of the drugs that he wasn't able to grow himself. The current belief is that he convinced all of the members of The Family to commit suicide—did you give him enough pills to make that happen?"

Paul's eyes sagged naturally, but the sadness expressed on his face made him look like a remorseful basset hound. He let out a long breath, running his shaky hand over his balding head, which was covered in age spots. "I'm tired," he announced solemnly. "I'm tired, and I'm dying."

Jenny looked into his eyes, feeling a stir beginning to grow within her. Unsure what to make of it, she remained still, almost afraid to move.

Paul shook his head. "No, I did not give Jove enough drugs to kill everybody who lived there. He didn't do it."

She felt nerves and agitation, yet she showed nothing outwardly. She wanted him to continue.

Paul's silence was long; it was obvious he wasn't quite sure what to say. "I'm going to die in here—and soon, if God can find it in Himself to be merciful. Not that I deserve any mercy." He struggled some more, clearly uncomfortable in his own skin. "It's funny—I'm in here on drug charges. My sentence was far too long for a drug charge, if you ask me, but this is where I belong. If they only knew the shit I've done, I would have been hanged a long time ago." He placed his elbow on the table, resting his forehead on his palm. It looked as if he wouldn't otherwise be able to hold his head up. "I did it," Paul said softly. "I killed those people."

Jenny felt anger consume her body. She began to stand up, the urge to yell *we trusted you* almost too strong to ignore. However, control prevailed, and she sat back down, pretending she was merely shifting in her seat.

Paul didn't seem to notice; he simply shook his head with remorse seeping out of his pores. "I was such a damn fool—so fucking high."

A long silence followed. Jenny fought her inner demons and waited patiently for him to continue, but he seemed to be done talking. With great effort, she made sure she spoke softly, remaining in control of what she was saying. "Why did you do it?"

The hand that had been supporting Paul's head fell to the table with a heavy thud. The skin around his eyes turned red, although he produced no tears. "I was mad," he proclaimed.

Trying to keep the conversation from shutting down, Jenny kept compassion in her voice. "Mad about what?"

There was a pause before everything Paul said. "That girl."

Out of respect, Jenny returned the long pause before asking, "What girl?"

"The girl that wouldn't sleep with me. I have no idea what her name was, but it was her turn to fuck me...and she wouldn't. She wouldn't even touch me, and I was pissed. I felt like it was her duty. It was part of the deal." Paul's eyes rose to meet Jenny's. "Long story short, I killed a shitload of people because a girl refused to fuck me for drugs."

Anger once again threatened to encompass Jenny. She had to divert her eyes from Paul's—they looked too familiar. She remembered seeing them when they graced the face of a younger man—a man she had regarded as a friend. Her body began to tremble with the urge to crash through the glass and strangle the bastard on the other side.

Paul went on, oblivious to Jenny's inner turmoil. "Can you believe that? The girl showed *morals,* and I killed them for it?" He shook his head again, clearly disgusted by his own actions.

Swallowing her hate, Jenny asked, "How did you do it?"

"I spiked their water supply. I put enough shit in there to kill a small army." The look on his face showed immeasurable shame. "I knew that no matter how sick they got, they never would have gone to the doctor. Jove didn't allow that. So I knew they'd just keep drinking the water until the dosage became fatal." He shook his head and muttered something Jenny couldn't understand.

"Well, you can make this right, you know," she added with professionalism.

"Make it right?" Paul mocked. "There's nothing in this world that will *make it right*."

"You can't *undo* it," Jenny noted, "but you can confess and give a lot of people some peace. There are people out there who still don't understand what happened. All we have now are rumors and speculation—Jove is currently being blamed for orchestrating a suicide that everyone else willingly participated in. That's not what happened. You can give Jove his good name back, and you can let some families know that their loved ones didn't willingly commit such a desperate act."

Paul's sarcastic tone showed he didn't agree. "You really think that will help?"

"I do, actually," she replied with conviction.

"They won't be any less dead."

"No, they won't be any less dead." Jenny once again swallowed the demon squirming inside her. "But they will be exonerated."

With a shrug, Paul said, "I'm going to hell. Whether I confess to this or not, I'm going to hell."

Jenny sat straighter. "Then why not tell the truth?"

He sat motionlessly with his head in his hand. An eternity seemed to pass before he finally said, "Then everyone will know the monster I really am."

"Everyone already thinks that of Jove, and he didn't do it."

After another lifetime of silence, he managed a subtle nod and whispered, "Yeah, I'll do it. I'll write up a confession."

Jenny felt herself relax, although there was a part of her that was still consumed with anger. "Thank you, Paul. It's the right thing to do."

He snorted and made a face, seemingly amused by Jenny's statement. With one last burst of life, he looked up at her and said, "You know the most fucked up part of this whole thing?"

"What's that?" Jenny asked, barely able to contain her hate.

"I went to one of the funerals…some kid whose family lived close by. And while I was there, guess who I saw?"

Jenny shrugged and shook her head.

"I saw that girl who wouldn't fuck me, alive and well and walking around."

Chapter 20

"Well, that didn't go as expected," Jenny said as she turned the key.

"What happened?" Zack asked.

Jenny looked squarely at her husband. "He confessed."

"He *what*?"

"Uh-huh. That was my reaction."

"Why in the world would he have killed them?"

"Sabrina." Jenny began to back out of the parking space. "She wouldn't sleep with him when it was her turn, and in his drug-induced delusional state, Paul concluded that everyone at Eden needed to be punished for that."

"Holy shit."

"I know. He spiked their well with what he called 'enough Nembutal to kill an army.' But, unfortunately for him, Sabrina had left Eden a couple of weeks earlier, so his intended target wasn't among the dead."

"Don't you think that's a little extreme? Killing a whole community of people because you got shot down?"

"Of course it's extreme," Jenny replied. "Drugs do some strange things to people. Anyway, he said he was going to make a more formal confession to help right some of the wrong he had done. I only hope he lives long enough to do it. He looked like he was on death's door."

"And after he dies, he'll get to face all of those members of The Family that he killed sixty years ago."

Jenny shook her head. "I'm not sure he'll go to the same place that they went to."

"You think he's going to hell?"

"Something like that." Jenny gestured to her purse. "Hey, can you please turn my phone on? I want to see if Kayla tried calling while I was in there."

Zack lifted her pocketbook from the floor of the car. "The fun just never ends on this trip, now does it?"

"Yeah, it's been a laugh a minute."

After looking at the phone for a second, Zack said, "One missed call from Kayla, one new voicemail."

"Ooh, can you play it?"

He pressed a series of buttons, including the speaker feature, and Kayla's voice came through the phone. "Hi, Jenny, it's Kayla. Devon did recognize that woman from the picture you sent; he said she was the person he was talking about. She sat next to him on the train. I don't know if Matthew is concerned for her safety like he was for Mary and Julia, but I don't want to tell him she died in the fire...not without you here to help me, just in case he gets upset about it for some reason." Kayla let out a sigh. "Well, if you could give me a call back when you get this message, that would be great. I hope things are going well for you in Georgia. Bye."

"That's good news, I guess," Zack concluded as he hung up the phone. "At least we know what person we're dealing with."

Jenny nodded as she thought. "I wonder why he's so concerned about this one girl."

"I guess it's time to find out."

"Are you sure you don't want to tell Dr. Wilson we're going back to South Carolina?" Zack asked. "I feel like we're running away."

Jenny shifted in the driver's seat. "Yeah, I'm sure. Devon's case is different than the others; he's a psychic, and the other kids weren't. This case shouldn't even interest Dr. Wilson, really."

Zack stifled laughter. "And the fact that the good doctor grates your nerves has nothing to do with it?"

Jenny smiled. "Nothing at all."

Her rear end was numb from the long drive, so she was happy to hear Zack say, "The station should be less than a mile from here on the left."

"It's certainly in a sketchy neighborhood," Jenny noted.

"It is now, but it probably wasn't back in 1961 when Jacqueline boarded the train. Remember, this train line is defunct; it wasn't before, so I imagine the businesses along this strip used to be a lot more successful than they are now."

She looked at the old, crumbling houses and shops that surrounded her. Perhaps this had once been a nice, new neighborhood full of promise; now it just looked like a place where people moved if they had nowhere else to go.

Soon, she pulled the car into an abandoned parking lot, complete with tall grass growing in cracks in the asphalt. The train station itself was covered in graffiti and littered with broken windows, just as the other one had been. She tried to picture the way it would have looked when it was new and not frightening, but that was too much of a stretch for her to envision.

They got out of the car and headed toward the platform. Jenny felt the tiniest twinge begin to stir within her, but it was fleeting, and everything seemed perfectly normal as she reached the concrete area next to the train tracks. She walked around in a few circles, unable to get any kind of reading.

"So far, I've got nothing," she announced. "Maybe Jacqueline didn't board the train here."

"It's the closest station to where she lived at the time," Zack said, "but that's no guarantee this is where she would have gotten on."

Jenny walked off the platform and stood on the tracks themselves, which also had long grass growing amongst the metal and wood. She looked in front of her in the northbound direction and watched the tracks disappear around a small curve. *This was the path,* she thought to herself. *This was the path that all of these people took to meet such a horrible fate.*

As they sat on this stretch of track, everything must have seemed perfectly normal for them—just another day on the train. Little did they know that this was the path to disaster, and for eleven of them, they were within an hour of their death.

A wave hit. Jenny closed her eyes, suddenly finding herself seated on a train, looking out the window. A couple stood there—Jacqueline Crespi and a dark-haired man who was trying to convince her to accept a present. She looked as if she didn't want it, but he persisted, and she eventually wrapped her arms around the gift with a roll of her eyes. The man kissed her cheek; the expression on Jacqueline's face indicated that it, too, was an unwelcome gesture. She got on the train without so much as a glance back in his direction, the gift tucked clumsily under her arm.

She took her seat next to Jenny, setting the large and awkward gift on the ground in front of her. The young woman flashed a quick, insincere smile in Jenny's direction before sinking back into her chair and allowing the look of irritation to once again take over her face. The train started to move, and Jenny noticed the woman didn't look out the window to return the overzealous wave of the man standing on the platform.

The vision subsided; Jenny opened her eyes to look over at Zack. "You said the youngest person to die in the train explosion was forty-four?"

"Yes," he replied, "that's what the article said."

"And you wondered which one of those people had an oxygen tank?"

"Uh-huh." He sounded curious about what Jenny was going to say next.

She stepped back onto the platform. "I don't think any of them *were* on oxygen." Squinting to keep the sun out of her eyes, she looked up at Zack. "I think that tank may have been part of a homemade bomb that was disguised as a present."

"You know, I was thinking there may have been a bomb, but I didn't say anything. I figured the investigators would have known what they were talking about when they declared it an accident."

"I can't imagine they had a whole lot to work with," she replied. "Remember, it took the fire crews a long time to get to the scene—the train was in the middle of nowhere when it exploded. It probably burned so long that it destroyed most of the evidence in the process."

"But what makes you think it was a bomb in a present? Did you see it in a vision?"

"I did...sort of. Matthew made a point of showing me that Jacqueline had a gift with her. It was big and bulky—large enough to hold a bomb, I would assume. But I also thought of something else. Do you remember when we first went out to lunch with Devon, and I asked him about the fire? This was before we knew it was an explosion."

"I remember."

"Well, at one point I was asking Devon something about how the fire started. He was playing with his tablet, and his response to me was, 'It's a present.' Then he said, 'Click.' At the time I thought it was just his short attention span kicking in and he was focusing more on his tablet than the conversation, but now that I've seen Matthew's vision, I get the impression that the present really may have gone *click*."

"Oh, shit," Zack replied. "Do you think she was a suicide bomber?"

Jenny shook her head. "A man on the platform insisted she take it, even though she looked reluctant to bring it on board." She folded her arms across her chest. "I think that man just wanted her dead."

"Who was he, do you know?"

"I assume it was her husband, but I don't want to jump to any conclusions. I will say that if it was her husband, she didn't look like she was all that happily married. He did, but she didn't."

Zack raised an eyebrow. "That may be a motive."

Sadness crept into Jenny's bones as she reached for her phone to call Kyle. "Indeed it may."

Jenny was all too happy to put her suitcase down in the hotel room and plop onto the bed. "It feels so good to lie down," she announced. "I don't know how riding in a car can be so tiring, but it is."

"Well," Zack reasoned as checked out the view, "you did get a confession out of a mass murderer and have a vision that may unlock a sixty-year-old mystery about a train explosion... perhaps that's contributing to your fatigue."

She responded with just a grunt, which was all she had the energy to muster.

Zack found the remote and turned on the television, getting comfortable on the other queen bed in the room. He scanned the channels as he propped the pillows behind his head.

Jenny could hear the brief snippets of programs as he surfed. "...in what is perhaps the largest mass murder in American history."

She sat up in bed like a shot, all the exhaustion instantly gone from her body.

The announcer continued, "Paul Thomas confessed earlier this morning to being the mastermind behind what was previously assumed to be a mass suicide in the small town of Bedford, Georgia. On June seventeenth, 1968, forty-five members of a hippie commune were found dead inside their home in what had appeared to be an intentional overdose; however, Paul Thomas has just admitted to poisoning their water supply in retaliation of a drug deal gone bad. Mr. Thomas is currently serving a twenty-year jail sentence for drug charges, which sources say is surely a life sentence due to his rapidly declining health. Under the circumstances, prosecutors have decided not to pursue charges in this newest case, stating Mr. Thomas will likely not live long enough to make it worth the taxpayers' money. Reporting live from Axworth Prison, this is Allison Kierney."

"He did it," Jenny said with awe. "He actually confessed."

The reporter from the desk asked a question. "Allison, do you think this may be a publicity stunt? People have been known to confess to crimes they didn't commit for a variety of reasons; could this be an instance of a man looking to get a little fame before he dies?"

"Kurt, that has been speculated," Allison replied. "The police are going to look into his claim to see how likely or unlikely he was to have done it, just to give the families of the deceased some answers. However, like I said, they will refrain from pressing charges even if they do find enough evidence against him. Paul Thomas is in very poor health, and he is not expected to live more than a few weeks."

"I've got to call Troy," Jenny said as she hopped out of bed. "He needs to contact the police."

"Doesn't he need to be made aware of this first?" Zack asked.

"That, too," she replied. "Unless he's watching the news." She dialed his number, pleased to hear his gruff voice on the other end. "Troy," she began, "are you watching the news by any chance?"

"The news? Naahhhh. It's always full murder and death and tragedy. I choose to stay away from that depressing stuff."

Jenny drew in and released a short breath. "Well, they've had a little break in the investigation in the Eden case." She looked over at Zack, who was making a face at her word choice. "Paul Thomas, the Bringer of Happiness, confessed to poisoning the water supply."

"Well, I'll be damned. What the hell would he have done that for?"

Another breath. "It seems Sabrina refused to sleep with him when it was her turn."

Troy remained uncharacteristically quiet for a while; Jenny imagined she had struck a nerve. "She told me that," he eventually said, "but I didn't believe her. I thought she was just saying that to make me feel better. I hated the thought of her doing anything with that ugly bastard. She was my girlfriend. She was pregnant with my kid. But we were so brainwashed at the time, I actually felt like it was her duty to sleep with him. It was right after that when she told me we needed to leave. She didn't want to go through any more of that shit."

"Well, it's a good thing you left, because he apparently started plotting his revenge at that point."

More silence indicated he was once again considering just how close he and his family had come to death.

"Would you be willing to contact the police and tell them what you know? They're trying to determine if Paul Thomas is actually guilty or if he's just confessing for attention. I bet you can give them some valuable information."

"I don't know about *value,* but I can tell them some stuff."

Jenny smiled. "It would be great if you could."

She finished her call and placed the phone next to the television. She turned toward Zack, who said, "Do you think maybe *you* should contact the police?"

"And say what?" Jenny asked as she sat back down on the bed. "I'm a psychic and I was temporarily overcome by one of the deceased?"

"Well, you knew they didn't take any pills, which would substantiate Paul Thomas's claim."

"I'm not sure they would believe me. Troy, on the other hand, was there."

"But you're a world-renowned psychic," Zack said with a smile. "Of course they'll believe you."

Jenny rolled her eyes. "I'd prefer to not be world-renowned, if you don't mind. Remember, there's a lunatic out there who has a bone to pick with me. I'd rather keep my whereabouts under wraps, if possible."

"They still haven't caught him yet, huh?"

"Not last I checked. Besides, Ed and Renee told me they'd let me know if he ever got arrested. They know I'd sleep a little more soundly at night if he was behind bars, and I haven't heard a thing from them."

"I doubt he's going to come after you. He's too busy hiding from the police."

"I hope so," Jenny added as the excitement of the moment began to wear off and fatigue crept back in. She slid sideways into a laying position, cradling her head in her bent arm. Enjoying the comfort and silence, a sense of dread filled her body when her phone chirped, signaling a text message. "Zack, can you be the greatest guy in the world and check my phone?"

"I suppose I can, for a small fee." He got up off his bed and looked at the screen. "It's from Kyle," he announced. "He says he found Jacqueline Crespi's sister."

Chapter 21

The morning brought a renewed sense of vigor; Jenny felt much more equipped to search for a killer than she had the previous evening. She called Kyle, who gave her the number of Amy LaRoussa, Jacqueline Crespi's surviving sister. They had been close in age, apparently, so Kyle was optimistic that Amy could provide some information about who might have wanted Jacqueline dead.

Jenny had snuck out to a local craft store while Zack slept in, purchasing some painting supplies and a canvas. She had set up shop in the bathroom, where she was able to turn on the lights without disturbing her husband. Periodically closing her eyes to retrieve the image in her mind, she sat on the closed toilet lid and recreated the face of the man who had given Jacqueline the present. She figured this would be useful information to pass along to Jacqueline's sister; hopefully Amy would be able to conclusively identify the person in the picture, and this mystery would be solved.

She was halfway through painting the picture when her phone screen lit up, displaying Kayla's name. "Hello?" she said softly. She hoped the echo in the room didn't give away her location.

"Hi, Jenny. I just wanted to check in and see if you had gotten anywhere."

"I have, actually. I'm sorry I haven't called; I fell asleep pretty early last night, and I've been busy this morning trying to work on a lead."

"A lead...that sounds promising."

"I hope it turns out that way," Jenny explained. "I got a vision last night of Jacqueline Crespi, the woman that Devon had recognized from the picture. She was boarding the train with a big, bulky present that a man had given her on the platform; Devon had mentioned a present way back in the beginning, and my guess is that it might have actually contained a bomb."

"A bomb?" Kayla's shock was easily detected through the phone.

"That's just my theory at this point; I really have no evidence to support it. But I once asked Devon who started the fire, and he said 'it was a present,' or something to that effect. I'm thinking that he was being honest with that reply—that a present really did start the fire."

"I'd love to ask him about that," Kayla said, "but I'm always afraid to bring it up. When he's acting like a normal five-year-old, I don't want to do anything to ruin those moments."

"I understand," Jenny said compassionately. "You might not need to ask him if my lead pans out the way I hope it does. I'm currently sketching a picture of the man who gave Jacqueline the present, and I have her sister's contact information. I'm hoping the sister can tell me who that man was and if he had a reason to want Jacqueline dead. Then maybe we can figure out who did this, which might be what Matthew wants from us at this point."

Kayla's voice was incredulous. "I just can't imagine hating someone so much that I'd be willing to kill a train full of innocent people to get back at them."

Jenny thought about the drastic measures that Paul Thomas had taken in order to exact his revenge against Sabrina. "There are indeed some sick people in the world."

"Well, if we can figure out who was responsible for this explosion, maybe Matthew will go away once and for all. Jenny, can I just tell you…I was absolutely devastated when I heard Devon talking about that train again. I thought for sure he'd be rid of all this after he met Mary. My heart absolutely *sank* when he mentioned that blond woman."

"I'm sure it did," Jenny said emphatically. "I know mine did when I heard your message."

Kayla let out an exaggerated sigh. "I guess I should let you go, then, so you can get working on that picture. The sooner you get it done, the sooner we can figure out who that man was and, hopefully, the sooner

Matthew will go away. God knows that moment can't come quickly enough for me."

Jenny smiled. "I won't stop until I'm done."

Jenny had lied. Her backside was so numb from the uncomfortable toilet seat that she had to take a break. She walked out of the room, closing the metal lock mechanism into the path of the door to keep it from shutting all the way. Taking the elevator to the lobby, she walked over to the large windows in the front of the building, looking outside as she dialed Amy LaRoussa's number.

"Hello?"

"Hi, may I speak with Amy please?"

"This is."

Jenny rubbed her forehead as she spoke. "Hi, Amy, my name is Jenny Larrabee; I know you don't know me, but I have been looking into the train explosion that claimed your sister's life back in 1961. I am under the impression that it wasn't an accident, and I'm trying to get to the bottom of who might have wanted to sabotage the train."

"Wait a minute...you think somebody blew up the train *on purpose*?"

This was not going to be an easy conversation to have, on many levels. "I do," Jenny replied. "Do you have a minute so I can tell you the whole story?"

After a detailed explanation that started with Devon and ended with the half-finished painting in the bathroom, Jenny asked, "Was Jacqueline's husband dark-haired, by any chance?"

"The man's name was Salvatore Crespi." Amy spoke in a tone that indicated she was not being condescending. "Yes, he was dark-haired."

"Did they have a good relationship, Jacqueline and Salvatore?"

"They did. He was devastated when she died; it nearly killed him, too."

Jenny couldn't discount the fact that Salvatore may have been a good actor. "So, you don't think he would have done this?"

"I—I mean," Amy began, "I would be very surprised to find out it was him. He does sound like the man you're describing, but I can't think of any reason that he would want to hurt Jackie." Her voice grew softer. "They were happy."

"Were you close with your sister?" Jenny thought that perhaps there could have been marital trouble that Amy just didn't know about.

"Very. We told each other everything."

Feeling stumped, Jenny remarked, "Well, I can honestly say that Jacqueline didn't seem happy to be with the man on the platform. The look on her face spoke volumes."

"Wow," Amy said in a whisper. "You can really see her face?"

Jenny hadn't considered that she was just able to do something that Amy hadn't done in decades. "Yes," she replied, keeping sensitivity in her tone, "she seemed lovely."

"She was lovely." Amy sounded distant. "I can't imagine anybody wanting to hurt her—especially not Sal." Her change in demeanor indicated she snapped into the present when she added, "Are you *sure* there was a bomb in that package?"

"No," Jenny admitted with a slight laugh. "It's just a hunch."

"Well, I certainly don't mean to discredit you—it's just that I have a really hard time believing she was an intended target."

"Believe me, I understand." Once again, Jenny was reminded of Paul Thomas's retaliation against Sabrina. "The problem is that when you're dealing with a lunatic, the victim has nothing to do with it."

Jenny couldn't help but feel a twinge of jealousy when she returned to the room and found Zack still sleeping. He was sprawled out face down on the bed, lying in a position that she hadn't been able to achieve in months. She found it a bit unfair that they had both conceived the baby, and they were both going to get to be parents after all of this, but she was the only one to make the physical sacrifices.

Although, she was the only one who could feel the baby's every move.

With that thought, she returned to the bathroom and continued her painting. It wasn't until she was almost done that Zack came staggering in, bleary-eyed, pointing to the toilet. "Are you using that?" His hair stood up in every direction.

"Only as a chair," Jenny replied as she got up. "It's all yours."

He noticed the painting and squinted at it. "Just how long have you been up?"

"A while. It's almost noon, sleepyhead."

"Noon," he grunted. "How did that happen?" Running a hand aimlessly through his hair, he lifted the lid to the toilet and went about his business—initially missing the target until he caught on and shifted his aim.

Jenny couldn't help but think about how the magic had all but disappeared from their relationship.

He finished up and flushed, once again looking at her picture. "That's really good. You have an amazing talent." He left the bathroom without washing his hands.

She stood still for a moment, digesting what had just happened. He was momentarily lazy, unkempt and gross, but he had paid her a compliment. Shaking her head rapidly, she decided that most men probably had the ability to be gross behind closed doors; she would focus on the compliment, which is something she never got from her first husband. In that regard, this was an improvement.

With a sigh of determination, she sat back down and put the finishing touches on her painting. Once she was satisfied, she snapped a picture of it, sending it with a note to Amy. She hoped that soon she would be getting a definite answer as to whom this man had been.

Her wish was granted almost instantly; she received a quick phone call from Amy. "Hello?"

"Wow," Amy replied. "I got your picture."

"And...?"

"That wasn't Jacqueline's husband." She paused for a moment before adding, "It was mine."

"He was *your* husband?"

"Uh-huh." Amy's voice was shaky. "My God, I cannot believe this."

Jenny was unsure of what to say. "Do you have any idea why he would do that?"

"Yes," she said definitively. "Jackie was coming to visit me. I guarantee I was the intended target."

"You think your husband would have tried to kill you?"

"There's not a doubt in my mind."

Jenny remained silent, inviting Amy to continue.

"I had left him just a few months before that and moved back in with my parents. The reason why I left was because he was too controlling—this is exactly the kind of thing he would have done if I defied him." Her voice once again reflected overwhelming remorse. "He killed all those people because of me."

"No, I wouldn't say that," Jenny replied reassuringly.

"I would. I had so many warning signs. I should have been able to see this coming. My entire family warned me not to marry him, but I did anyway. I was eighteen and as stubborn as they come. And look what ended up happening."

"You couldn't have predicted this."

"My family did. They all told me it would come to this, but I thought I knew better. God, I was so stupid. I actually found his jealousy to be *endearing* at first, if you'll believe that. I thought, *wow, this guy cares about me so much that it destroys him when I'm not around.* Everybody around me tried to tell me that it wasn't healthy—that it was psychotic, not charming. Even I started to get a little wary of it when we were engaged, but I figured that once we got married and I came home to him every night, the jealousy would subside. He would see that I loved him and there wasn't anything to be jealous about." She let out a loud breath, clearly frustrated with herself. "But it turns out my family was right. Things only got *worse* after we were married. I couldn't even *talk* to another man without him getting upset about it. It got to the point where I couldn't take it anymore, so I left."

"I don't imagine he took the news very well."

"No, not at all." Anger permeated her voice. "He stalked me, even though the word *stalking* wasn't a term back then. He was everywhere I went. He followed me, showed up at my door at all hours of the day and night—and when I went to the police about it, they said it wasn't against the law for him to ring my doorbell."

Jenny nodded slightly. "This was before all the stalking laws were put into place."

"Exactly, so I was stuck. But one day, he seemed to disappear. It was completely out of the blue, so I was skeptical of it at first, but he really did stop harassing me after that. I figured that he'd found another woman to obsess over." Her voice became quiet. "This was a few weeks before the train explosion."

Jenny's shoulders sank. "I guess he hadn't found somebody else."

Amy sounded as if she had started to cry. "I guess not."

"Would he have even been capable of making a bomb?" Jenny asked. "That can't be an easy thing to do."

"He was pursuing a degree in chemistry; he was more than capable. I just never would have associated him with my sister's train exploding. He must have driven all the way down to South Carolina to give her the bomb to give to me. It didn't even cross my mind that he would have done such a thing, although now that you say it, it seems perfectly reasonable."

"He knew your sister was coming to see you?"

"He knew everything about me. I don't know how he did it, but he always seemed to know where I was going to be, and when."

"Stalkers find their ways," Jenny said.

"I guess so." Another heavy sigh. "I just feel positively awful that all of those people died because my ex-husband wanted to get back at me. My God, I should have listened and never gotten involved with him in the first place. What a fool I was."

"Listen," Jenny said compassionately, "I chose the wrong guy the first time, too, and looking back, I can recognize that I overlooked a *ton* of warning signs in the process. A lot of us do it. I was just lucky in the sense that my husband didn't hurt anybody when I left him. But that's what it was—luck. It could just as easily be me in your shoes right now...but that's not a reflection on you. It's one-hundred percent him."

Amy's voice was little more than a whisper. "He killed my sister."

And so begins the guilt, Jenny thought. Had the bomb detonated when it was supposed to, Amy would have been the victim, but due to a crazy twist of fate, Jacqueline and ten others paid the price. That notion was sure to haunt Amy for the rest of her life. What could Jenny possibly have said at that moment to help alleviate Amy's guilt? Nothing...so she simply changed the subject. "Did he come back to bother you any more after that?"

"No...I never saw or heard from him again. It's like he dropped off the face of the earth."

"Do you know where he is now?"

"If there's any justice in this world, he's either dead or in jail."

Jenny cleared her throat. "Well, I know a man who is very good at finding people. I bet he can track your ex-husband down, wherever he is."

"Good," Amy said. "If he is still alive, I want to see him rot in jail for what he did, provided he's not there already."

"Well, I can get Kyle working on this right away. The only things I'll need to know are his name and his birthdate, and then he can get this process started."

"Fabulous. He was born on May fifteenth, 1941, and his name is Roger Hillerman."

Chapter 22

"I'm still stunned," Jenny announced after she'd recounted the story to Zack. "I can't believe *Jove* was responsible for blowing up that train." She made finger quotes as she said Roger Hillerman's fictitious name.

"It is crazy," Zack agreed, "but it fits, if you think about it. Amy was married to a smart but very controlling man. Jove was a smart but very controlling man."

Jenny looked at him with a sideways smile. "I believe the phrase you are looking for is *intelligent delinquent*."

"Okay, he was an *intelligent delinquent*. Either way, it makes sense that they were the same person."

"I agree it makes sense, but the odds that the cases were related are just so slim."

"Stranger things have happened."

Jenny blew out a breath. "I guess. Anyway, Kyle is working on finding out where he is buried. I would ask Delilah, but I don't want to talk to her about that yet."

"Do you plan to tell her what he did?"

Shrugging and shaking her head, Jenny said, "I don't know. I'm not sure what I want to do about that. I just got through telling her that I cleared her great-uncle Roger's name. Do I really want to go back and announce that I discovered he was guilty of something else?"

"That's a tough one. I think you're right about not saying anything yet. You can always tell her later, but you can't un-tell her once you've said it."

"That's what I'm thinking." She sat back against the pillows on the bed, looking at the picture she had painted of the man who went on to be Jove. "It's just so messed up, you know?"

Her phone signaled a call was coming from Kyle. She put the phone to her ear and simply said, "That was quick."

"Hey, Jenny," he replied with a laugh. "Yeah, the information you were looking for wasn't too hard to find. Again, though, I'm sorry I didn't make the connection earlier. I saw Amy LaRusso had been married before, but I didn't recognize that name as one of the people from Eden…which is sad considering I had just researched him not too long before that. I'm getting old, I guess."

"It's no problem, really," Jenny said. "They were two separate cases; I wouldn't have expected you to be looking for a connection."

"Well, I'm glad you discovered it. You picked up my slack. Anyway, I have discovered that Roger Hillerman is buried in a place called Ridgewater cemetery, not too far from where Eden was located. I can text you the specific address."

"Thanks, Kyle."

"No problem. Can I help you with anything else?"

"Can you carry this baby for me? She's getting huge and I'm about done with this."

He let out a chuckle. "I'm not sure the wife would let me. Besides, I'm carrying enough extra weight around the middle; I don't need any more."

"Oh, well, I tried," Jenny said with a smile. They hung up the phone, and seconds later she received the address of the cemetery. She jotted the information down on the hotel's notepad before dialing Kayla's number.

"Hi, Jenny," Kayla said. "What's new?"

"Well, I don't want to get ahead of myself, but I think we might be able to get rid of Matthew once and for all…is there any way you and Devon can come down to Georgia?"

Kayla's voice immediately became determined. "Let me get my purse."

Zack took Devon out to a playground while Jenny and Kayla stayed back at the hotel room. Jenny was using the only chair in the room while Kayla sat nervously on the edge of the bed. "It's a bit complicated, but I think I finally have the whole picture," Jenny began.

"I'm ready," Kayla said. "Let me hear it."

"It's all about a man named Roger Hillerman. Having looked into his history a little bit, he was born in Georgia in 1941. He was a rather unremarkable, middle-class kid, but he was very smart; he ultimately went to Sherman College in Pennsylvania to study chemistry. Shortly after he moved there, he met a local girl named Amy Mills and quickly became obsessed with her. He was extremely jealous and possessive, but unfortunately, Amy was only about seventeen at the time, and she mistook that behavior for love."

Kayla closed her eyes and nodded.

"They got married a short time later, but it didn't last. His controlling ways became too much for her, and she moved back in with her parents. As you can imagine, that didn't sit very well with Roger. He began to stalk her, but back then *stalking* wasn't a term. She went to the police to report his harassment, but they told her that he wasn't doing anything illegal. Then, one day, the stalking stopped—out of the blue. She didn't believe it at first, but after enough time went by, she figured he must have met someone else. She never heard from him again.

"However, the stalking hadn't really stopped; it had just changed in nature. It seems he went from following her to trying to kill her. We believe that when he stopped following her, he started making the bomb that was designed to kill her."

Upon hearing the word bomb, Kayla hung her head. For the first time, it appeared she was able to make the connection between Roger Hillerman and Matthew Ingram.

Jenny continued, "He apparently caught wind of the fact that Amy's sister, Jacqueline, was going to take a train from South Carolina to Pennsylvania to visit her. He must have driven all the way to South

Carolina, disguising the bomb as a present and giving it to Jacqueline on the train platform. I saw that scene in one of my visions, and it makes perfect sense now. Jacqueline didn't look happy to see Roger at all, and she was reluctant to take the gift from him, but she ultimately agreed. I'm sure he told her it was a present for Amy, and it must have been designed to go off when she opened it. Unfortunately for Matthew and the others on board the train that day, it apparently went off prematurely, causing an explosion on the train.

"After that incident, Roger went into hiding. He and a group of friends took up residence at the farmhouse his family owned, and they started living off the grid. He became the leader of this little commune, which they called Eden, and could probably be described better as a cult than a community. Roger changed his name to Jove and insisted the other members change their identities as well. One of the other rules was that all residents cut ties with their families, which I originally thought was to ensure the members never left the cult. In hindsight, though, it may have had more to do with the fact that Roger didn't want anyone to connect him to the train explosion. If investigators figured out it was him, his name and face may have been plastered all over the news. However, if he went by Jove and nobody around him had contact with the outside world, he would have been safe."

Kayla's eyes were wide. "Isn't that the other case you were working on?"

"It is. Can you believe it?"

"I can believe anything these days."

Jenny imagined that was the truth. "Well, Roger's cult grew to be forty-seven strong, consisting mostly of hippies and draft-dodgers. They lived off the land, using bartering as a means of exchange instead of money. Their drug supplier, Paul Thomas, used to give them LSD in exchange for the cult's marijuana, mushrooms and sexual favors."

"Oh, my."

"Indeed. Except one day, a cult member named Sabrina refused to sleep with him when it was her turn. She was in love with another cult member and carrying his child, so she didn't want to have anything to do with Paul Thomas...at least, not in that way. To retaliate, a couple of weeks later, Paul put Nembutal in their water supply, resulting in the deaths of everyone who lived there. Ironically, Sabrina—the one who refused to sleep with him—had left the cult with her boyfriend just before the poisoning. Once again, a lot of other people paid the price, while the intended target walked away unscathed.

"Strangely enough, Roger Hillerman was accused of masterminding that overdose. It was ruled a mass suicide, and, being the cult's leader, he was considered the brains behind the operation. For decades, Roger Hillerman's name has been mud. Just recently, Paul Thomas has confessed to that crime, and Hillerman's name was cleared...for about a day. Now, as you know, we realize he actually was a murderer, just in a different way than we had suspected."

"But the man is dead," Kayla said as more of a statement than a question.

"Yes, he's dead." Jenny smiled and raised her eyebrows. "He was murdered."

"So, do you think if we tell Matthew this, he will go away?"

"I'm hoping so. I have even found the place where he is buried. With your permission, I'd like to take Devon there and actually show him the grave site. My hope is that it will provide enough closure for Matthew to move on."

"Well, let's do it, then." Kayla stood up off the bed. "I am about done with this whole thing."

"Why are we here?" Devon asked from the back seat.

"We're going to show you something," Jenny replied as she navigated the car through the cemetery's narrow, one-way streets.

"Are these dead people?"

Jenny glanced back at him in the rear view mirror. "Yes, but they're at peace. All but one, maybe."

He didn't reply. He simply rocked back and forth as much as the seatbelt and booster seat would allow.

Zack and Jenny had found the headstone earlier in the day and marked it with a bright-colored flag, so she knew right where to park. She turned the car off and looked at the wide-eyed little boy in the back, fighting the nervousness that coursed through her veins. "Devon, honey, I have a picture I'd like to show you, if that's okay."

He continued to sway. "What's it of?"

Without answering, she removed the towel that had kept the painting covered and simply held it up so he could see. The fidgeting suddenly stopped; Devon studied the picture with scrutiny. "That's the man," he ultimately said.

"What man?" Jenny asked.

"The man with the present. He gave it to the yellow-haired lady."

"What present?"

"The present that went *click.* It started the fire."

Nobody in the car said anything for a long time.

Devon broke the silence. "Do you know who he is?"

"His name is Roger Hillerman," Jenny explained, "and the present was actually supposed to go to his wife. He was angry at his wife, and he wanted to hurt her. The woman with the yellow hair was the wife's sister, and she was supposed to pass it along. Unfortunately, the present started the fire earlier than it was supposed to, and that's why you all got hurt."

"Did he get punished?"

Jenny smiled. "Yes, honey, he got punished. And, in fact, his grave is right over there. Do you want to see it?"

Devon only nodded.

They all got out of the car; Kayla immediately took Devon's hand, walking him silently over to the marked grave. "Is that it?" he asked. "The one with the flag?"

"That's it," Kayla said.

Devon let go of his mother's grasp and took a few steps closer to the headstone. He squatted down to get a closer look at it, staying in that position for what seemed like an eternity. Eventually, he looked over his shoulder to the nervous adults behind him and stated, "He ruined everything."

Kayla hung her head; Jenny managed to stay strong enough to speak. "I know he did, but he paid for it. Somebody else killed him shortly after the train fire."

Devon turned back around, his focus once again on the grave. After several moments he stood up, walking toward his mother. He looked up at her and said, "I can go now."

Jenny wasn't sure who had just spoken: Devon or Matthew. "What do you mean *you can go now*?"

"I mean, I can leave this place. I don't have to be here anymore."

Jenny was desperate to know who was talking, but she was still unsure. "Where do you want to go?"

"The good place," he replied, turning to look Jenny in the eye. "Where Julia is."

Devon walked slowly over to Jenny, who knelt down to look at him at his level. "But first, I want to thank you," he said sincerely.

Jenny smiled, taking hold of his hand. "No need to thank me. I'm just glad you got your answers."

Without another word, he wrapped his little arms around her neck in a tight hug, which Jenny returned. Eventually, he whispered into her ear, "Tell Mary I love her."

Closing her eyes to battle her tears, Jenny replied, "I will."

After holding the embrace for a few moments, Devon let go and turned to his mother. "Mom?" he began, "can I have my tablet?"

Two months later

"Oh my God, I can't do this anymore," Jenny exclaimed.

The labor nurse spoke reassuringly. "You're making good progress."

"Making good progress," Jenny mumbled, unconcerned with being rude. "You've been telling me I've been making good progress for two hours now. If that was really true, I'd have had this baby an hour and a half ago."

"It takes time," the nurse replied patiently. "The baby has to get past your tailbone, which isn't easy to do…especially when it's your first baby."

"Can't you just take it?" Jenny asked. "It's clearly not working this way."

"A caesarean is not something we take lightly. We only do that in extreme circumstances."

"I think this is extreme. I've been pushing for two hours." Another contraction hit Jenny like a ton of bricks. "Shit," she said as she began to push again. Zack held one of her feet as the nurse held the other, giving her some leverage as she strained with all of her might to the doctor's count. After three exhausting pushes, the contraction subsided.

"I'm so done with this."

"You've had a long labor, I'll give you that," the nurse said, "but you're in the homestretch now."

Jenny glanced at the clock—she was on hour number twenty-three. She'd had neither food nor sleep in a very long time, the epidural was wearing off, and she was about as grumpy and tired as she could be.

"Homestretch. You really can't just take it? Then I'd be done."

"You're very close," Doctor Patil assured her. "It won't be long now."

Jenny was not amused by the statement; they had said it too many times before. "Give me a time frame."

"Within twenty minutes."

"Twenty minutes is too long. Oh, dammit!" Another contraction ravaged her body. She managed three more pushes before the pain went away.

"That was a good one," the doctor said. "Give me a few more like that and we'll have ourselves a baby."

...To be continued in Haunted.